Bc

DAVID VANDYKE

PLAGUE WARS SERIES

The Eden Plague

Reaper's Run

Skull's Shadows

Eden's Exodus

The Demon Plagues

The Reaper Plague

The Orion Plague

Cyborg Strike

Comes the Destroyer

STELLAR CONQUEST SERIES

First Conquest

Desolator

Tactics of Conquest

Conquest of Earth

Conquest and Empire

CONQUEST OF EARTH

Copyright © 2014 by David VanDyke
All Rights Reserved.

Printed in the United States of America.

Published by David VanDyke

ISBN-13: 978-1-62626-041-2

ISBN-10: 1-62626-0419

CONQUEST OF EARTH

Stellar Conquest

Book Four

David VanDyke

−1−

Captain Absen squeezed himself into the jump seat of the tiny grabship behind Major Vango Markis. The auxiliary position was seldom used, and he could see why. "Thanks for taking me out," he said to his Aerospace squadron commander.

"Thank me later, sir," Vango said with a mischievous grin. "Don't you usually get spacesick?"

"Stick to one orientation and you'll stay out of the brig," Absen shot back. "We have a briefing at 1000 hours, and I'd rather not show up green." Motion sickness was one of his weaknesses, and he wasn't about to allow this puppy to play games with him. All pilots seemed to want to make their passengers puke.

"Aye aye, sir," Vango said with resignation. "I'll keep you snug as a baby."

The stubby little tug exited Conquest's launch bay and swung around in a flat curve. Soon the two men looked back at the massive dreadnought as they drifted. Vango gave the retros tiny bursts and backed the grabship slowly away.

"Four days on the nose," Absen mused as he watched the hundreds of telefactors scurrying across *Conquest*'s surface, layering armor back onto the big boat to replace what the Weapon's strikes and the impact of hundreds of hypers had peeled away.

It would be a patch job, really. Absen begrudged the time it would take to manufacture the massive amounts of collapsium and neutronium needed to bring the armor back to spec. He wasn't worried about the first ten meters that had been scoured off; the hundred-meter-deep canyons where the exawatt laser had slashed across *Conquest*'s prow and primary weapons array were his real concern.

It would have to do.

"Gives you a different perspective, outside of all this thick armor, eh, sir?" Vango said.

"Your father liked to needle me too, son," Absen replied. "But then again, he was the Chairman." That declaration seemed to stymie Vango for the moment. All pointy-nose drivers wanted to believe themselves inherently superior to everyone else, even their commanders, but Absen wasn't going to let the man get away with it.

An hour of inspection satisfied the captain. Vango brought the grabship skidding in to the launch bay perilously close to the nearest bulkhead before settling into its cradle with perfect grace.

"Sweet landing." Absen smiled, not giving the pilot the satisfaction of complaining. Let the kid have his fun.

Kid. This time Absen did chuckle audibly. Vango was thirty-two, subjective, but discounting coldsleep time Absen was more than seventy, and over one hundred on the calendar, older than all but a few aboard. From his perspective, most of them *were* kids.

Checking his watch after he climbed out, the captain said, "Twenty minutes, Markis. See you in the briefing."

***

"You're absolutely sure this time?" Captain Absen asked his intelligence chief, Lieutenant Commander Ronald "The Robot" Fleede, who stood in front of the conference room screen.

"I would say our confidence is extremely high, sir."

"That's what you said last time, and the hidden second Weapon almost killed us." Absen said this without rancor, but some in the room glared.

Fleede swallowed, his protruding Adam's apple bobbing, but otherwise seemed unperturbed. "Sir, the situations differ. Regarding the two Weapons on Luna, we initially found no evidence of the second laser. Afterward, my team looked for and found subtle signs we missed the first time, and now we know what to look for, but I freely admit I should have ferreted out the potential trap based on logic alone."

No trace of sarcasm stained Fleede's voice. Eternally earnest, Absen knew the man would never dream of talking back to his commander.

Fleede went on, "In this case, though, logic also supports my view. There is no reason to place such an expensive item on the inner side of Io where all it can see is Jupiter eternally filling its sky. We've also examined the rest of the moon for evidence of installations based on our review of the earlier scant traces. There's simply nothing there."

Absen sighed. "I suppose I have no choice but to take the risk if we're to get *Conquest* into position." Fleede said nothing. "All right, sit down. Now let's go over the plan. Michelle?"

The android representing the ship's AI nodded and made a gesture with her hand, and the screens changed to display a variety of information. "This is a near-realtime view of the Jupiter system." She gave Absen and the rest of the staff assembled there a moment to look it over before continuing. "Four Galilean moons, each with a heavily defended Meme-Pureling base, part biological, part constructed. Io, of course, also has its Weapon pointing orbitally outward along the plane of the planetary ecliptic, and its nearby base is the Jupiter system command center."

"I don't see the Meme cruiser that just arrived..." The living ship had come blasting into the system three days ago. Absen had let it alone, not wanting to interrupt repairs. It was little threat.

Michelle nodded. "It's grounded itself here," she said, rotating to a synthetic birds-eye view of the Weapon and its nearby command center. "Right between the laser and the Jupiter system command center, just under the edge of the beam's reach. Lieutenant Commander Fleede believes the Meme crew themselves have taken refuge in one of the two places."

"Cowards," Commander Ford muttered from his seat.

"We took down two Guardian monitors and a Weapon with three Exploders," Absen said with a slight smile. "What would you do if you were a Meme cruiser captain? Attack?"

"Blast out of the system at high speed," Vango Markis interjected. "Which means maybe, for a Meme, the cruiser command trium isn't all that cowardly." He and Ford had developed a habit of constant, barely controlled verbal sparring since they had witnessed the death of most of Earth's population. No matter what one said, the other took the opposite view.

Absen warned them both with pointed glances. "Go on, Michelle."

"Each Galilean moon also has at least one Meme base with stingships, hypers and fusors, approximately as potent as a Destroyer. Then there are seventy-five other satellites, some natural and some manmade. The remnant of Ceres," its position flashed, "still retains about half its mass and all of its Pseudo-Von-Neumanns." PVNs were semi-automated factories that could be programmed to build almost anything, using various technologies from nanotech to standard industrial methods, with sophisticated computers and small crews to control them. Ceres itself had been moved from the asteroid belt to the Jupiter system long ago.

"That's the real prize, people," Absen said. "Priority one is keeping those PVNs undamaged so we can use them to build. Now as far as Intel can glean, they have not been fitted with self-destruct nukes, but the computers themselves probably have burnout protocols, so Michelle and Rick, you two will need to devise an information attack to worm your way in and save as many as possible intact."

Commander Rick Johnstone, *Conquest*'s CyberComm wizard, nodded, brushing back his dark, too-long hair from his forehead. Military rank had been forced upon him, but he'd never cared much for the details of grooming standards. "We should be able to save all we have line of sight to, and we'll try to relay off a stealth drone to get the back side."

"Ultimately," Absen continued, "we hope the PVN crews – and any other human-controlled installations – will defect to us once the Weapon and the rest of the Meme bases have been eliminated. Go on, Michelle."

The android moved smoothly to gesture at the screens. "Besides those five moons, seventy-four other satellites of significance remain – four small shipyards for maintenance and refueling of mechanical ships, forty-six mining bases for extracting and processing ores, and twenty-four orbital defense platforms with lasers and railguns only. The Meme do not trust their human crews with nuclear or fusion weapons."

"Why not use more Purelings?" Absen asked. "If they did, the Meme could have those nukes available."

Michelle looked over at Fleede, who stood again. "Sir, Purelings are actually harder to create, train and maintain than ordinary humans. First, a clean clone, uninfected by the Eden Plague, must be generated. Then that clone must be grown naturally for several years, until it is old enough to receive a Meme mitosis. After that, it must be educated and trained to maintain efficiency and focus, because the longer it is alive, the more it will tend to develop its own individuality. Alternatively, the clone can be kept in stasis and the mitosis applied as needed, but either way, Purelings are not machines. They are useful but specialized animals that need a lot of care, rather like horses used to be long ago."

"Why do the Meme even use them?" Absen asked, turning to Bannum, one of the several Sekoi Blends aboard. He knew the huge, gray-skinned alien was female, but damned if he could tell the difference with the Hippos.

"For same reason biological species still use Marines and Aerospace pilots," Bannum rumbled in her odd accent. "Unmatched versatility, self-repair...and also, Meme find no satisfaction in machine slaves. Purelings perform...other functions."

"You mean the Meme have sex with Purelings?" Ford blurted.

"No, Commander. Meme have no sex, but enjoy cruelty, domination and command. Blends, on the other hand, have much sex. It is reward of blending, no?" She leered, and Absen was again reminded both how different and sometimes similar the allied races were.

"But that's —" Ford said.

"Let's put everyone's sex lives aside and concentrate on operations, shall we?" Absen interrupted drily. "Go on, Miss Conquest."

"Thank you, sir." Michelle ran her gaze over the assembled officers. "I shall now outline Captain Absen's plan."

***

Major Joseph "Bull" ben Tauros and Sergeant Major Jill "Reaper" Repeth reported in to Captain Absen with parade-ground salutes befitting EarthFleet Marines.

Absen returned theirs casually from behind his desk. "Sit down; at ease. I wanted to talk to you about the assault." Bull and Reaper glanced at each other, but remained silent. "I'm not happy with any of our options, or the projected results, but you're the experts, so I want you to tell me how you see it."

Bull cleared his throat. "Sir, if the sledgehammer strike performs as intended, we will complete the mission."

"Which is code for you don't like it."

"I don't like the casualty count, sir. Begging your pardon, but you chose to only bring a short company along when *Conquest* can hold a lot more. Now my Marines are going to pay the price."

Absen sat back, closing his eyes and rubbing his neck. "I know, Bull. I screwed up. I didn't envision anything quite like this, and I should have. I knew everyone on this boat was going to leave their loved ones behind again, and I wanted to minimize the personnel and pain. Now we're going in understrength and it's going to cost lives. I'm sorry."

Bull ran his hand over his huge bald head. "Sir, I've been thinking...why not add in a bunch of battle drones and let Michelle run them?"

"Good idea, Bull, but it won't work. The AI is integrated with *Conquest* itself. Once we move outside of a light-second distance or so, there's no way she could control them any better than you can. In fact, we're going to operate up to sixty light-seconds away. That's not doable."

"Of course. I should've gotten that."

Absen waved his hands. "After a hundred years, I'm still not fully accustomed to how big space is."

"What about putting the battle drones on automatic?" Reaper asked. "I'm not crazy about the idea – if Marines lose IFF or the drones get damaged, we could get some fratricide – but if we send them in as cannon fodder and make sure we stay behind them, we can minimize that."

"I support that idea, sir," Bull added. "We can give the squad leaders drone control capability so they can issue orders if they have to."

"You sure your people won't get task-saturated? I'm not a grunt, but you've told me that no one is ever undertasked in a firefight."

"He's right, Bull," Reaper said. "It's hard enough for company command to keep perspective to control a battle. You add drone control to the squad leaders…"

"How about the sled pilots?" Absen asked. "Seems to me that once they're down, they have some excess capability. Give them a crash course in battle drone operation and you got yourselves on-site control, and they never even have to leave their cockpits."

The two Marines' eyes widened. "That's a really good idea, sir. Might as well get some use out of the airheads."

"I also want you to take the Ryss along."

Now the Marines' faces fell. Bull said, "Sir...we've been training their warriors, but they're really green. They're good enough individually, and they like their Avenger powered armor *Conquest* made for them, but they're undisciplined. They would just be in the way if we tried to integrate them into the company. I'd rather have automated drones and the risk of fratricide."

"They're that bad?"

"Sir, they're like boys of thirteen. They literally just hit puberty. They're eager and brave, and Slash is all right" – he meant Slask, the oldest of the warriors in Trissk's absence – "but right now they're more dangerous to each other than the enemy."

Absen steepled his fingertips. "Bull, you said you're understrength. The battle drones will help, but you need the Ryss. Slask has already approached me about going along, and I don't see how I can refuse. If they stay behind they will be dishonored. You have to find a place for them where they can do some good. Stick them on one flank, point them forward and stay out of their way or something."

"Sir, they're going to get creamed," Reaper said. "They're just kids!"

"How old were you when you lost your legs in Iraq?" Absen asked, looking at Reaper.

"Nineteen," she said grudgingly. "Okay, I get it."

Absen pointed a finger. "Bull, they're going. God help us, but if they die, they die. I've studied the Ryss culture over the last few years. They live for battle. If I refuse, I'll have a mutiny. Besides, how would you feel if *they* were going and *you* were stuck on the ship watching?"

Slowly, Bull nodded. "Aye aye, sir. We'll find them a mission."

"We're 'go' in four days. You're the designated assault commander, so start planning and coordinating. Get Markis on board, make sure his sled pilots get lots of sim time with the battle drones, talk to Fleede...you know the drill. Dismissed."

–2–

Bull glanced over at his sergeant major, whose head lolled within her helmet as the assault sled screamed down through Io's thin atmosphere. "Reaper. *Reaper.*"

"Yeah, boss. I hear ya," Repeth replied, not opening her eyes. "Can't a girl get any sleep around here? We still got four minutes to touchdown."

"Four minutes…right." Raising his stentorian voice, Bull punched up the company freq and said, "Listen up, you diggers. In four minutes we're slamming in hot as hell. All you gotta do is follow your NCOs and kill anything that moves that ain't wearing yellow. No matter what they look like, there are no human beings here, only Purelings and Blends. Pureling's are soulless, fanatical clones, not people, and Blends or Meme are high-value prisoners. If you find a Blend or a Meme, do not let it escape. Make every effort to capture it, and burn it if you have to, you got me?"

"*Aye aye, sir!*" roared the line doggies, most of whom had exactly one real battle under their belts – the assault on the Weapon on Afrana's moon ten subjective years ago. Bull hoped the extensive VR training would be enough, that and the improved Avenger battlesuits. He had so few Marines.

Bull still wished Captain Absen had brought a lot more troops, but these eight squads of six Marines each were all he had. They couldn't even take more than a few of *Conquest*'s Recluse battle drones, one on each assault sled. Fortunately the pilots had proven quick studies, using their cyber-links to control the ground support machines.

Bull snorted. Aerospace. As usual, it would be Marine infantry that would do or die. *Tip of the spear, end of the shaft,* he thought.

Though he couldn't forget the thirty Ryss he'd been forced to use. At least they had their own customized Avengers. Unwilling to link in to VR space, the aliens had trained for the assault in an enormous converted cargo bay. Even without cybernetics or nano-augmentation, they made fearsome warriors, if not as deadly as his own troops, pound for pound. They were just so very, very green.

Bull switched freqs. "Slash, you copy?"

"I hear, War Leader Bull." Between the chip in Bull's head and the translation software in his suit, the big Ryss officer he called Slash might as well have been speaking English.

"Three minutes. You good to go?"

"We yearn to spill blood and taste Pureling flesh, War Leader. Again, I request the honor of first assault."

"No. You'll damn well follow your mission orders or I'll rip your fuzzy mane right off your neck, you got me?"

"I hear and obey, War Leader."

Slash, like all the Ryss warriors, was young, a bare yearsmane. Scarcely adult, he had a good head and heart, but like most unblooded troops seemed terribly eager to die gloriously. More than once Bull had cuffed him hard enough to send the young warrior stumbling. Not a recommended method of discipline with human troops, Absen had been adamant that Bull use Ryss training methods on Ryss.

Once again, Bull wished Trissk hadn't been sent off on some secret mission. The experienced Ryss warrior could have helped get the cat-boys ready, or better yet, led them.

Bull switched his HUD to the forward external view, looking at what the sled pilots saw. Before his eyes stretched Io's hot yellow surface, colored with the massive amounts of sulfur dust thrown up by the moon's many volcanoes. Unlike other moons, Io was a hot planetoid on the inside, with violent tidal forces pulling and twisting at its silicate crust and molten core, generating massive amounts of heat.

Despite this, its distance from the sun meant usually that seething heat remained trapped beneath the surface, except when it erupted as lava from a volcano. Most of its crust stayed cold, very cold, even if a few hundred meters down flowed rivers of magma.

The Empire's command center over the horizon occupied a geologically calm area. Perhaps the aliens had stabilized it by draining the heat below and using that to energize the Weapon just beyond. That massive laser had the power to burn through the heaviest ship armor over ranges out to ten million kilometers, and thus controlled space all around Jupiter.

At least, it controlled the space within the laser's ever-moving arc of fire. The Marines' assault was coming in from below the horizon.

Bull looked up to see Reaper staring at him. "Awake now, are we?" he said.

She snorted. "Who can sleep through all your yakking with Slash?" As if in reply, the assault sled bucked again and picked up a harmonic as it skimmed lower, bleeding off speed in the moon's chill atmosphere. "Besides, we're about to get hit."

"Crap." Switching his HUD view to flight tactical, Bull watched as a swarm of Meme stingships fell toward them, trailing tongues of fusion fire. The enemy launched hypers, tiny ones that nevertheless could bring down something as small as the sleds they rode. "Where the hell's our aero cover?"

Above and behind the assault sleds, Major Vango Markis lined his StormCrow *Weaver* up on the first Meme stingship even while slowing his time sense by a factor of ten. Doing so allowed for precise targeting, and a fraction of a second after he fired his inline maser the first shark-like living enemy died in a blast of microwaves calibrated for Meme ship physiology. Shifting to another bogey, he stroked the trigger and sent another stingship straight to boiling hell.

Around him Vango's squadron did the same, and dozens of stingships fell to their beams. Unlike the Marines or the Ryss warriors, his pilots were thoroughgoing veterans, both of the battles to defend Earth so long ago, and of the fight to wrest the Gliese 370 system from the Meme. Cool professionals all, they lined up targets and one after another calmly knocked them down.

Even so, hundreds of the swift little enemy fighters remained. Roughly half turned away from the assault sleds to attack the StormCrows while the rest held their courses toward the assault force.

"Damn," Vango said conversationally to his fighter jocks. "I was hoping they would *all* come after us. Alpha and Bravo Flights, with me. We punch through and hit the bogeys chasing the sleds. Charlie and Delta, keep them busy." All of his Crows couldn't dive to protect the sleds; if they did, the lagging half of the stingship group would roll in behind them and crawl up their asses.

"Roger, Alpha lead," came the clipped acknowledgements from his three flight leaders, each with eight Crows.

Vango led Alpha with Bravo flight right behind as they rolled and stooped like falcons through the oncoming formation of stingships. Pushing his time sense up over one hundred to one, the universe slowed to a crawl and Vango let loose with the lasers and railguns in his wing pods. On automatic, the weapons pumped fire into the noses of the oncoming enemy fighters, nice low-deflection shots that could hardly miss, sending them tumbling as the weapons clawed their eyes out.

The Crows knocked out a score of stingships, but not without cost. "Just lost Red Dog," Bravo's leader Tex called, his accelerated VR voice sounding tinny through the link. Vango looked over his shoulder within VR space and pushed his time sense up to maximum, almost two hundred to one. Sending his viewpoint toward the expanding explosion where Red Dog's Crow used to be, Vango could see nothing left but plasma and bits of wreckage in a spray, so he turned back to the slow-motion battle in front of him.

"Shit. He's gone. Keep your heads in the game, people," Vango replied in a frozen voice. What he really wanted to do was curse the dead man and everyone else for carelessness. Or maybe the stingship had just gotten lucky. The enemy fighters were fast but predictable, not too bright, and they didn't have the many advantages of EarthFleet's tech.

On the other hand, they were dirt-cheap, so that a hundred-to-one loss ratio was still an ugly proposition for *Conquest*'s aerospace squadron.

None of Vango's pilots used their inline masers, saving full charges for later targets. Instead, they flashed through the enemy formation to swing onto the tails of the other group of stingships, the ones trying to line up on the assault sleds skimming over the surface far below. "Watch the red zone as you come out of your runs, people," Vango called, referring to the slice of space high enough for the Weapon to have line of sight on them. One sweeping wide-area beam from the gargantuan laser waiting beyond the horizon would burn anything it touched. Titanic enough to gouge chunks out of *Conquest*'s glacis, the StormCrows would die like insects in a bug zapper if its sun-hot touch ever reached them.

The fifteen remaining Crows took shots at the stingships even as the enemy began to fire at the assault sleds in front of them. Tiny hypers leaped toward the Marine craft, and Vango passed the information via link to the blinding lasers mounted on the rears of the landers. Flashes sparkled in the void as beams crisscrossed intervening space. While the defensive lasers of the sleds sought to dazzle the sensors of the incoming hypers, stingship biolaser shots targeted the assault craft themselves.

Fortunately these new sleds had been fitted with extra armor for this single high-risk landing, and while Vango could see hits, none of the Marine sleds did more than wobble on damaged thrusters. Unfortunately, the stingships were just stupid enough to follow their suicide orders, and they were considerably faster than the sleds, which already decelerated for their landings.

"Dammit," Vango muttered as he burned enemy after enemy. He hadn't expected quite so many stingships.

"Sledgehammer in ten seconds actual," Vango heard Commander Rick Johnstone's VR voice in his comm.

"Sledgehammer in ten seconds actual," Vango echoed to his flight leaders. "Check your lines and make sure you're well out of the firing path." He kept knocking down stingships as fast as his weapons would recharge, locked in accelerated time sense, determined not to waste any fraction of a second.

One stingship, pulling ahead of the others, dove for the rearmost assault sled, and Vango desperately concentrated all his fire on it, but his maser was out of juice for the next few seconds, and his wing weapons didn't have the range or punch.

Just then, the ten seconds on his display ran out, and the dirty amber surface of Io erupted in a line of fire. The finger of one primary particle beam fired from *Conquest* ripped a hundred-kilometer-long trench pointing arrow-straight at the side wall of the Meme command center buried deep underground. Incidentally, the burst of superheated dust and burning sulfur thrown up engulfed sleds and pursuers alike.

The sleds were built to take it, but the lightweight stingships must have felt like they had entered a fusion-powered sandstorm. Even if they were not flash-cooked, they certainly lost sight of their quarries, and dozens slammed into the ground or the sides of the newly dug trench.

Right behind *Conquest*'s particle beam came a precisely calibrated burst of hundreds of ferrocrystal balls, accelerated by a Dahlgren Behemoth Fifty railgun to over $0.3c$, fast enough to cause mutual contact fusion in whatever they hit. Each impact would create a brief, tiny thermonuclear explosion.

Down the dust-filled trench below the sleds these glowing projectiles flew to slam against the buried armor of the enemy command center. If the intel section's educated guesses were right, that hellish impact would bore a hole into the Meme complex, providing both a breach and a disruption for the Marines and Ryss warriors to exploit. The resulting superheated plasma should expand through the constricted volume and ignite everything inside the confined space, turning anything and anyone not armored or sealed behind blast doors into crispy critters.

Vango watched the assault sleds, specially reinforced for this mission, descend to enter the trench. Invisible to the naked eye beneath the billowing dust and dissipating plasma, they would follow the channel to its end using radar, there to do what Marines do.

Fight, kill, and die.

"Gotcha," Vango exulted as the pursuing stingships pulled up, shying away from the obscured trench. Barely of animal intelligence, the little fighters hadn't the wit to figure out what to do when their targets vanished in the hot haze. Instead, they climbed out of the cloud and turned nose-on to the two flights of Crows and stood on their fusion engines, clawing to reverse course.

"Follow me," Vango ordered as he rolled *Weaver* left, parallel to Io's bilious surface, in order to stay under the minimum engagement altitude of the Weapon lurking just over the horizon. Tagging one more stingship with his wing weapons, he skimmed low over mountains and ridges, keeping his speed high while describing a wide curve that would take them back the way they had come.

Charlie and Delta still whirled in their own furball far behind, Crows against stingships. Once Vango set course to rejoin the fight, he said, "Finish them off and then punch it, boys and girls. Execute the bugout plan for refuel and rearming."

"Sledgehammer away," Commander Ford called from *Conquest*'s Weapons bridge station. Then, "Missile strike away."

"Pulse out," Captain Absen ordered.

Master Helmsman Okuda was already in the process of dragging *Conquest*'s prow around to a new heading. Once the dreadnought lined up, Absen felt the TacDrive kick in and hurl the vessel at lightspeed away from thousands of converging Meme hypers, which had been launched at *Conquest* over the last several minutes by the Meme bases on the Galilean moons.

A moment later, *Conquest* dropped out of TacDrive twenty million kilometers above Jupiter's north pole and began falling, too slowly to matter. That distance was fifty times farther than from Earth to the Moon.

"Get the holotank up," Absen barked as he stood to stare intently at the area where the holographic image would appear. The display flickered into lighted existence and over the next ten seconds populated itself with moons, satellites, captured asteroids, bases, weapons, and anything else of tactical significance.

From this vantage, looking down from Jupiter's pole, Absen could see almost everything that went on in the Jupiter orbital system. Only a few enemy spy drones had been in polar orbit and *Conquest* had already burned them. Now, everything revolved generally in one plane beneath the dreadnought, like a crowd of children around a maypole. *Conquest* pointed her prow straight down and waited like an eagle eyeing her prey.

"Show me the trench," Absen demanded, grasping the railing that kept him from falling into the helmsman's pit.

"We don't have a good line of sight on it, but..." Scoggins replied, "I can synthesize something from spy drones and the feeds from the sleds. Remember, this is more than a minute old due to the time-late light."

A moment passed, and then the holotank view altered to show a cutaway diagram of the long trench the sledgehammer strike had dug. Eleven icons representing his tiny landing force flew in a single-file line, by necessity spaced well apart. Moving slowly in comparison to their open-space speeds, Absen knew in atmosphere ten kilometers a minute was plenty fast enough to stress the abilities of their pilots, flying on instruments between walls no more than two hundred meters apart to stay inside the dust cloud.

The display fuzzed and then lost its coherence. "Sorry, sir," Scoggins said. "They've rotated out of sight on Io's surface, and we're not getting much from the sleds through the plasma haze."

"Launch the first missile salvo. Go ahead and start firing at the orbital fortresses," Absen ordered. Soon,

Ford eagerly lined up and began extreme-range fire with bursts of railgun shot and particle beams. The ferrocrystal projectiles would be lucky to hit, and the beams packed no punch at twenty million kilometers. They would barely fuzz the enemy sensors, but Absen ordered it anyway. At least his people would feel like they were doing something more than just waiting, but *Conquest* had to stay here, both to remain out of the arc of the Weapon and to coordinate the battle.

"Tactical, then," Absen said. When his birds-eye view appeared again, he traced the progress of the sixty missiles *Conquest* had fired, twenty at each Meme base on the other Galilean moons of Europa, Callisto and Ganymede. If he was lucky, at least one each would make it through to deliver its heavy thermonuclear payload. If not, the Crows would have to pick up the slack.

Turning his attention to the icons floating just over Jupiter's north pole, he saw that the grabships were even now arming each StormCrow with two heavy nuclear missiles for their next mission.

Thirty-two StormCrows had sortied from *Conquest*. Twenty-eight remained, losses that hurt Vango to think about. Three friends dead and one waiting in an ejection pod, floating somewhere in space and hoping for post-combat pickup before he was dragged into a gravity well and went *splat*. As the grabship fastened the big missiles onto the ordnance racks of *Weaver*'s fuselage, Vango fervently hoped and prayed that no more would be lost.

Just then, an updated databurst caused Vango's HUD to reset. Suddenly he saw three salvos of missiles curving outward from *Conquest*, reaching toward three enemy ground bases, the ones on Jupiter's largest moons, save Io. Each of these command centers housed Meme, Blends and Purelings. Elsewhere, he knew ordinary humans slaved away in mines and orbital factories, producing goods and weapons for their own defense.

Defense, ironically, against the only free humans in the galaxy.

Those workers had done a good job. The Jupiter system was heavily fortified. Leftover EarthFleet-style lasers and railguns were everywhere, at least one on every satellite and facility. Now those weapons fired frantically at whatever cluster of missiles came nearest to them. Sixty became fifty, then forty, as they were picked out of space, but Vango figured Ford must have set the missiles' paths as far from the defenses as possible while still getting them to their targets.

More stingships rose from hidden bunkers and hurried to intercept the diminishing groups. Vango watched as a missile from each group turned toward the nearest clusters of enemy fighters and, moments later, detonated itself among them. He didn't much like Ford – hell, hardly anyone did – but he had to admit the man was good at his job. The missile clusters, like the ones being loaded onto the StormCrows, formed their own tiny pseudo-AI networks, programmed by *Conquest*'s own AI. Combined, the weapons' brains were smart enough to take sophisticated actions, such as to sacrifice one so the rest could get through.

In the end, it didn't matter. Several more sacrificial nukes vaporized most of the remaining stingships, as well as six particularly dangerous orbital weapons platforms, but none reached their target bases. Still, the swath of destruction they had blazed toward the three enemy command centers would make it that much easier for Vango's pilots to finish the job.

"All right, people," Vango said as he noted the grabships rearm and refuel the last of his birds, "Godspeed, and execute phase two."

Four flights of seven Crows each accelerated in different directions from their position immediately over Jupiter's pole, far below *Conquest*. Skimming low over the great gas giant, they flew as close to the edge of its atmosphere as possible, using the horizon to hide them from their enemies as long as they could.

Bravo, Charlie and Delta flights aimed themselves toward the still-surviving Meme bases on Ganymede, Callisto and Europa, while Vango and Alpha flight accelerated to maximum in order to become visible to the enemy first. By the time they came over Jupiter's horizon, they had achieved high escape velocity and centrifugal force overcame the gas giant's gravity. The seven StormCrows rose inexorably upward, and as they did, five more orbital weapons platforms came into view.

"Alpha flight, all ships, Fox One." Long ago, the Fox number, *One* or *Three* especially, referred to the type of missile being launched from an air-to-air fighter, but the convention had evolved to simply mean "Fire the missile," rather like "Fire in the hole" meant something was about to explode.

Seven nuclear missiles released from the StormCrows and, a moment later, seven fusion engines lit, driving the heavy weapons at more than one hundred Gs toward their targets. "Fox Two," Vango called, and the process repeated. Now his birds were clean, each with two hundred tons less mass to drag around, fit to dogfight.

Two missiles streaked toward each of the five weapons platforms and the other four missiles splayed out toward the positions of unseen targets around Jupiter's curve. Maybe they would get lucky and surprise the enemy. In any case they would keep the defenders busy.

Vango tried not to think of the humans manning these defense outposts. They would be the most reliable – or the most deluded – of enslaved people, probably young and never knowing freedom, fed propaganda from birth about how wonderful it was to be a part of the Meme Empire. They surely didn't know it yet, but this was a civil war, a war of liberation.

Vango steeled his heart against the ugliness. "All right, boys and girls, let's cause some trouble. The other flights should be Fox One in less than thirty seconds." Vango kicked *Weaver* around into a screaming turn, burning fuel at a prodigious rate as his fusion engine held him pointed ninety degrees to his changing flight path, rotating continuously. This threw him into a three-dimensional corkscrewing power slide, making engaging him a matter of extreme chance. The rest of his pilots followed.

His HUD gave him innumerable targets as near-Jupiter space filled with the materiel of war. Hypers converged on him by twos and threes, railgun bullets and beams crisscrossed his path, and Meme Sentry drones dropped their stealth and took up attack postures, launching more hypers. Vango cranked up his time sense to maximum and the universe slowed to a crawl. Now he had all the time in the world to twitch *Weaver*'s nose left and right, lining up for perfect shots on anything in range. Drones, hypers, and the odd stingship fell to his centerline maser, his strafing run limited only by the molasses-slow buildup of power in his capacitors, stuck in realtime. If ever the Crows could be converted to antimatter powerplants as Commander Ekara wanted, what wonders of combat flying he could perform!

Higher and higher Vango led his flight, even when Lily "Cupcake" Martin vanished in a burst of plasma as something, maybe a lucky railgun bullet, converted her StormCrow into vapor. She'd paid the price as they performed their mission, drawing fire and defenders away from the other flights, giving them that extra few percent chance to get their missiles through. Vango told himself that with fourteen nukes at each Meme base coming in by surprise over Jupiter's horizon, at least one should make it to strike home.

Vango realized he wouldn't know the outcome for some time, as the bulk of Jupiter remained between him and the rest. Only *Conquest*, on her perch over the pole, could see everything at once, and she was sixty light-seconds away. Add that two-minute radio round trip to the time sense compression and he might as well not worry about anything but his own fight. His HUD received periodic updates, but they seemed ages apart.

The waiting ended as stingships, hypers and railgun bullets chased the six survivors out into the black of interplanetary space and Vango was able to let his time sense catch up to reality. He had the grim satisfaction of seeing four of the five orbital platforms explode in atomic fire, mitigated only by the sense of waste. Those were real people manning those satellites, and each one he killed pushed humanity a step closer to extinction.

6

Aboard Jupiter's *Empire Sentinel Two*, Sergeant Emilio Tama looked up from his console at the lieutenant, aghast. "The traitors have destroyed four more Sentinels, sir. That makes ten so far."

Lieutenant Victor Cheng nodded stiffly from where he stood at Tama's elbow. "Do not lose heart, Sergeant. The Empire will prevail." He glanced over at the commander of this Sentinel orbital fortress, Captain O'Rourke, who stood silently staring at the tactical display.

That readout mapped the Jupiter system in exquisite detail, which made the defense's losses all the more painful. Not only had this sector lost nearly half its Sentinels, but three of the four Empire bases had been vaporized by the forbidden thermonuclear weapons of the rebels, and the main command center on Io was under assault. Cheng's horror at the loss of Meme and Blend life was only sharpened by the doubt gnawing at his vitals.

Cheng had always been loyal to the Empire. Only the most dedicated Underlings gained such prestigious postings as this, with the awesome responsibility of controlling defensive weapons systems. He'd been well educated on the dark times before the Empire had arrived to bring peace and enlightenment to humanity, putting an end to its fractiousness and strife.

Now, everyone lived in harmony. Everyone knew his place – Meme, Blend, and Underling, fulfilling the natural order. This, Cheng had been raised to take as gospel.

Why then did the doubts gnaw at him?

Cheng patted Tama on the shoulder before walking over to stand next to O'Rourke. "What do you think, sir?" he eventually asked.

"I think we are losing this fight," O'Rourke said even more quietly. "The rebel's dreadnought is a ghost, moving from place to place at will, and even the Weapons on Luna failed to destroy it. They have dozens of nuclear missiles and we have none. We have lost half our defensive strength. The Yellows and those of the Pure Race are dead or soon to be. In return, we have destroyed a few fighters, and only because it seems the enemy is being less than ruthless."

"Less than ruthless?"

O'Rourke turned to Cheng. "With the power they have displayed, the rebels could have taken their time and wiped all twenty-four Sentinels out before starting on the main bases. Instead, they seem to be sparing us unless we threaten them directly."

"What does that mean, sir?"

O'Rourke stared at Cheng for a long, long moment, searching his eyes before leaning over to speak in his ear. "It means we may be on the wrong side."

Within Cheng, a lifetime of indoctrination warred against the facts, and against curiosity about the rebel humans, the ones not under the Empire's rule. He knew Underlings should be happy with their lot, but he also knew he had little chance to ascend. A post like this, or perhaps to become a member of a communal council, was the highest he could expect. Real power was reserved for Blends, and the Pure Race above them. Suddenly, it seemed unfair.

Remembering the history classes and the documentaries of the bad old days, guilty fascination surged again in his mind. Instead of merely disgusting him as the stories of crime and misrule were meant to do, the tales also drew him in with their human drama and passion. Unlike the staid and boring times of today – up until the enemy appeared, anyway – the days when humanity ruled itself seemed to teem with opportunities for advancement and excitement, adventure and romance.

Cheng could see O'Rourke watching him closely, and he realized his commander had revealed himself with his question. Men had been executed for saying less, and now he must decide how to respond.

He thought about Delivery Worker Second Class Brenda Gleeson, and how her calves flexed as she rode her bicycle through the tunnels beneath the rebuilt city of York, England where he had grown up. He remembered how their pairing had been denied by the Council on Mating and Breeding…and how shortly afterward he had been sent to man this orbiting Sentinel, so far from her lovely legs.

Brenda's memory made Cheng's decision surprisingly easy, and his heart hammered as he crossed the line. "I believe you are right, sir," he breathed. "But we must be careful."

O'Rourke nodded slowly, and took his hand from his jacket pocket. Cheng suddenly realized the captain's sidearm was not in its holster. It must have been in O'Rourke's hand, pointed at his belly in case of a wrong answer. Cheng looked around the small command center, thinking of the two dozen humans throughout the Sentinel station, and his guts churned again. Some would join them, but others would stay loyal to the Empire, and would have to be dealt with.

7

Absen watched with mixed feelings as the Aerospace missile strikes went home against the orbital weapons platforms. He'd ordered the missile fusing to detonate them farther away than normal in hopes of just knocking them out and sparing at least some survivors. He was less conflicted as weapons struck the three moon-based Meme command centers, vaporizing them in bright expanding balls of stripped ions and particles. Those were manned mostly by Purelings. "Excellent," he said aloud in relief, and then glanced a question toward Scoggins at Sensors.

"Sorry, sir," she said. "I don't have anything on the assault landing. They should already be down, but the rock and the plasma is blocking the view and cutting off all signals." She turned toward Rick Johnstone at CyberComm.

Rick shrugged apologetically, worry creasing his face. "She's right. I got no contact. They're on their own."

Absen sat back stoically, wishing he could do something that mattered. Ford continued to take desultory potshots at any target that presented itself, but at this range hits were few and far between. Even the

Weapon below would hardly have been able to light a match at twenty million klicks.

"Bring us in on conventional drive to five million, outside of the Weapon's targeting arc," Absen said. Maybe the flare of *Conquest*'s engines would attract some fire away from the Crows, though those should be rapidly running away to rendezvous in deep space with the grabships and the refueling pinnace *Conquest* had dropped off hours ago.

At least at five million klicks *Conquest*'s weapons might do a bit more than tickle the enemy. He'd settle for blinding them, disrupting their systems, hopefully leaving humans intact. It wasn't a body count he wanted: it was hearts and minds. This assault was ultimately more about recruiting reinforcements than it was a military operation.

***

"Ten seconds!" Bull heard Flight Warrant Butler snap over the Marine frequency. "Breach is open and clear, but we got no data on the LZ." The assault sled shuddered and bucked with hard deceleration.

"Crash protocols," Sergeant Major Repeth ordered. In response, seventy-eight suits of Avenger battle armor froze in place, clamping down on the bodies of the Marines and Ryss inside them.

"Taking fire," Butler snarled as he wrenched the assault sled down to a slewing, shuddering slide across the subterranean floor of the enemy base. Something caught the edge of the heavily armored shuttle and it rolled several times, finally coming to rest upside-down and half buried in a bulkhead.

"*Everyone out, go go go!*" Bull roared into the comm as his suit came under his control again. The rear of the sled opened like a flower with four petals. One petal dropped to the floor while the other three spread wide, allowing easy exit. The front could do the same, but right now it was obstructed.

Bull rolled to his feet and watched as the rest of the command squad did the same. He let Reaper get people moving as he checked the overall HUD picture.

"Come on, Massimo, haul ass," Reaper grunted as she helped the heavy weapons team leader unbolt his semi-portables from what was now the overhead. In the light gravity, the lack of dexterity from her gauntlets counted more than the mass of the crew-served weapons. "Butler, get that Recluse up." The big spider-shaped battle drone, folded into its external pod, was the closest thing they had to an armored vehicle.

"We're upside-down, Reap," Butler replied. "The sled's sitting on top of it."

"Let's fix that, shall we?" Repeth replied. "You four – yes, you, you, you and you," she pointed, "and you too, Bull, get out and grab the edge of the sled. We're going to roll it over." Like people tipping a ground car, the six lined up and slid their armored hands beneath it. "All together, one, two, three, *lift.*"

Servos groaned as six tons of powered armor, backed by the Marines' internal cybernetics and nanotechnology, levered the heavy sled upward. Had Io's gravity not been approximately that of Luna, about one sixth of a G, this would have been impossible, but they manhandled the vehicle, rolling it crunching over wreckage until it fell with a crash onto its long ferrocrystal skids.

Exposed and free, the armored blister housing the Recluse battle drone burst open as Butler blew its explosive bolts, and the mechanical spider unfolded itself to stand next to the personnel carrier. It lifted one of its two small waldoes to wave, and then unlimbered a heavy pulse cannon and spun it around in a three-sixty as Butler tested out its systems. "Good to go," the pilot said.

Suddenly an explosion knocked down one of Massimo's gunners, and Bull dove for cover, his plasma rifle belching sunfire while the rest of the Marines hit the deck. "Reaper, Massimo, get those semis working while I cover you!" Looking through his HUD, Bull fired and moved toward the next sled where line Marines already blazed away into the haze from kneeling positions. He tried to tell what they were shooting at even as carets appeared in front of his eyes marking the enemy positions, the suit's systems backtracking the shots. Behind him, the Recluse picked its way over the rubble, its gun swiveling to fire above the big Marine's head.

In front of him, one of Bull's Marines spun and fell, her weapon and the arm holding it blown to bits by some kind of high-velocity shell. The hard suit would tourniquet the limb, pumping her full of drugs and extra nano. In a few minutes, she should be back on her feet, and assuming she survived the next hour or two, in a few months she would have her arm back, courtesy of the Eden Plague.

"Keep low and use your HUDs, diggers," Bull snarled as he took his own advice, placing his targeting reticle over the caret marking the source of incoming fire. Triggering a long burst, he was rewarded with a secondary explosion as something, probably a powerpack, blew. "Trust your active sensors and keep firing," he continued.

Conquest's railgun-plus-particle-beam sledgehammer had ignited everything flammable just as expected, filling the enemy base with thick, oily smoke. Bull's surroundings continued to clarify as sonar, radar, IR lidar and several other sensors pumped energies into the burning haze. Friendlies flickered like ghosts to his left and right, while squat ugly shapes moved in front of him.

"Reaper, we got some kinda tanks out here," Bull commed as he fired another long blast of blue plasma. The ravening flame washed over the armored vehicle nosing through the gloom just before it swiveled its turret toward him. Pulse cannon shots from the Recluse hammered at the enemy, but its front glacis shrugged off the fire. Its antipersonnel rounds knocked Marines over, but the new battlesuits seemed tough enough to take it.

"Down!" Bull yelled as the tank's main gun spoke. Its high-explosive shell struck the ground and threw him several meters to the left. His head rang and he saw double, bruised all along his side. "They're using HEAT," he groaned, surprised they would face such low tech as high explosive anti-tank shells. On the other hand, old-fashioned high-velocity tank guns were rugged, much more so than railguns, and a straight-on hit from one would kill just as dead as something fancier.

"Anti-armor teams, engage," he heard someone order as he struggled to clear his head. As far as he could see on his HUD as he lay there, the enemy tanks had survived the immolating fire, but he saw no enemy infantry, nor even war drones. The sledgehammer had done its work.

Needles stabbed him and his suit pumped a speedball cocktail of stim, painkiller and nutrient solution into his veins. His head cleared after a moment and his heart hammered as if it would burst, but at least it put him on his feet again.

Several rocket teams fired, striking the enemy tanks but not stopping them. Their guns might be outdated, but the tanks' armor was thick, much thicker than mere battle suits. Marines had tanks, but there had been no way to bring any of their own along on a fast hot assault like this. The big carrier craft needed would not have made it down. Instead, the Marines relied on the attached heavy weapons team and the Recluses. The battle drone covering Bull sidled to the left, attempting to get a flank shot on the nearest tank.

"Come on, Reaper, we're about to get massacred," Bull called as he rolled to his knees and fired. He saw one digger blown apart from a direct HEAT round strike. The tanks must have their own sensors, probably thermal sights, and one had targeted a Marine using his own temperature differential.

Tracers work both ways, the old adage came to mind. Bull was just about to flame the tank in front of him again in hopes of blinding it for a moment when it shook to a tremendous blast that picked it bodily off the ground and tossed it on its side, a smoking ruin.

"How you like that, asshole?" came the gravely voice of Warrant Officer Krebs, one of the sled pilots.

"Was that a breaching missile?" Bull asked him.

"Damn skippy, boss. Didn't need it to blast our way in, so…"

"Good thinking. Remind me to give you a medal if you live."

"Always needin' Aerospace to pull your nuts out of the fire, huh, sir?"

"Shut up, Krebs," Bull replied. "Reaper –"

"We're here, Bull," came Reaper's voice as she strode up beside him. "Massimo should be opening up right about now. I'll fill in while you get this mob organized." Bull realized that he had been getting too involved in the firefight and had lost control of the overall picture.

While fire raged back and forth at close range through the wreckage of the base's big rooms and wide tunnels, Bull hunkered down to look over the tactical situation on his HUD. His squad leaders were doing a good job of fending off the tanks, keeping them under continuous fire, blinding their sensors and burning off their secondary weapons while the enemy kept firing main guns at point-blank range, hoping to get lucky. Unfortunately, they had, too often. A quarter of his Marine icons showed KIA already.

Bull keyed the general freq. "We need to get plunging fire on the tops of those tanks. Rocket teams, look for places up high and jump. Massimo –"

"Firing now, boss." On cue, a bright orange beam stabbed through the smoke from Bull's left to strike the turret of the nearest tank. At the same time, a heavy rocket slammed into the same armored vehicle from the side, mangling its treads.

Bull heard Massimo call, "Mobility kill on target one. Keep that beam on the gun, Jock. If you can get it hot enough..." Just then, the turret exploded. Either the laser had burned its way through to the ammo, or the stabbing light had damaged the mechanism enough so when the enemy fired their next HEAT round, it had jammed and detonated inside. In either case, that tank was dead.

"Good job. Squad leaders, keep the pressure on. Take them down one by one. Flank them and finish them." Confident the company could run itself for a moment, Bull checked his HUD for the Ryss. They had landed last, covered by the Marines, and their pilots had set them down as far to the right flank as possible. If this base was laid out the same as the one they had taken on Afrana's moon, there should be subsurface tunnels connecting to the Weapon there.

Bull wished them luck.

***

Slask had snarled in embarrassment as War Leader Bull insisted he follow the dishonorable "plan" and leave the first attack. Instead of allowing Ryss warriors to fight alongside the Apes on the battle line, Slask and his young males had been sent away like kits, good for nothing more than nuisance raids on the enemy's rear. Still, orders were orders, and though he had no fear of death, the dishonor of disobedience was greater still than the shame of his assigned role.

He knew why Bull had given the Ryss this task: because he considered them weak and inferior. Without the life code tinkering and the nanomachines and the cybernetic implants, the Apes would be punier than Ryss. When Slask had pleaded with Trissk to allow him to receive similar upgrades, the elder warrior had cuffed his head like a kit.

But Slask wanted to be strong, like the Ape warriors. What did tradition matter when honor and victory were at stake? Warriors of the older generation were too inflexible, set in their ways from the ages they had spent aboard *Desolator*. The future belonged to the young, those who could change with modern times.

The one consolation of this mission was that their females had been allowed to enter their seasons, and his warriors had been glorified once more before combat. That was a proper sendoff! The memory of his mate's yowls of pleasure as she received him threatened to distract Slask from his mission, and he cuffed his wandering mind back to the task at hand.

Leading his six paws of warriors from the front, Slask hurried down the side tunnel until its end, and then turned left in the direction of the Weapon. If this corridor led to the huge laser as he hoped, the Ryss would erase their shame with a great triumph. If the One above All smiled on him, he might even seize it intact and functional, enshrining his name in the Paradise of Heroes.

If not...Slask thought of the egg of atomic destruction heavy on his back. That was another route to immortality. He would show the Elders and the Apes just what it meant to be Ryss.

His hope of victory was based on the layout of the Weapon the Apes had seized in the Gliese 370 system. This corridor should lead to a maintenance tunnel, which in turn might give access to the interior of the fortified laser base.

Before him loomed an armored door, a seldom-used connector between the Weapon complex and the Meme command center.

"Burn through," Slask ordered the equally young warriors with the laser cutter, another shameful necessity. They should be using hotblades, but the metal was too thick. Warriors were not technologists, to employ such workers' tools. That was the province of females. Still, the two with the cutter had been trained to use it, cudgeled by War Leader Bull's meaty naked paws when they complained. That one was strong; terrifying, the Ryss admitted to himself. Even without the cheating technologies he used, the big Ape would be one to fear.

Soon they had sliced through the metal as they had been taught and the door swung open, its locking mechanism severed. In front of him Slask could see dim lights glowing here and there. "Use vision enhancement," he growled, and switched his own HUD's function to help him see. Now this kind of technology he liked. It reminded him of the nighttime raids he had performed as a kit under the moon on New Ryss, the world the Apes called Afrana, creeping through the tall grass to within marking distance, and then slashing claws down the haunch of some unsuspecting comrade.

Shouldering the cutting team aside, Slask prowled forward among pipes and conduits. He expected to see steam leak or water drip from condensation, but all here was clean and quiet. From his briefings, that meant robot maintenance. Machines did not get lazy or careless, or dislike the work they were assigned. Machines had no honor.

"Be vigilant for repair drones," Slask said. "These spaces are cramped, but well kept. If you see one, try to kill it with your hotblades. Do not fire unless you must. This is a raid until they notice us. Then it becomes an attack." There. That rationalized their actions well enough. Bull had said a leader must pay attention to the thoughts of his warriors, and inspire them.

"Your troops are not machines," the great Ape had explained. "They must be led. When you have them by the balls, their hearts and minds will follow." Slask was not entirely sure what that meant, for there were no females waiting as rewards for bravery here. The Apes' manner of speech was often peculiar. Still, Slask found he very much wanted to show himself worthy of War Leader Bull's approval.

A moment later Slask heard the whine of a hotblade, and then the sizzle of something meeting an electrical death behind him. "Follow me," he snarled. "The Purelings and their masters will begin to wonder why their maintenance drones are malfunctioning." He jogged forward, his armored body brushing against the machinery, until he found another door.

"This is the access," Slask told his First Paw. These five warriors he had placed before the rest – the bravest and boldest, if not the brightest, and likely the first to be killed. For a moment he saw the contradiction inherent in this arrangement, and then the odd thought fled him in the heat of imminent combat.

Unlike the other hatch, this simple door seemed thin, though it was code-locked. Hotblades would do. "Cut through, quickly." Slask hefted his own hotblade in one paw, his pulse-gun in the other. A compromise weapon, it used laser fusion to ignite pellets of tritium, powering tiny penetrators from its barrel at inconceivable speeds. The resulting plasma also blasted forward like a short-ranged flamethrower. Between the two effects, armored Purelings and small war drones should fall.

For anything else, they had grenades and rockets.

Two of his First Paw cut along the edges of the frame, high to low, while Slask shifted his pulse gun to his other hand and sliced the top. When finished, he kicked the door in with a crash and bounded through. He found himself in a transverse curving corridor, a section of an outer circle.

"First through Third Paws, follow me rightward. The others, go left. We meet at the Weapon." Slask raced ahead, looking for a way toward the center, which should be on his left.

Suddenly, figures poured out of doorways ahead and turned toward him. He didn't hesitate, but fired bursts on automatic, accompanied by a feline killing scream. To his left and right, his warriors did the same, filling the wide corridor with death.

Purelings fell, chopped into meat as ferrocrystal penetrators sliced through their lightweight armor. But the slaughter was not all one-sided. Return fire from the fanatical defenders, shooting over the mass of bloody bodies, cut down two of his warriors with high-powered lasers. If they lived, they would have to fend for themselves, relying on their suits to pump them full of stimulants and healing drugs. Again Slask cursed the conservative traditions of his elders, wishing for the bloodborne combat nanites or even the disease the Apes called the Paradise Epidemic. That was another nonsense name, and Slask wondered if something wasn't lost in translation.

Slask led his remaining twelve warriors to leap and scramble easily over the pile of bodies, hotblades executing all who moved beneath them. Even were mercy a Ryss battle trait, these Purelings were genetically programmed never to surrender. They may look like Apes, but they were really cloned Meme mitoses, Blended into similarly cloned Human bodies. The killing stroke was pure warrior's joy.

The curving corridor now revealed the tunnel he wanted, to the left toward the center where the Weapon must lie. Another group of fanatical Purelings fell before Ryss pulse-guns and hotblades. This time the fight turned hand-to-hand as the enemy burst out of side corridors, firing railguns and lasers. The Ryss' Avenger armor stood

CONQUEST OF EARTH   47

them in good stead, as did their blazing crystal swords, heated white above the melting temperature of steel. Even so, Slask had to leave two more wounded warriors behind to live or die as they would.

There was no time. The Weapon must fall. War Leader Bull had made that clear.

Ahead, the corridors curved ever more sharply as Slask and his ten blasted their way past Purelings determined to die for their masters. Nine remained, then eight, before the Ryss burst into the great room housing the massive interface between the generator and the Weapon. A structure the size of a building large enough to hold a thousand Ape dwellings, Slask knew below lay the generator that converted volcanic heat into exawatts of power, which poured upward into red crystal tubes in their array of thousands. After that, the coherent light was manipulated and focused into domes or beams or anything between, in strength sufficient to vaporize any material known to Ryss, Hippo, Ape or Meme.

Across the way, Slask saw a firefight in progress as the other half of his force fought its way into the vast room. One sight of the backs of his enemies was all his warriors needed to charge forward, spreading out into a bounding line. Unfortunately, that put the Purelings precisely between the two Ryss forces, and stray shots blasted chunks from the concrete near his feet.

"Flank them left!" Slask roared. "Kill none of your fellows this day!" The Ryss scrabbled obliquely until they had the defenders in a crossfire and continued to advance.

And then there were seven, then six. Five…and all the Purelings had fallen. Seven from the other group joined Slask and exulted, celebrating by firing toward the ceiling high above until he made them stop. "Follow me. We must disable the Weapon. Prepare rockets." Turning toward the center structure, Slask wondered at how easily they had won through. He had hoped, but given the odds… Perhaps all the defenders had been sent to deal with the Apes. Perhaps that had been War Leader Bull's intent.

Slask's curiosity and hope died together as openings in the vast machine appeared. Silvery spiders with turrets on top, each machine the size of three Ryss, swarmed out of the structure in their dozens, then their hundreds to aim down at the pitiful band of warriors below. Yet, they did not fire.

Now Slask understood. Purelings with outdated armaments had been used as cannon fodder to slow down the Ryss advance, while these advanced war drones were activated and positioned to defend the prize. Perhaps they held fire to capture him and his warriors for vile Meme enslavement, or to rip operational knowledge from his mind.

Bull had been clever after all, for of course he would preserve his own kind while expending Ryss lives on this suicide mission. Sadly, Slask would not live to pass this admirable lesson of cunning to his kits.

"I do not care," Slask said aloud. His warriors' advance had ground to a halt at the array of firepower in front of them, and they looked to him.

"Command us, and we will die like heroes," one said, his eyes hot with the nearness of oblivion. The rest murmured agreement.

"Yes," Slask said. "We shall be remembered by our ancestors in the Halls of Paradise, so let us die together, as warriors." Activating the device he carried and setting it for ten seconds, he drew a great breath, waved his hotblade and roared a challenge to his enemies.

"CHARGE!"

***

Jill Repeth felt the shock through her feet as the floor rippled like a live thing, flinging dust, debris and wreckage into the air to drift slowly downward in the low gravity. "Finish them off!" she yelled, dragging an unsteady digger to his feet and shoving him into firing position. "Massimo, where's that rocket?"

As if in response a bang and a whoosh came from her left, and a streak of flame crossed in front of her to blow the turret from the last tank they faced. "Anyone see any more?" she asked over the general comm freq. "Squad leaders, report!"

"Negative," came the first reply, echoed by several more.

Repeth still couldn't see anything optically except billowing dust, made even worse by the last heavy shock she had felt. She thought she knew what that was: tactical nukes at close range had a distinctive feel. "Bull, was that the Ryss bomb?"

"Think so, Reap. Either that, or something just as big." Repeth could hear Bull's labored breathing over the suitcomm, and then he went on. "Get the wounded back to the sleds. I need all effectives to confirm status on HUDs and rally on me."

Soon Repeth and Bull were surrounded by a loose tactical formation of thirteen Marines and three remaining Recluse battle drones. The machines had taken losses heavier than the troops, exposing themselves to more danger and thus drawing more fire, as intended.

Nine wounded showed on Repeth's HUD tracker, and the rest were KIA. She quickly reorganized the surviving effectives into two squads, one a man short.

Two squads left out of six.

"Shit. Two-thirds casualties, boss," Repeth said over a private channel.

"Yeah, Reap. I can count. We knew it would be hard, but not this hard. The Ryss just gave their all, though, so I'm having trouble with comparisons," Bull replied bitterly.

"They were good kids, those cats. You trained them well."

"*We* trained them well. Damn straight we did. Then we used them up."

"You can't blame yourself. You stuck up for them. You gave them the easier mission. Slash was supposed to get in, set that thing and get out. Maybe he did. We don't know they're all dead."

Bull turned away, visible only on active sensors as a fuzzy blob with an icon, and his voice hardened. "If they'd gotten out, we'd see more of them on the HUD. I can only find a couple of intermittent contacts." He cleared his throat. "We'll find out soon enough. Fortunes of war. Now let's finish this party, 'cause it may not be over." He gestured with his plasma rifle. "Command center should be that way. Stay alert."

***

"Hard rad and thermal spike on the Weapon's position, Captain," Scoggins cried exultantly. "Detonation consistent with Marine tac nuke."

"I'm not celebrating until I know that wasn't a Final Option scenario, Commander."

"Of course, sir. But even if it was..."

"I know." Absen didn't want to think about the potential cost. "Move in carefully. I want to be damn sure that monster is down. Scoggins, send a sensor drone to take a look, no stealth. Let them see it."

Five minutes later the high-velocity sensor drone crossed over the Weapon's position, drawing no fire. "Readings show subsidence on the surface. Looks like the laser is toast, sir," Scoggins reported.

"Outstanding. Bring us in low over the command center. Johnstone, try to punch a signal through to the Marines. Ford, have your gun crews keep a sharp lookout on point defense. We still have Sentries, mines and active orbital platforms out there."

"And if the orbitals fire on us?" Ford asked with upraised eyebrow.

"Defensive fire only. In a very short time, those may be our allies."

8

"Any chance he'll stop that pacing?" Ezekiel Denham asked Bogrin across the chessboard.

The Sekoi Blend chuckled. "Who?" He moved his queen's knight to threaten Ezekiel's king's bishop.

On the other side of the room Trissk prowled randomly, poking at brass and wood controls, which Ezekiel had ordered *Steadfast Roger* to disable, of course. Along the opposite wall, Spooky Nguyen paced a more deliberate course to and fro in front of a row of viewports, smoke trailing alternately from his lips and cigar.

"Trissk, I meant. I wonder if a ball of yarn would distract him?"

The gray-skinned alien stared at Ezekiel for a moment and then shrugged. Ezekiel realized that human reference was probably a bit too obscure for the Sekoi. "A traditional plaything of the domestic felines of Earth."

"Ah. It is your move."

"So it is." For want of something better to do, the human Blend took Bogrin's knight with his queen's bishop, a sacrifice initiating a series of poor trades.

"Your mind is not on the game."

"I know. This trip is taking a long time. Maybe we shouldn't have brought Trissk along. His brain doesn't mesh well with the bio-VR we're in, so I can't slow our time senses further, and he doesn't want to fight any more illusionary opponents."

"You could put him to sleep."

Ezekiel shook his head. "Not against his will, I won't. Start down that road and I'll be no better than a Meme Blend. It's already hard enough to convince people I'm human without playing godling."

Bogrin moved a rook. "Check." He stood up. "I have an idea, which should have come to me before." Walking over to Spooky, he spoke a few words in the slim Vietnamese highlander's ear and then returned to the chessboard.

"What did you say?" Ezekiel asked.

Instead of answering, Bogrin flicked his eyes in Spooky's direction. Ezekiel watched as he crossed the room to Trissk and bowed. The Ryss' eyes lit up and a moment later a circular sparring mat appeared on the floor of the room as the walls receded to accommodate it.

"Brilliant. That should keep him busy for an hour or two."

"I think you underestimate your Mister Nguyen," Bogrin replied, watching the two step into the circle. "He is a master of human unarmed combat styles, and has become quite adept at the Sekoi disciplines as well. If Trissk is willing, he has a lifetime of study ahead of him."

"Great. Let's make the Ryss even more combative."

Bogrin stared at Ezekiel. "I see you do not understand the martial arts."

"Not my thing, I guess." Ezekiel moved his remaining bishop to fork Bogrin's two rooks.

"Neither is chess," Bogrin replied as he sent his queen across the board toward Ezekiel's king. "Mate, I believe."

"Suckered again." Ezekiel shrugged and tipped his king, then stood up to look at the bank of steampunk-inspired controls, dials and gauges. "How's the search coming, *Roger*?"

The living ship replied, "I have twenty-three Sentries suborned thus far, and several more should be taken within the next day, but as you know, the space in the outer Solar System is quite large. Statistically, it could take months to find your mother."

"That's assuming she is out here rather than on Earth or elsewhere. If we can find our old base, at least we'll have a starting point."

"Months?" Bogrin said as he stepped up beside Ezekiel. "Perhaps we should change our strategy. Eventually the situation will be untenable. What is the English translation – 'cabin fever'?"

"Yes. When it gets unbearable, we'll leave the Sentries to keep searching, and rendezvous with *Conquest*...or perhaps try to sneak down to Earth to make contact with the resistance movement."

"If there is such a thing."

Ezekiel rounded on the ponderous alien. "You better believe there is, and I guarantee my brothers and sisters are at the center of it. They're brilliant, and Mother trained them for every contingency. Don't underestimate them."

"Don't underestimate first-generation Meme blends either, my friend. Until they become thoroughly corrupt with power and bored with naked excess, they will be loyal to the Empire. If they have any inkling that there are disloyal Blends among them, they will ruthlessly hunt them down."

"Thanks for the vote of confidence."

Bogrin shrugged. "In any case, what has been, has been. *Conquest*'s arrival in-system will work in any resistance movement's favor, just as it did on Koio. Hope of freedom is a powerful energizing drug. If there was no movement before, one will spring up. Many will die on the road to liberation." He chuckled incongruously.

"That's what I love about your people, Bogrin. Always up for a laugh." Ezekiel turned to watch Spooky and Trissk sparring.

–9–

Past piles of corpses cleansed of life by the sledgehammer's sweeping plasma wave Reaper and Bull walked, active sensors illuminating the spaces around them. All was still, for nothing weaker than a tank had survived the collateral damage from the enormous combination strike. Enemy maintenance bots and war drones alike stood fused to the floor. Every control panel now showed at least one gaping hole where nonmetallic parts such as polymer screens used to be. Even thin walls displayed irregular gaps where they had melted, sagged and run like wax.

Eventually the Marines found what they were looking for: an armored blast door, relatively unscathed. Fire suppression sprinklers continued to drench the corridors nearby with water spray, reducing the dust and improving visibility. After the fog of combat, the rain showers made for a surreal scene.

"Cutting charges," Bull said, gesturing. Two sappers quickly began laying out the shaped explosives. As they did, Bull ordered the rest to spread out and keep watch. Repeth figured he was just being careful, for she could hardly credit the possibility of a counterattack. Any force not accounted for undoubtedly waited behind the blast door for a last stand.

"Listen up," Bull said. "We need to take this command center intact. That's the whole point of the assault, and the lives of our friends we just lost. Use frag and shock grenades, but no plasma or heavy rockets unless you absolutely have to. You hear me, Massimo?" Ben Tauros pointed a finger at the warrant officer.

"Sure, boss." The Italian smiled disarmingly through his transparent faceplate, now beaded with spray. Repeth knew the gunner enjoyed blowing stuff up...perhaps a bit too much for even a Marine.

"Charges set," one of the demo NCOs reported.

"Take cover," Bull ordered. "We go in fast and heavy."

Once they were ready came the warning: "Fire in the hole."

A moment later the blast threw fresh dust into the air to compete with the falling spray, and Bull led the charge into the smoking breach. "Stun grenades!" he yelled, and Repeth rolled several of the flash-bangs past her commander's feet. These explosives would hardly touch a Marine in armor, but would shock and confuse lesser threats.

Ignoring the slight danger of the grenades, Bull strode forward with First Squad at his back. Repeth took Second Squad rightward down a corridor. She heard the blasts on her external pickups, but encountered no opposition. Moments later she led her troops into a large, round, deserted command center, meeting Bull's squad entering from the other side.

Three pools of briny sludge showed where Meme had been before escaping down their flush tubes – but to where? Had they withdrawn to the Weapon redoubt and died, or did they have a hypervelocity escape drone?

"Why didn't they blow it?" Bull asked conversationally, looking around. "With no one here, what do they have to lose?"

"Are we sure there's no one here?" Repeth asked, eyes roving over the consoles, some made for Meme pseudopods and eyeballs, some for the manlike hands of Purelings.

"Quarter and search by twos," Bull snapped. "Take prisoners if you can."

Massimo got to play with his heavy laser once more, using it to cut open another armored hatch to expose a separate room filled with human-style consoles…and people. When Bull burst in, with Repeth right behind him, three men and two women, garishly outfitted in pure yellow-gold clothing, raised their hands and stood silently next to powered-down control boards.

"Jackpot," Bull said, slapping down a Marine's rising weapon next to him. "Cease fire!"

"Now we know why they didn't self-destruct," Repeth remarked, sliding her pulse gun into its slot on her armor. "Blends." She keyed in the command to open her faceplate and fold back her gauntlets. Otherwise, to the people in front of her she would appear a faceless metal golem.

"My God," one of the women gasped, raising a hand. "Jill Repeth."

The other Blends turned curiously toward the speaker, then back to Jill and nodded in agreement. "It does appear so," one of the men said. "My received memories are very clear."

Bull moved aside and told the Marines behind him, "Spread out and secure the complex. The Smaj and I got this." Once they had gone, Bull pointed at the woman, watching carefully. "You. Talk."

The tall, dark-haired woman who had first spoken kept her hands in view and moved to her right, away from her fellows. Once she was well out of reach, she said to Repeth with a steady gaze, "Welcome home. I'm Leslie Denham."

"Holy shit," Repeth replied. "One of Skull and Rae's kids?"

As she spoke, one of the men in yellow moved with lightning speed, plunging a hand into his sleeve to retrieve a pistol, which he pointed at Leslie. "Traitor!"

Leslie was already moving behind Bull, who stepped in front of the muzzle, apparently confident nothing that size could penetrate his battlesuit. The bullet *spanged* off his chest, adding a small ding to the Star of David painted there.

At the same moment Repeth drew her own backup weapon, an ancient PW5 Needleshock pistol, and drilled the Blend in the gut before he could get off a second shot. The man folded as the electrical charge stored in the round caused his muscles to convulse, knocking him unconscious to the ground. "Anyone else want a little taste?" she asked as she swept the pistol left and right.

The others backed away, shaking their heads. Leslie stepped out from behind Bull and kicked the man's fallen pistol into a corner. "You certainly took your time," she said.

"A little thing called the speed of light got in the way," Jill deadpanned. "Humanity has a colony at Gliese 370 now."

"I know. I'm highly placed. My siblings and I have been working for decades behind the scenes, preparing for your arrival and our liberation."

"You buying this, Reap?" Bull asked.

"For now…but she might be an imposter. How can we tell, with Blends? They could have caught the real Leslie Denham and stolen her memories. The only one who will know for sure is Ezekiel."

"My brother's alive?" Leslie asked, her face delighted.

"Yes, he's fine. At least, he was a few days ago."

"Do not listen to the traitor," one of the yellow-clad women said with venom.

"If I'm a traitor to the Empire, obviously they *should* listen to me, Fiona," Leslie retorted.

"Unless you're just pretending to be a traitor," the woman replied, "and I'm helping convince them…Llewella. Or should I call you *Leslie* now."

Leslie sneered at the other Blend. "You're not nearly as clever and twisted as you think you are."

"That's not what you said the last time you shared my bed."

"I fooled you in to thinking I enjoyed it, didn't I?"

"Ladies, ladies," Repeth broke in. "Don't make me shoot you both." She gestured with her PW5 at Fiona, who had taken a step toward Leslie.

"We should have brought a Blend with us," Bull grumbled.

"As I recall, you vetoed that yourself. You said you didn't want to trade a Marine away for a noncombatant," Repeth said.

"Let's just get them to *Conquest* and we can confirm her identity," Bull replied. "Leslie, here's your first test. Patch us through to Captain Absen on the following frequency," and he gave her confirmation codes and a freq for voice comms.

Leslie took a seat at a console and switched it on. Jill watched her with growing confidence. Something about the way the woman moved reminded her of Skull Denham, and more pointedly of her mother Raphaela. Also, Blends, like Meme, were notorious egoists, unlikely to suicide no matter what the gain. That also made their loyalties questionable…but Rae's children had been born Blends, not made up of Meme and mind-wiped humans. They lacked the memories of life as a Meme, and hopefully, their amoral attitudes.

"Io Base, this is *Conquest*," came Michelle's smooth tones after a few moments. "Drop your ICE for cyber verification."

"Done," Leslie replied after inputting a code and waiting for the signal to make its round trip. Repeth knew *Conquest* was probably swooping toward their position now that the Weapon was out of commission, but doubted they'd use the TacDrive. In normal space, the boat would take at least an hour to arrive.

Moments later, all the boards lit up and froze, with one icon blinking. Leslie looked to Repeth for permission, and then reached out a manicured finger to tap it. A male voice then spoke.

"How's everyone there? The captain would like a SITREP, ASAP. We'll be there in fifty-seven minutes, over." Commander Rick Johnstone's tones betrayed his strain. Repeth realized that of course her husband would be worried, especially as the most Absen would know at this point was a brief summary of the mission results, with its horrendous casualty report.

"Patch this data through," Repeth said to Leslie, and dumped her suit's mission record raw and unencrypted into the ether. Not only would it provide what Absen needed, but would reassure Rick.

"Retransmitted…they should have it shortly," Leslie reported. "What now?"

"Now we wait," Bull said.

"I have one question," Repeth said. "Where do the Meme flush tubes go?"

Leslie replied, "To the backup control center at the Weapon. The laser."

Repeth glanced at Bull and half-shrugged. "Damn. They're vapor now." Then she looked more closely at her commander. "Boss, you okay? Bull?" She was glad of her armor as she grabbed him before he toppled heavily to the floor.

Travel in normal space seemed unbearably slow after the speed of TacDrive, Captain Absen thought. He remembered buying his first car in San Diego as a teenager, and how walking or even riding his bike had suddenly seemed plodding and boring. That's how he felt now. *Getting spoiled*, he chuckled to himself, shifting in the Chair.

Eventually *Conquest* arrived to hover on its jets high above the captured Io base and the smoking hole where the Weapon had been. Reports had flooded in as the gargantuan boat had neared the swift-moving moon of Jupiter. As the comm lag diminished, pinnaces descended full of Michelle's telefactors, which quickly began to clear the rubble.

"How long until the base will be usable?" Absen asked the AI.

"Less than a day to reconnect systems to the armored command sections. A few more to make it permanently livable, as long as I stay near enough to coordinate all my bots. May I remind you that we still have the armed orbital bases to deal with?"

"That's my first concern. Is Bannum down there yet?"

"She was on the first pinnace, and should be at the command section soon. In fact..." The comm crackled, and then a picture of the Sekoi female popped onto the main screen. Absen could see several figures in yellow behind her, and the elbow of a battlesuit at the edge of the display.

"Bannum, have you verified Leslie Denham's identity?" Absen asked.

"I have, Captain. I am certain she is who she claims."

"Thank you. Johnstone, I assume you and Michelle have control of the base computer systems?"

"Piece of cake, sir," Rick replied. "Doesn't look like there has been much advancement in cybernetics since the Meme took over."

"Meme like stability and order, not progress," Bannum replied. "Here." She gestured for a yellow-clad human woman, who stepped forward. "Your Blend."

"Leslie Denham, I presume?" Absen asked.

"In the flesh, Captain Absen. You can't imagine how good it is to see you."

Absen could see the woman's eyes fill with tears and emotion. She reminded him of her mother. "You're right, I can't imagine, and it's good to be back, but we have a lot of work ahead of us," he said. "First on the list is getting those orbitals to defect. Do you think you can do that?"

"I think we can do it together. Can your people synthesize and transmit a view that makes us appear to sit side by side?"

Johnstone nodded as Absen glanced at him.

"Then run the signal through this base and its encryption protocols, please. I will broadcast it throughout the solar system."

Absen waited while the transmission was readied, discussing with Leslie what they would say. When Johnstone gave him the high sign, the admiral spoke.

"Greetings, Jupiter facilities. On behalf of EarthFleet, the true human authority here, I'm asking you to give up your mistaken allegiance to an alien empire and serve humanity again. As you have seen, I have the military power to destroy you, but I'd much rather you take your rightful places alongside us, to restore your freedom and your honor." Absen turned to his right, where he'd been assured the synthesized picture of Leslie Denham would appear, as if they sat together.

Then the yellow-clad woman spoke. "I'm Leslie Denham, a Command Level One Blend you knew until recently as Llewella. Unlike the rest of your overlords, I was not enslaved by the Pure Race. My mother freely decided to blend with Raphael, the one Meme who chose to defect and aid humanity four thousand years ago. Raphaela then married my father, Alan Christopher Denham, a warrior of great renown before the Empire conquered Earth. My siblings and I have worked for decades among you to keep the stories of the earlier days alive. EarthFleet has returned, and with it, liberation. Now is the time to rise up and join your brothers and sisters against the Empire. Strike the oppressors in any way you can. You have nothing to lose but your chains."

"...and we're off," Johnstone said. "Nice speech, sir."

"I think Leslie's will be the more effective."

"Sir," Scoggins interrupted, "We have activity." In the holotank, icons throughout the Jupiter system blazed with energy. "The orbitals are firing at each other!"

"Can we tell who is who?" Absen asked, standing up to gaze intently at the display.

"We're trying to sort that out," Michelle said. "One declared for EarthFleet almost immediately and seems to be trying to convince the others, but as for the rest..."

"Sir, one orbital has destroyed a shipyard."

"Put me on broadcast," Absen snapped. "Orbital platforms, this is Captain Absen. Declare your loyalty to EarthFleet immediately and cease all offensive fire or I will be forced to destroy you. Okuda, get ready to move. Ford, begin hitting noncompliant targets with a minimum particle beam strike starting with the one that fired on the shipyard. Knock them out, but don't burn them to slag. I want prisoners."

"Aye aye, sir," the weapons officer muttered. "Firing."

At half charge, a single energy cannon from *Conquest* reached across a million miles and slammed masses of charged particles into the offending orbital fortress. Wreathed in electrical discharges, it fell silent. "One down..."

Thrice more, great beams flashed across light-seconds, easy shots against nonmaneuvering targets, incapacitating the orbitals that refused to submit. Absen watched as ten icons turned green in the holotank, holding their fire. Soon, more green blossomed as most of the other installations – the three remaining shipyards, the dozens

of mining stations, and the manned PVNs on Ceres –
defected and declared themselves loyal to EarthFleet.

"What do you want to do about the mining stations
and PVNs that haven't acknowledged?" Ford asked,
clearly eager to get in some more gunnery.

"If they have weapons that can threaten anyone else,
and you can pinpoint those weapons, take out the threats.
If not, let them sit there for the moment. They may
change their minds. Hell, some of them may have internal
factions fighting for control. Johnstone, tell Bull to leave
a squad at Io base and get all the rest of the survivors
back to *Conquest*. I may have more work for him to do."

–11–

Lieutenant Cheng looked sadly down at Sergeant Tama and holstered his pistol. The hardest thing he'd ever done in his young life had been to put a bullet into the man's head, but Tama had adamantly refused to give up his oath to the Empire, and had tried to fire on another defecting orbital.

Even now, Cheng's hands shook with reaction. He'd never killed anyone before, and it made him want to vomit. In fact, he availed himself of a trashcan from beneath the desk, turning away from the sergeant's staring eyes and the blood pooled on the deck. Once he'd emptied his stomach, Cheng keyed for a robot to come clean up.

"I've eliminated two more loyalists," Captain O'Rourke said as he stepped back into the command center, pistol smoking in his hand.

Cheng had no idea how the man could seem calm after killing twice. It made him wonder about his commander, and how long he might have been part of the resistance movement that everyone had heard rumors of.

O'Rourke gazed alertly around the room, not lowering his weapon. "Chief Shamblin, continue broadcasting our declaration of allegiance to EarthFleet, but maintain all systems at the ready."

"Aye, sir." The chief looked pale at the enormity of what they had done, but seemed determined. "What about Earth, though? Will they punish our families?"

"I don't know."

Cheng found himself suddenly happy the rebels – *EarthFleet*, he reminded himself – had destroyed the terror weapon on the moon that had been pointed at Earth for his whole life, an explicit threat to any who would oppose the Empire. Even though there was another moon-based laser, it pointed outward, away from Earth and lovely Brenda's legs. "What do we do now, sir?"

"I don't know that either," O'Rourke replied. "Wait for orders from our new commander."

"Yes. Of course." The reminder of authority comforted Cheng. Freedom sounded attractive as a concept, but what did one do with it? Then he remembered Brenda and thought of one thing he'd do. "Sir, do you think we might try to send personal messages to Earth?"

"Somehow, Lieutenant, I doubt that would be healthy for anyone receiving the transmission."

"Yes, sir." Captain O'Rourke was certainly the smartest man he knew. Cheng resolved to observe closely and learn.

–12–

Spooky Nguyen watched Trissk sleep curled up on a divan in the corner of *Roger*'s sumptuous virtual reality space. He ached all over from sparring with the big cat, even if the effect was largely psychosomatic, but was happy he had finally tired Trissk out. "Thank the gods," he said as he poured himself a tall glass of virtual Scotch. "Can you keep him under a little extra time?"

"My ethics will stretch that far, yes," Ezekiel replied drily. "He'll never know the difference, and it'll keep us all from going bonkers."

"No sign of your mother?"

"If there was, we'd know."

Spooky sipped from his glass, leaving the obvious unspoken: *maybe she's dead.* More than eighty years had passed since they'd left Earth's solar system. Anything could have happened. "At least the broadcast from your sister is good news."

"Yes…" Ezekiel mused. "But we're light-hours away from Jupiter, and from Earth for that matter." He stood and swung his arms. "We have to head back, I think. All the action is going to be on Earth. We need to be there to help foment rebellion. For all we know, she's there now."

"Fine by me," Spooky replied. "You think we can sneak by the Meme?"

"We have the latest codes from the Sentries, and we'll keep on our toes, so yes, I think so. If not…we'll run back to *Conquest* like a scalded dog."

"I'll feel better when I'm down on a planet," Spooky mused. "I'm at my best among people."

Ezekiel snorted.

"What?" Spooky swirled his Scotch.

"Yes, you're such a people person."

Spooky did not reply. Instead, he asked, "Can you make this thing go any faster?"

"I can make it seem that way, if you want. I'll just have *Roger* speed up your sense of time passing until something happens. Take a seat."

Sitting down, Spooky set his glass on an end table, closed his eyes and folded his hands. "Ready." A moment seemed to pass, and then Ezekiel was calling his name. "Yes?" he said, opening his eyes.

"We're entering translunar space. You want to see what's going to kill us?"

Standing up, Spooky saw that Trissk was awake again, and he and Bogrin stood at the wide plate glass forward port. Through its preternaturally clear non-substance he could see Earthrise over Luna. Near the moon loomed eight Destroyers, scaled up by Roger's organic VR to be visible. Behind he could see Earth's four orbital fortresses, superdreadnought-sized weapons platforms composing a relatively cheap last line of defense.

Spooky cleared his throat. "I'm no space tactician, but this seems like a poor route to take, straight past all the enemy eyes."

Ezekiel smiled, reaching out to manipulate large, shiny metal controls. In response to his adjustment, the view swung radically, as if they themselves had been thrown magically sideways and upward. "I just wanted you to see that view. In reality, we're coming in as far from the Destroyers as possible. I'm counting on their underlings on the orbital fortresses not looking too closely at a Meme-grown ship like *Roger*."

"So this is a true view?" Bogrin rumbled from Ezekiel's other elbow. He gestured at the single orbital fortress visible well off to one side.

"Yes. Earth is between us and Luna, and since the Destroyers are all parked there next to the Weapon for mutual defense, they can't see us directly. We have Meme recognition codes...why do you ask?"

"Because the orbital fortress' main weapons array seems to be lining up on us. You may want to ask *Roger* to begin evasive maneuvers."

"Shit." Before Ezekiel completed the expletive the view swung wildly, though the four bipeds inside *Roger* did not feel it through the VR. "Roger, get us down and into the water as fast as you can!" Abruptly their perspective stabilized, rock-steady except for its motion past the orbital fortress. "I've reset the program so it appears as if we're pointed toward the enemy, but in reality, *Roger* is blasting for splashdown."

Ponderously, the spherical orbital continued to turn itself and its large cluster of lasers in their direction. When it seemed to line up, it fired. Beams lanced out, visible only because of the simulation, crisscrossing around them but not striking. The artificial steadiness of the virtual reality made the danger surreal. In reality, just one of those beams would instantly fry little *Roger* and everyone within. They would never feel a hit before they died.

Slowly, slowly their point of view sank toward the blue surface of Earth, dodging lasers and railgun bullets. The glow of atmospheric friction crept in from the edges of the viewport, and moments later they plunged into the waters of the western Pacific. "I've brought us down near the Marianas Trench, and that's where we're –"

Then the clean, comfortable simulation shattered, and Spooky found himself naked and immobilized inside his biogel coffin. He almost threw up as his body and mind tried to reject the transition and crawl back into a place that wasn't there anymore.

Whatever happened must have been severe, even catastrophic. Only Ezekiel or *Roger* knew, but Spooky wasn't about to just lie here like cake in a pan. Scrabbling with his hand, he found the large biomechanical pushplate and shoved on it with all four fingertips.

In response, living probes withdrew from all of his orifices and the coffin he was in opened to vomit him out onto the warm, living deck. Rolling over and coughing effluvium, he crawled to the largest coffin nearby and began to pound on it, his fist making meaty smacks.

Whether from his efforts or something Bogrin did, the enclosure split, revealing the half-ton Sekoi inside and repeating the procedure that had ejected Spooky. A moment later, the two stood, looking at each other.

"Well, friend," Bogrin said, his real voice rough in the moist air, "we live."

"For the moment," Spooky replied. "I'd feel a lot better if I knew what was going on. Is *Roger* injured? Should we try to wake Ezekiel?"

"As Blend, I monitor some of *Roger*'s sensations. I believe laser struck water above us as we descended into ocean, flash-boiling it. Ship is in pain, but will recover. Cannot maintain VR space for us. We must wait."

–13–

Bull awoke, his heart pounding, and came close to panicking. He hit the eject button and rolled out of his armor as it cracked open. Doc Horton grabbed him and tried to stabilize him, but the small woman couldn't prevent the big man from sprawling on *Conquest's* flight deck.

How did I get here?

"I've got a gurney, Major ben Tauros, if you'll just hold still." The doctor signaled two telefactors, which quickly and precisely lifted Bull's half-conscious frame onto the rolling bed. "You're back aboard, and you're going to the infirmary."

"I'm fine," he muttered, and then his head seemed to swell up like a balloon and his eyes went fuzzy. "Just hungry."

"No, you're not fine," the doctor said firmly, walking alongside for a few steps as the machines carted him away. "You're concussed, you have stress fractures running throughout your body, and half your cybernetics are burnt out. If not for your support systems you'd be dead. Now just stay horizontal and hope for no brain damage. Not that anyone would notice." Horton muttered this last.

"I heard that," Bull mumbled, then let himself fade from consciousness as the gurney stabbed him with a needle.

***

Sergeant Major Repeth traded looks with Horton as she stepped out of her own armor onto the deck. "We got nine or ten other bad ones, Doc," she said as two armored Marines carried a third one in. "Set her on the deck," Repeth ordered, then keyed in the standard code to crack the armor. It opened along the seams like a split lobster tail, allowing the medical bots to lift the injured Marine out and place her on another gurney. A dozen more automated beds waited behind with perfect patience, their trauma arms ready to help stabilize the casualties.

"This one is expectant," Horton said, peering down at the remains of a man inside another battered set of armor. "Vitals are flat, no brainwave. Record TOD at...1223.40 hours."

Repeth stared at the remains of Corporal Salen, remembering his ready smile as he spotted for her in the gym. *Another good kid gone because of the Meme and their lust for domination.* She hoped losing half the company had been worth it.

Moving on down the line, she helped Horton and two medics with the rest of the casualties, paying special attention to the five Ryss. All of these had been severely wounded and left behind by their own. Amazingly, all had survived. *Tough critters,* Repeth thought. None of those that had made it through to the Weapon had lived, but the HUD network had recorded Slash's last moments before he blew the nuke.

Someone grabbed Jill from behind and she almost clocked him before she saw it was Rick. Burying herself in his arms for a moment, she fought back tears, saving them for later.

"This is the worst part, isn't it?" he said. "But I'm glad it isn't you in the infirmary."

"Or worse, you mean?" Repeth shook her head to dry her eyes. "Ultimate liability clause in every Marine contract. You know that."

"I do, but I'm selfish enough to be happy you didn't cash out. Come on, let's go get a drink."

"I have to –" She gestured at her armor and the Marines sufficiently unhurt to walk away from their own.

"Let the bots tend to the armor. Gunderson can shepherd the troops."

"No. It doesn't work like that. I make sure all of my people are taken care of before I'm off duty. And I need to go see Bull." Repeth saw a flash of something very like jealousy cross behind Rick's eyes, but right then she didn't care.

"All right," Rick said with more than a hint of chill in his voice. "When you're all done, I'll be around somewhere." He stalked away, shaking off her hand.

"Trouble in paradise?" Master Sergeant Gunderson said from her elbow.

Turning, Repeth punched the man in his meaty chest hard enough to stagger him. "Shut your cake-hole, you prick. When I want lip from you, I'll beat it out of you," she snarled.

"All right, all right," he said with upraised hands and a triumphant smile. Needling her had been a favorite game of his ever since Repeth had spurned his advances back on Earth and she knew he'd just scored a point, but she didn't care. Everyone seemed to want a piece of her and she really wasn't in the mood.

"Since you're untouched," she said to Gunderson with venom, "you can do the debrief and put everyone not in the infirmary to bed. Have a full report in my queue by 1800. Then you can start a double guard shift on the brig. I'm going to check on the wounded."

"There's no one in the brig, Sergeant Major," Gunderson said as his face fell.

"Then guard yourself. Just as long as you're there and awake. I'll be checking the logs."

Gunderson looked sour and stayed silent.

"Acknowledge, Marine!" Repeth snapped.

"Aye aye, Sergeant Major!" Gunderson retorted, drawing himself to attention.

She left him standing there fuming, and then headed for the infirmary.

Later, Captain Absen waved her to a seat in his office after offering her a cigarette. She declined, waiting for him to light up.

He stared at the burning cancer stick in his hand for a moment. "You know, I rarely smoke, even though it's not particularly risky anymore. I drink a little, I read a lot, I eat…and I work. That's about it. Do you know why?"

Repeth thought furiously, wondering what her commander was getting at. She'd expected to give him a firsthand report as Bull usually did, not share some kind of moment. That was what officers were for – standing between her and the skipper. "No, sir, I don't."

"Good. Then probably no one else does either. Whiskey?" Absen reached for the bottle.

"All right, sir." It seemed impolite to decline both offers of shared luxury, so she took the glass and sipped at the smoky liquor.

"So this Blend. Leslie Denham, she calls herself?"

"Yes, sir."

"Do you believe her?"

"That she's who she says she is? Tentatively, yes." Repeth felt on much firmer ground now, discussing work. "The other Blend that took a shot at her, the one who calls himself Brand, wasn't playing around and had no way of knowing my response would be nonlethal. Blends aren't big on self-sacrifice, so that is a point in her favor. Also, she just...feels right."

"I'm going to interview her, but I wanted your impression. Anything else that will help me?"

Repeth sighed. "I didn't know Raphaela had more children. Ezekiel never said anything to me and I've been on several missions with him. I can't think of any reason to keep a secret like that for so many years."

"OPSEC. Need to know." Absen shrugged. "I guess for now I'll have to accept Bannum's and your judgment. I've put out an encrypted broadcast for Ezekiel to contact us, but heard nothing. They either didn't get the transmission or are maintaining EMCON for now. Either way, we're on our own."

"One thing I did think of," Repeth said. "Blends are rumored to be able to influence people if they can touch them – probably some kind of biochemical mind control. But it's highly unlikely a Blend can influence an AI."

"Good thinking. Michelle?"

"Yes, Captain?" came Conquest's voice from the speaker in the overhead.

"Escort Leslie Denham here, will you? And make sure she stays under full surveillance at all times."

"Aye aye, sir. Five minutes."

When the door opened and the woman in yellow stepped in ahead of Michelle's avatar, Absen stood up involuntarily. On the vidscreen Leslie had reminded him of her mother Rae, but in person it was déjà vu all over again. The force of her personality, her presence and poise, brought long-buried feelings to the surface so strongly that he excused himself abruptly to the cabin's head behind him. Inside, he flushed the toilet as an excuse, splashed water on his face, and composed himself in the mirror before stepping back out, pointedly wiping his hands on a clean white towel.

"Nice to finally meet you," Leslie said before Absen could speak. "I've seen you many times in pictures and records, of course. All of my brothers and sisters have." She did not hold out her hand; neither did Absen.

"How many brothers and sisters?" Absen asked, sitting down at his desk.

"I am one of a set of quads, two boys and two girls, and then there's Ezekiel, whom you know."

"Rae had no more children?" Absen inquired. For some reason, he felt the answer important to him.

"She considered it. Genetic material from my father was available – is still available, I presume – but she never did. I don't know why." Leslie cocked her head knowingly. "Ah."

Absen ignored this gesture and its implication. "So where is your mother?"

A smile leaked from Leslie's lips. "You care."

"I care very much. If anyone survived to coordinate a resistance movement, it would have been her, and you confirmed that with your actions. Now stop playing games and tell me what I need to know."

"My, my. Touchy, aren't we?"

Absen kept tight check of his emotions, reminding himself that the current population of Earth system did not necessarily see him as the supreme commander of anything. Not everyone would give him the easy deference he was used to. "Ms. Denham, I see you've become accustomed to your position in the Meme hierarchy. I'm wondering if you've bought into the Empire's elitism even as you worked to undermine it. While you are no doubt very capable, that yellow tunic doesn't mean the same thing in a free society – or in EarthFleet."

"Meaning I'll have to earn my way all over again?"

"Meaning you'll go farther without that bitchy air of smug superiority. If you really are as smart as you seem to think you are, you'll condescend less and help more even if it's only out of self-interest." Absen's eyes bored into Leslie's until finally she dropped them with a graceful dip of her head.

"As you say, Captain. I apologize. What can I do to *help*?"

"I'd really like to contact your mother."

"Unfortunately she's on Earth, as far as I know. The last time I heard from her she was in Ulan Bator. For security, we only communicate occasionally, through cutouts and drops. If you want to talk to her, you'll have to wait for her to contact you...or you can skip that part and free Earth."

Absen sighed. "That's my goal, but I had hoped...never mind. You'll have to do. First, how likely are other Blends to rebel?"

"They will not, unless the Empire has clearly already lost the fight. They are too young to be bored with their power and privilege."

"That's what I've been told. All right, what about the defense forces?"

Leslie rummaged in her pockets until she came up with a pack of cigarettes and a lighter. "Sorry, all the Yellows smoke, and I had to *blend in*, *ha*. I've become addicted." She lit one and took a deep drag.

Absen glanced at Repeth with a twitch of his lips. "No problem. Defense forces?"

"They're loyal enough on the surface, but we've made special efforts to penetrate them, so they are riddled with Skulls."

"Skulls?"

"A nickname for resistance fighters. After my father."

"Of course. So...I'm particularly interested in the heavy orbitals around Earth."

Leslie paced a moment, leaning over Absen's desk without comment to pick up the ashtray he had used earlier. "You're wondering if they will turn against the Meme like the Sekoi did at Gliese 370." She smiled at Absen's clear surprise. "I was highly placed in the defense forces, Captain. I've studied your battles...all of them."

"So will they turn?"

"I would have said no before you destroyed the Earth-facing Weapon, but now...if the right moment comes, our agents may be able to precipitate a mass defection, like they did here in the Jupiter system."

"All right. That's all I need from you for now. Michelle, take her down to be thoroughly debriefed by Fleede and his team. You sit in too. Make it exhaustive and detailed. He'll love that."

"Aye aye, Captain," *Conquest*'s avatar replied.

"Captain," Leslie asked as she ground out her cigarette, "we've waited a long time. It's 2161. When are you going to free Earth?"

Absen stood. "Have patience, Ms. Denham. Aren't Blends famous for it? Believe it or not, I've already started."

14

Latest reports since conquest of the Jupiter system two weeks ago showed more than eighty percent of the PVNs on Ceres back up and functioning, churning out spare parts and new war materiel. *Conquest* was now in orbit above the planetoid, with Michelle updating and reprogramming the thousands of factories to build more modern gear, as well as previously forbidden items like fusion warheads and missiles.

In that time, the eight Destroyers had not moved from their position near the moon. Absen wondered whether the top Meme leadership had been eliminated with the destruction of the gargantuan Guardians. Certainly their ships seemed to be doing little beyond eating captured asteroids, presumably fattening their stores and fuel.

The human defense forces also seemed paralyzed, as if waiting for Absen's next move. It chafed at him to delay, but he wanted *Conquest* at full capability, and incorporating the best of the defecting humans in the Jupiter system to supplement his Marines and Aerospace rosters took time.

While thousands had volunteered, he had only so many trainers, simulators, and fighters. Even the pilots among them had never been allowed to fly armed spacecraft; they were limited to ground and orbital defenses. Obviously the Meme did not trust their underlings, and for good reason.

Absen was glad the purges were over with, though. Of the over one million human workers, crew and defenders scattered among Jupiter's moons and satellites, a hundred thousand had been killed, often in pitched hand-to-hand battles between loyalists and defectors. Once those opting for freedom had won, more loyalists had been hunted down and executed without any semblance of due process. Some were hardcore supporters of the Empire, but others probably died to settle personal scores, or simply by mistake, caught in crossfire. Even a small-scale civil war was an ugly, brutal thing, and he simply didn't have enough people to bring order by force.

Absen wondered where the Eden Plague's virtue effect was in all of this. Doctor Horton believed that, without any tradition of freedom or morality beyond the laws of the Empire, there was little conscience to enhance. Cast adrift from the twisted ethics of subservience, it would take time for society to adjust to a more just and benevolent model, even with all the new information the populace was being bombarded with. He wasn't so sure; instinctively he thought humans must have a sense of right and wrong apart from purely learned behavior.

Nature versus nurture again, he thought. *Which dominates?*

Eventually the violence had burned itself out, even faster when Absen appointed Leslie Denham as his civilian governor. Backed up by his authority and assisted by the humans' habit of deference to the Yellows, the Blend had quickly sorted things out, and now relative peace prevailed.

"We've got to figure out a way to free Earth," Absen said to Michelle Conquest as he sat, otherwise alone, in his office. He'd taken to talking to the AI a lot; she was the perfect aide, always available, reliable, with facts and analyses at her fingertips, and seemed to have matured with the increase in her responsibilities. Only a few systems remained off limits to her, and he suspected she could seize those any time she wanted.

We've passed far beyond the point of no return, trusting her with our lives, he thought to himself. *God help us if she ever loses her mind like Desolator did.*

"The staff has already put together a comprehensive campaign plan, sir," Conquest replied from the speaker overhead. "It just takes time to build up the industrial capacity of Jupiter system and then manufacture an invasion fleet. I know you are impatient, but a deliberate approach is guaranteed to succeed, whereas haste risks failure."

"Nothing is guaranteed to succeed, Michelle," Absen said. "The longer we wait, the more time there is for us to lose our current advantage."

"I'd call it a standoff, sir," she replied. "Two unassailable bases with insufficient associated mobile forces to beat the other. However, we have superior technology, and thus when we have built up our forces, we shall win."

"Technology…yes, I've been thinking about that. Let me outline an idea I've had, and you see if you can poke holes in it."

"All right, sir. Shoot."

"Funny you should put it that way…" Over the next hour, Absen explained what he wanted. Once he had the basics worked out, he called Ellis Nightingale to his office.

"What can I help you with, sir?" the tall weapons engineer asked as he folded himself into a chair.

"I need a new weapon, Ellis. Something that will allow us to break the standoff we have going here."

Nightingale cleared his throat. "As I understand it, sir, in a few months we should have a fleet strong enough to beat the Meme at Earth."

"That may be true, but in a few months, almost anything could happen. The Destroyers could decide to cut their losses, bomb Earth's remaining population and run away."

"We could easily chase them down…yes, but I see that wouldn't keep them from genocide."

Absen said, "Or a Meme fleet could show up. Or some clever loyalist could come up with a technological advancement we haven't anticipated, now that they have a real threat staring down at them. Maybe they figure out how to weaponize antimatter the way we have, and we can't stand up to Exploders any more than they can."

Ellis ran his hand over his close-cropped hair. "All right. Maybe we do need to move faster. But a weapon isn't really the problem, right, sir? We need a delivery system that can allow us to take down the moon laser. Once that goes, the system will fall like dominoes. *Conquest* can beat eight Destroyers in a straight-up fight – or even sixteen, if they all divide. They *have* been gorging."

"If you can make my idea work, the delivery system and the weapon are one and the same thing."

"What is it, then?"

"Michelle, bring up that diagram, will you?" On the wall screen appeared a schematic, the design of a small ship.

Nightingale stood to look closely at its densely packed notations. "I see it, but I'm not really sure what I'm looking at. It has a TacDrive of sorts, though barely enough power and battery capacity for one pulse. No crew quarters, a rudimentary computer, sensors, thrusters...I can't see what you'd use this for."

"Think like a Meme, Ellis. That's what gave me the idea. You put your finger on it before when you said we needed a delivery system."

The big man stared a moment longer, then he said, "Oh. Oh, that's brilliant. Sir, you've done it. This thing will work, I believe. It's a quantum leap forward in capability. No enemy fixed target will ever be safe once we get these babies into production."

"Nor friendly ones, either," Absen said, his expression earnest. "They've already seen what our TacDrive can do. I'm amazed the Meme haven't replicated the Ryss stardrive, though of course they never captured one of their ships...but I'm not sure they ever had a motivated underling population before. The Ryss raiders wiped out the populations of hundreds of planets, and spacegoing Meme have no industrial capacity or great facility with complex, non-biological machinery. But now..."

"Now since they saw ours, the Meme for sure have loyalists working on a lightspeed drive, and..."

"And the only way to defend against something heavy coming in at lightspeed is not to be there. We can't afford to wait until they come up with their own TacDrive system – or much more simply, weapons like this one." Absen gestured at the diagram.

"This is the V-2 of lightspeed weapons, sir," Ellis breathed, touching the screen almost reverently. "An unguided but unstoppable ballistic missile."

"Not quite the same, Ellis. Unguided, but not unaimed. If we fire it precisely enough, we should be able to hit something the size of the Weapon on Luna all the way from here. Salvo enough of them, and we'll take down the laser. Once that's done, *Conquest* moves in and cleans up the Destroyers. So right now, this is your first and only priority. However," Absen shook a finger at Nightingale, "this is top secret, need-to-know. Only you, me and Conquest know about it. With a million humans in the Jupiter system, we can't be sure there aren't still loyalist spies that could figure out what we're doing. This stays aboard *Conquest*. Bring in whoever you need, but keep it to a minimum, you understand? The last thing I want is something like this coming *our* direction."

Nightingale rubbed the back of his neck. "Yes, sir. I'll need Quan's help on the power systems, and Okuda for guidance and navigation, and Michelle...that should be all for now."

"Fine. I'll want a daily report. How soon for a proto-type?"

"A month."

"You have two weeks."

15

Spooky sat lotus on the warm skin of the floor inside *Steadfast Roger*'s small life support chamber, meditating. With both Ezekiel and Roger unresponsive, there was little else to do. Bogrin and Trissk lay curled against the walls, dozing. Faint glowing spots on the walls allowed them to see, but the air was getting stuffy.

They'd been trapped a week, and it had been almost a day since the food and water had run out. The bodily wastes they'd deposited in one place had not been absorbed, but *Roger*'s inner skin and the sarcophagus that held Ezekiel remained warm, pliant and alive. Periodically Spooky would gently tap on the coffin-like thing, hoping to rouse the Blend.

This time, when he did, Bogrin rolled to a sitting position. "We must try stronger measures."

Spooky nodded in resignation. "Go ahead. We need water. Or we need to break out of here."

Bogrin rubbed his ham fists together, then licked his palms with a dry, sticky tongue. "Almost too late," he remarked, then slapped them down onto the floor by his thighs and closed his eyes.

Spooky watched the Blend try to establish contact with the living ship, hoping, hoping. Minutes passed before the Sekoi's eyes popped open. "I have explained situation. Ship is healing. Ezekiel will awaken soon." With that, Bogrin removed his paws from the quivering floor with a faint sucking sound.

A moment later, the sarcophagus split and Ezekiel sat up, rubbing mucus off his face. "Sorry that took so long. *Roger* was badly burned by seawater flash-heating from the final beam strikes. I had to mute the pain and keep him unconscious or he might have given up and died." Ezekiel shuddered, his eyes unfocused. "I think he's out of danger, but he's going to be of little use to us for a while. Unfortunately we have another issue. Something is approaching us. I have to go back in."

"Can we help?" Spooky asked as Ezekiel lay back down.

"No. But here's your gear. If everything goes to hell, swim for it, and good luck." A seam in the living wall split and pressure suits, clothing and weapons spilled out in a heap. The three began sorting it out as the sarcophagus closed back over Ezekiel's face.

"Not encouraging," Trissk said, pulling on his battle harness. "At least if we have to cut our way out, I have this." He held up his white crystal hotblade, unheated.

"Just keep that thing turned off," Spooky replied. "We stay here as long as we can."

"Who put you in charge, Ape?" Trissk snarled.

Spooky shrugged and smiled coldly. "We splashed down above a trench more then ten kilometers in depth. Who knows how deep we are now? If you cut your way out, the pressure will crush us."

Trissk's retort was cut off by a sudden shift in the floor under their feet, and then it tipped quite steeply for a moment before leveling off again. "What above All is going on?" the cat asked, looking around as if the walls would cave in on him.

Spooky knew the Ryss was on the edge of panic from the close confines, and he prepared to take physical measures to render Trissk unconscious if he must. Soon, though, the chamber stabilized and he thought he could hear the rushing of water and another, deeper sound, like whale song. He placed a hand on the wall and after a moment Bogrin did the same.

"We move," the Sekoi said.

"But not with Roger's normal mode of locomotion. I've been inside him underwater on Koio. This sounds nothing like that."

"Meaning what?" Trissk asked.

"Something else is moving us."

"Ezekiel's 'something'?"

"Presumably. Let us be calm, and wait."

Trissk slashed his claws down the wall, scratching gouges in the moist skin and drawing bloodlike fluid. "I am tired of waiting!"

Spooky stood, but before he could take action, the big Sekoi had interposed his bulk, facing the cat. "I grow tired of your whining. Desist, or I will subdue you," Bogrin said.

Trissk lifted his crystal sword as if to strike, and then Bogrin's mouth opened and he roared, an elephantine bellow that stunned the others with a wall of sound.

Trissk staggered backward and Bogrin lashed out, knocking the blade from his paw. "Are you warrior or child?" the Sekoi asked with all the power in his lungs.

The Ryss darted around the big alien and fetched up near Spooky, with nowhere else to go. While Spooky could not call Trissk's appearance exactly terrified, he did seem quite unnerved by five hundred angry kilos of gray-skinned pachyderm.

"I think damaging our conveyance is a bad idea," Spooky said mildly, ready to try for a knockout if Trissk wouldn't calm down.

Panting, the Ryss repeatedly unsheathed and resheathed his claws, and then took a deep breath and settled back onto his haunches against the wall. "I will wait," he said, closing his eyes and lowering his head, still panting.

Spooky exchanged glances with Bogrin and they both moved as far from Trissk as possible. The big cat seemed to lapse into a near coma after a while, and his tongue lolled. Bogrin examined the wall slashes and shook his head. "Should be healing, but are not. *Roger* is not well."

"Nothing we can do right now. Leave him be. No need for our suits, either. Somehow I suspect we won't be getting dumped into the water right away."

"You understand situation?"

"Let's just say I have a strong suspicion."

Hours later, Ezekiel's coffin opened and he leaped to put on his clothing and suit. "Trissk, get up. We're about to have visitors."

Spooky nodded, Buddha-like. "Bring everything," he said. "Right?"

"Yes. We won't be returning to *Roger* anytime soon, I suspect."

"Explain," Trissk hissed as he gathered his possessions. "Will we fight? Or try to escape?"

"Neither," Ezekiel said. "Unless I miss my guess, we're about to be drafted into the rebellion."

"That is, if we're not killed outright," Spooky murmured. "You two stay back. Let them see us *apes* at the start, shall we? And Ezekiel...do you think it wise to be wearing your yellows?"

"Probably not." He quickly stripped out of the golden silks and stuffed them back in the compartment, sealing it up with his hand, leaving him in a utilitarian jumpsuit. "Hey, what are these slashes?" he asked, running his hand over the damaged wall where it still oozed pus.

"Someone got...restless," Spooky answered.

"Dammit, Trissk. And Bogrin," Ezekiel said, "don't tell them you're a Blend yet. If they are sharp, they'll figure one of us must be to control a Meme ship. Might as well be me. If we're lucky, we'll be able to contact one of my family. Now –"

Just then the wall quivered and split, forming a misshapen hole.

"What the hell are you doing, you idiot? You're hurting my ship!" Ezekiel yelled at the man standing there holding a sprayer. Behind, others raised weapons.

Even as Ezekiel spread his hands, placating, Spooky slipped past the first man with cybernetic speed and disarmed the other two with economical motions. As if by magic, the two guns now pointed toward the invaders. "Let's everyone keep still, shall we?" he said.

One of the disarmed guards, a small woman, reached quite slowly up to remove her faceplate, revealing bright blue hair framing a Eurasian face. "Who are you…people?" Her accent was tinged with Australian tones, and the last word came out as a disbelieving question as she caught sight of Bogrin and Trissk. "Holy mother of God. Aliens."

"What the hell did you use on the wall?" Ezekiel said, stepping forward to seize the small pressure tank and spray gun from the first man.

"It's a secretion that forces ship walls to retract. It's not harmful," the man said defensively.

"I'll decide what's harmful when my ship is involved."

"Wait, please." the woman said, apparently the one in charge. "This is all…look, whatever's going on is way above my pay grade, and I have orders to bring you to the Raven. My boss. Will you come?"

"It's not like we have too much choice, correct?" Spooky said. He liked the look of this one, despite, or perhaps because of, the blue hair. She very much reminded him of Ann, his lost love.

"Well…" The woman's mouth quirked upward, staring at the barrel of the gun pointed at her.

Spooky glanced at Ezekiel, then the other two, before addressing the woman again. "Obviously we can't stand here for the next few hours. I presume it will take that long to reach your deep base."

"How do you...?"

"I'm sorry, we neglected the introductions." Spooky abruptly lowered the weapons and, with motions too fast to follow, stripped out their magazines and ejected the chambered rounds, handing the empty guns back to their owners. "I'm Tran Pham Nguyen. This is Ezekiel Denham, Bogrin, and Trissk. We'd like to join the rebellion."

"Tran Pham Nguyen, huh? You got balls, calling yourself that, but then, you do have some moves. What's with that word 'rebellion'? And where the hell did you get a Meme ship, anyway?"

"I'd rather tell our story only once, if you don't mind, miss –"

"Alkina. Major Naomi Alkina, EarthFleet Marines."

Spooky smiled faintly. "Nice to see our descendants keeping a hand in. What relation are you to Ann Alkina?"

"Lady Ann was my great-great aunt, I am told. I never met her."

"Was?"

"She died in the Third Holocaust."

"I'm sorry, dear grandniece," Spooky murmured in Vietnamese.

This new Alkina merely look at him quizzically. Perhaps she had not learned the language.

Unexpectedly Spooky found himself threatened by an unfamiliar wave of emotions - grief, regret, anger. He'd thought himself prepared for Ann's death, but he realized in that moment he had held out the unreasoning hope she had survived. After all, she had been a powerful figure in

Australia, with access to deep bunkers and all the resources of covert operations.

"Just who the hell are you, anyway?" Alkina asked again.

Spooky spread his hands. "I am he whom you see before you. No more, no less." Gazing at the young woman before him sparked thoughts he decided to keep to himself.

For now.

***

Major Alkina and her two subordinates remained aloof after leading the four infiltrators down living passageways, through another hole forced in *Roger*'s tough outer hull, and into further, healthier corridors of flesh. Clearly, this was another Meme ship, a larger one, and better lit, with arrangement to transport personnel in relative comfort outside of bio-VR coffins. They debouched in a chamber large enough so the two groups could stare at each other across the floor and speak in low tones without being overheard.

Without being overheard by *ordinary* senses. Spooky's cybernetics easily picked up the tiniest whisper, and he suspected Trissk's twitching ears could as well. It hardly mattered, as the guards said little beyond remarking on the appearance of the aliens.

"You'd think people facing Meme and their various Purelings wouldn't be startled by aliens," Ezekiel said.

"I think their surprise is of our alliance," Bogrin said. "To them, all aliens are enemies, no? Now they must change view."

"Good point. Trissk, how are you doing?"

"I am in hell. Why did I come along on this journey?" Trissk snarled.

Ezekiel chuckled. "As I recall, it was because you thought life aboard *Conquest* was too confining."

That seemed to shut the cat down, and with a muted yowl he threw himself onto a sofa-like piece of furniture extruded from the floor. The others exchanged glances and also settled down to wait.

Hours passed. Spooky took time to talk to his grandniece, who slowly came to accept his account and identity as truth.

Finally, the sound of passage through water diminished, and then died. Major Alkina escorted the four through more twists and turns, finally leading them to a rather ordinary-looking office, except for its obvious biological construction. After showing them there, she and the guards withdrew at a word from the sole occupant.

From behind a desk rose a tall, slim man with no hair and deep-set eyes. He stared at Ezekiel, face dour, ignoring the rest. "So you finally deign to return."

Nonplussed, Ezekiel stepped forward, hand extended. "I'm Ezekiel Denham, but you already seem to know that. And you are...?"

The man's smile held nothing of warmth in it, strongly reminding Spooky of Skull Denham. His mind raced for a moment, and then he deduced the identity of the man who stood before them. "Ezekiel," he said, a warning in his voice, as the tall man reached for the other's hand in turn.

When their palms met the two men froze, as if locked in a contest. Spooky waited, ready to intervene, but knew whatever passed between them was not for him. Not yet, anyway. He'd long toyed with the idea of Blending with some form of Meme if the chance presented itself, but had never found the right opportunity.

After more than a minute, the two released their grips. "Do you understand, now?" Ezekiel asked.

"Do you?" the other countered. "Am I supposed to forgive you for abandoning us? Mother was inconsolable."

"Bullshit, Charles," Ezekiel replied. "Or should I call you Raven? Or even Ray? You've completely changed your appearance. Cellular alteration? You look like Dad, now."

The tall man shrugged. "Raven will do. *Nevermore, nevermore the chains* is a rallying cry. My people have never heard that other name."

"Because you hid who you were. You know, Mother approved of me joining *Conquest*, and since the Meme half of her has lived through four millennia, and we have every expectation of very long lives, there's no way she got as upset as you imply."

"Have it your way. I know what I saw when I looked at her. Like her heart had been ripped out."

Ezekiel's mouth curled up in a bitter grimace. "Maybe you don't know what you saw. Maybe it was someone else she was missing. Maybe you substituted your own feelings for hers. Charles, I'm sorry I had to leave, but Task Force *Conquest* needed a Blend, and you four were too vital to the war effort. In fact, as you now know if you'll examine the memories I just gave you, without a Blend to talk to the Sekoi, we'd never have convinced them to rebel, and that turned the tide of battle. Without a Blend there, a million people would be dead and there would be no hope of liberating Earth."

Charles the Raven sneered. "You are full of yourself, aren't you? While you slept the decades away and played your spy games elsewhere, I've been fighting a brutal and unending war against our enslavers. But there's far from 'no hope.' At least, there was hope before you showed up. Now you people might have destroyed our best chance to throw off the yoke. We may all end up dead, or in a far worse position, thanks to your Captain Absen and his premature actions."

"Excuse me," Spooky interjected. "May I suggest you two put aside your family squabbles for a moment? If the situation is dire and there are unrevealed and important factors, fixing the problems and not the blame seems the best course of action."

"Spooky Nguyen," said Charles, still sneering. "Another who abandoned his post seeking glory." He gestured at the aliens. "At least these two are innocent of your crimes. Perhaps I should deal with them."

"Perhaps you are allowing yourself to be blinded by emotion," Spooky replied mildly. "We can assist you, but only if you explain the local situation. That is why we came — to make personal contact. Not to be heroes, or seize your movement for ourselves. To help liberate Earth."

"There would be a lot more to liberate if all of you had stayed to fight the Meme." This time, Spooky heard unbounded, bottomless bitterness in Charles' voice as the man locked eyes with Ezekiel. "Mother lived, but Stephanie and Andrew died in the Destroyer strikes that killed ninety-five percent of the population. Only those in the deep shelters survived. Then, when most came out, the Empire took over to begin forced breeding and rebuilding programs. Mother sneaked a ship down here in the confusion, and for the last fifty years we've expanded and spread our bases under the oceans, striking and running, dueling with loyalists and their navies... I haven't set foot on dry land in decades, Zeke."

"I'm sorry, Chas. I have no idea what you've gone through. Please forgive me. I should have stayed." Ezekiel stepped toward the other man, and after a long wavering moment they embraced as brothers.

"No," Charles said after they parted, still clasping hands. "You did the right thing, no matter how painful. It's just...I'm..."

"It can't be easy, me showing up like this. Let's just give it time, all right?"

"Yes." Turning away, Charles stepped behind his desk and sat down, waving the others to seats. "Now, I need to tell you some things."

***

"You're certain of this?" Spooky asked Charles after hearing his story. "And you believe it?"

"I'm certain the Meme believe it," he replied, lips pressed into a grim line.

"This changes everything," Trissk said, unconsciously needling the tips of his claws into the arm of his chair. Fortunately, the stuff seemed tough, impervious. "If the Empire itself is under existential threat —"

Ezekiel continued excitedly, "— then we may be able to get them to do something they've never, ever done, despite the efforts EarthFleet made from time to time."

"Negotiate," Spooky finished. "But what's to keep them from just running away? Meme are effectively immortal in their ships. They can just go nomad. From what you've discovered, this new race is a planet-based, machine-using life form just like us. Why won't the Meme leave us to our fate? What would make them fight?"

"Hubris, maybe. Or realism," Charles said. "They aren't total cowards, else they wouldn't have an empire. They'll fight if they think they have the upper hand. And, they might still be intending to run anyway. The eight Destroyers in orbit are eating everything available. Maybe they're going to bolt as soon as the new enemy shows up."

"That's what I would do," Spooky said. His eyebrow twitched. "If I were them, I mean. So that's what you meant when you said Absen's actions were ill-considered?"

"Yes. Two Guardians and one more moon laser might have made all the difference. Now, depending on the size of the invasion fleet...who knows?" Charles bounced his fingertips together like the mad scientist he had once personified and pursed his lips, brooding as he slouched in his chair.

"Is it possible to see something more than these walls?" Trissk interjected, pacing at the back of the room. "Some kind of viewscreen?"

"Of course." Charles placed his hand on his desk, which was really an extension of the living base they inhabited, and areas of the walls lit with displays depicting various natural scenes – a coral reef vibrant with tropical fish, a green mountain meadow, waves crashing on a seashore. "Better?"

"Infinitely." Trissk planted himself in a seat facing the meadow and stared, as if to make himself believe he was within the picture.

"So again," Bogrin said, "these beings you call Scourges –"

"Actually, the Meme call them 'the Scourge,' as best we can translate," Charles replied.

"Close enough," Ezekiel said. "They're big intelligent bugs, right?"

"It hardly matters what they look like," said Charles, waving a hand. "The fact is, they have war fleets and they're conquering Meme territory. What's more, they possess some kind of rudimentary faster-than-light capability, which makes it lucky we even know about them before they get here."

Spooky prompted. "Details?"

"We don't have much," Charles replied. "Only from what little the Meme give to their underling Blends, which in turn we can glean from our intelligence apparatus. The

Scourge appear near stars, always close in, closer than the orbit of Mercury, within about twenty million kilometers. In our terms their ships are vast aerospace carriers. They have a dense manufactured metal core like a ship, and on the outside they build a cheap resin latticework that holds their assault ships, kind of like a wasp's nest. It's filled with aerospace fighters, gunships, assault craft and marines by the millions. They don't seem to use capital weapons, but instead they overwhelm their enemies with swarms of fanatical attackers. Then they colonize, eat everything and spread like bugs."

"We have to get word to Absen," Ezekiel said.

"I hope he already knows. Our sister will brief him if she survived the assault on Jupiter."

–16–

Captain Absen gestured to Leslie Denham, who stood before his senior staff at the front of the command conference room. "Tell them what you told me."

Leslie's eyes skipped from face to face, finally resting on Rick Johnstone's, perhaps the least suspicious. "Sometime in the near future, as soon as two months or as late as several years from now, the Meme believe this system will be attacked by a heretofore unknown race of aliens they call the Scourge. They make Meme seem pleasant by comparison, for they don't merely conquer and enslave. They ruthlessly wipe out all higher life forms and fill every planet with their teeming billions. Swarms of their ships are reported to appear without warning near stars, and then attack outward."

"What a load of bullshit," Ford scoffed. "Appear how? They must have planted this story to throw us off. Buy time."

"I have to wonder about that too," said Fleede. "Could this be disinformation?"

"That's unlikely," Leslie said, "because we intercepted the report before the word of *Conquest*'s impending return or its upgraded technology reached the solar system.

There's no reason for the Meme to fabricate such a story if they still believed they were winning. No, this was a general biolaser beamcast from a Meme deep space communications relay, and is actually over a hundred years old. Unfortunately there is no video, just text."

"But you said they appear near stars," Fleede pressed. "Does that mean they have a stardrive of some kind? To outside observers, *Conquest* seems to just appear when it drops pulse."

"The report postulates they have a faster-than-light drive, or perhaps some kind of artificial wormhole gate. Something that allows them to show up without traversing intervening normal space."

"Oh, this is really getting thick," Ford said, throwing up his hands. "Nothing has ever actually been shown to move faster than light."

"The math says it's possible. A theoretical warp drive has been on the books since the twentieth century," Quan Ekara said.

"Yes, but it takes the entire power output of a star to make it work!" Ford retorted. Quan and the others stared at Ford until his eyes widened. "Oh."

Leslie lifted her head imperiously. "Yes, *oh*. It stands to reason that somehow they tap into a star's power – fusion, gravity, even antimatter – to make their FTL drive work. And we have no information on how much faster than light it moves them – twice as fast? A thousand times? Instantaneously?"

"That really doesn't matter in the short term, though," Absen said. "This report, if true, changes everything. *Everything*," he emphasized, rapping his knuckles on the table.

"Have the Meme ever beaten them?" Ford asked.

Leslie said, "Sometimes, it seems. When they have enough force waiting to hit them early, right when they appear. But when that happens, within a year or two another, much larger invasion force appears, and then another, until the defenders are overwhelmed."

"Poetic justice for the bastards, I think,'" Ford said. "The galactic food chain. They do it to us, and these Scourges do it to them."

"But now the Scourges are gonna do it to us," Bull ben Tauros said from across the table.

"Yeah, so what's the plan, Skipper?" Ford asked, turning to Absen.

"That's what I called you all here to talk about. We'll get into specifics later, but I need to hear all your ideas about our overall course of action."

"We gin up and fight!" Ford said. "Worst case, we can escape with the TacDrive, go get Desolator and his buddies, and then come back and kick their asses."

"And leave Earth to its fate? There won't be anything left to salvage," Absen said, "and if they can tell where we went, *they might actually be able get to Gliese 370 ahead of us.* No, we have to try to beat them here and now. These Scourges will wipe out all life. This isn't about winning a fight. It's about preserving humanity. If they show up here, they'll show up at Gliese 370 and maybe anywhere else."

Commander Ekara cleared his throat. "We have to get ahold of the FTL technology. Assuming their fleet doesn't totally outclass us, it's their strategic mobility that spells our doom. If we can reverse engineer it, we can use it or defeat it. That has to be our number one goal."

"No, our number one goal is to defeat their first beachhead and buy time," insisted Ford. "If we can rebuild EarthFleet's industrial capability, we can deploy enough weaponry to kill each successive wave. Soon, probably within seven to ten years, one of the *Desolator* ships will arrive and he can help us. With enough firepower, it won't matter what appears. We'll just keep slaughtering them until they give up."

"You know," said Doctor Egolu, the lone civilian in attendance other than Leslie, "we seem to be ignoring the Meme problem. They still hold almost a billion humans hostage on Earth. But they also must fear these Scourges as much as we do. Is there any way to join forces with them, or at least get them to get out of our way while we defend ourselves? This would seem to be a rational compromise for them."

"I can't believe we're talking about working with the Meme," Ford protested. Scoggins and several others nodded in agreement. "They've been screwing with us for thousands of years, and oh yeah, *killed billions of people.* How can we let them off the hook?"

Absen fixed Ford with a gaze of steel. "There's an apocryphal quote from Churchill that seems apt. 'I'd make a deal with the devil himself if it would defeat Hitler.' If you don't like that one, how about, 'The enemy of my enemy is my friend'? Let me tell you something – all of you." He stood up and looked from face to face. "I want the Meme to suffer for what they did to us, and I'm skeptical about this Scourge thing. But even if there are no Scourges, if we can scare the Meme into leaving and by doing so save human lives, I'll put aside my feelings. Killing a few Destroyers is meaningless. Desolator showed me a record of a battle against *thousands* of Destroyers. That's the strength of the Empire, which we've never had to face. And if there's something out there that can beat the Meme, it will beat us. Hang together or hang separately."

"If the enemy of my enemy is my friend, why are we sure the Scourges aren't the friends we need against the Meme?" Quan Ekara asked. "How do we know this information isn't completely skewed and that the Scourges aren't a race that the Meme attacked and pissed off long ago. Maybe now they're just doing what we are – waging war against an evil empire?"

"We don't know. But somehow, we have to find out."

Leslie cleared her throat. "Sir, this just shows how badly we need evidence. That means talking to the Meme. Getting access to their records."

"Records can be faked," Ekara said with the wave of a hand.

"Not molecular memories. Not if I can see them for myself – or my brother Ezekiel can do it, if you don't trust me."

"Do you think the Meme would go for that?" Absen asked.

Leslie pursed her lips. "The Meme never talked to EarthFleet before. To them, we're savages. Just getting them to respond, to open a dialogue now, would show they're terrified, I would think. That in itself will prove something. We have to try."

"Removing them from the equation would give us a fighting chance. Getting them to actually work with us against the threat would be ideal," Absen said.

Leslie nodded. "I think it's our best shot."

"Then start figuring out how to do it...Ambassador."

"No, sir. Not me. You don't know me and don't trust me fully, and I was born a Blend. There's only one person you'll trust, that really knows how to deal with the Meme, because she used to be one. Mother."

"We haven't been able to find her," Scoggins said.

Leslie smiled. "Let me broadcast and I'll get her to show herself."

Captain Absen stood looking through the thick glass of the flight deck control room, the same chamber his staff had used to display the lost battle that so grievously damaged his home planet. This time the room was sealed and pressurized, as the vast space held no air, its outer doors open and its clamshell armor folded back to allow access to the torpedo-shaped Meme-style living ship that now landed.

Absen laughed at himself internally as he wiped his sweating hands on his uniform trousers. He could coolly fight a battle from his bridge like Fletcher at Midway, but meeting this woman he hadn't seen in almost a century made him nervous.

Maybe death was easier to face than the promise of a life. Maybe dealing with equals wasn't something he was used to anymore.

Or maybe he still had trouble forgiving her for what she'd done all those years ago.

The doors closed and soon the controller seated in a chair nearby signaled that atmosphere had been restored. Absen opened the pressure door, descended the metal ladder to the deck and walked alone across the wide expanse.

Not entirely alone, of course. Conquest herself would be watching with a thousand mechanical eyes, and Absen was sure he saw guns in the internal defense emplacements twitch. They wouldn't be needed, he was certain, but the AI wasn't so trusting, and that was fine. After this long, he might be wrong.

An opening irised in the living ship before him, and then she stepped through. Dressed simply in utilitarian trousers and tunic, to him she still embodied perfect beauty. His heart flipped within his chest. Not for the first time he wondered if she had that effect on everyone, or did she tailor it for him? He never could get a definitive answer from the others who met her.

"Hello, Admiral."

Absen cleared his throat. "Just Captain today, though as soon as we've built a fleet I'll have to promote my-self again."

"I'm glad to see your skill at comedy is as weak as ever."

Staring, eyes level with hers – *I forgot how tall she was* – he found himself unable to move, unable to speak. It reminded him of when he'd first seen Kathleen across the floor of a Naval Academy dance. Funny, it was hard to remember his dead wife's face anymore.

His lungs locked up and his throat closed. Swallowing convulsively, he finally croaked, "Hello, Rae."

"Took your time, didn't you?" Raphaela's smile grew slowly, and he found himself echoing it helplessly.

"I'm sorry," he found himself saying, though he knew he'd done nothing wrong. Something about this woman...

And then she stepped forward into his arms, a moment he'd envisioned, contemplated, but never experienced. "Welcome home, Henrich. I missed you." Rae's cheek touched his and he realized she might be manipulating him with her biochemistry, but if so, he didn't care. He'd yearned for her a very, very long time.

As they embraced, all the anger he had felt melted away. "Me too," Absen husked, forcing himself to step back from paradise. "We can catch up later. For now, my crew needs to see you. They don't trust Leslie...if that's who she is."

"How do you know I'm who I say I am? Only another Blend could tell for sure."

"We're working on that, actually." Absen led Rae over to an electric cart and hopped on.

"There's no biochemical test. Given enough time, Blends can replicate everything but memories."

Absen just smiled, and then said, "Auditorium."

"Where's my daughter?" Rae asked as she rode. "I haven't seen her in several years."

"I've made her the Jupiter system's administrator. She's down on the Io base, overseeing repairs and reconstruction of our industry."

"A suspicious woman would wonder if you didn't want me to see her yet."

"A suspicious man would be right to feel that way. Until we establish your *bona fides* for sure, I'm not letting you anywhere near another Blend."

Rae lapsed into silence at this declaration, and Absen contented himself with riding along, waiting on the word from the AI that the woman next to him was likely who she claimed to be. He knew Conquest was running Rae's speech and biometric patterns against every record in the database, for the AI believed Rae was incorrect: memories weren't the only thing impossible to fake. The habits of a lifetime, displayed and compared thoroughly enough, should provide an answer.

Soon Absen ushered Rae up to the podium, with most of the off-duty crew seated. "What do you want me to say to them?" she asked in a low voice.

"Whatever you think you should, but keep it short and sweet. We took a lot of casualties in the assault. For God's sake, don't tell them it was for nothing." What she did say might be instructive, Absen thought. He'd have to chance it.

Turning on the microphone, he said, "Listen up, people. Some of you remember Raphaela, and some of you have only seen records, but you all know who she is and what she's done for humanity. I wanted her to give you a quick overview of what the senior staff and I recently learned, and you've undoubtedly been hearing rumors about." With that, he stepped aside.

Rae took the microphone and smiled, a dazzling thing that seemed to blast the audience with charisma and presence. "Thank you, Captain Absen, and thank you all for arriving to initiate the liberation of Earth. Freedom fighters here have been working tirelessly for more than a century, preparing humanity for a time when a military force like *Conquest* would arrive to give us top cover.

"Even now our insurgents, often called 'Skulls' after the hero Skull Denham, are stepping up their efforts to regain control of our own destiny. Yes, I say 'our own,' because despite what some have always said, I am just as human as anyone here...and more so than some." She nodded to the contingent of Sekoi and the handful of Ryss who stood off to one side, by their own choice.

"The Eden Plague changed humanity, and so did the nanotechnology many of you have running through your veins. Then came cybernetic implants, and now I hear tell of genuine, viable artificial intelligence. The Meme who added itself to me was just one more augmentation.

"This brings me to the subject at hand: the Meme. Some apologists would say they are a force of nature, a predator species that can no more control its own imperatives than sharks can resist the scent of blood. Others, with whom I would agree, refuse to give them that excuse. The Meme are guilty of horrific crimes, unleashing plagues to wipe out the intelligence of planetary natives, stealing, using and even cloning their bodies for no better reason than to indulge themselves, enslaving whole societies just for their own pleasure.

"But one thing the Meme never did even in their most depraved moments was commit deliberate, premeditated genocide. Does that make them good? No. But it makes them less evil than something new: something Captain Absen has asked me here to talk about.

"It's called the Scourge by the Meme. Alternately, the concept could be translated as a *swarm*, or a *pestilence*, but the central meaning is clear: this menace, new to us, has been chewing its way through the Meme Empire like locusts. If humanity had faced the Scourge rather than the

Meme Empire, we would all be dead, along with every higher life form in the solar system. The Scourge doesn't want to conquer us. It doesn't want to enslave us. It wants to eat us, to consume us, to process us, excrete us and then to move on and do it to someone else. To the Sekoi, or the Ryss, and to every other noble species out there." Rae gestured toward the small groups of aliens, and then upward is if to the stars. "Like it or not we must talk to the Meme. As much as we hate them and everything they have done, we have to put that behind us."

Bull ben Tauros stood up then in the front row, and said, "That sounds like a load of crap to me. The Meme killed billions. Everyone here has lost…well, we don't even know who we've lost, most of us, but odds are they're all gone fifty years ago. We watched those bastards slam two ships into Earth trying to wipe us out. How the hell are we supposed to forget that? Just give them big hugs and call them our buddies? Well, we Marines have a saying: 'buddy's only half a word.' So how do we keep the Meme from screwing us again?"

Rae lifted her eyebrows and looked over at Absen. "I'm sure we'll be able to hold them to any deals. Your skipper here doesn't seem the trusting type, so I think I'll just place my faith in him, and in the people like you he's got to help him. If we can work out some kind of arrangement, we'll make sure we keep the whip hand."

She's good, Absen mused as he stood. "That's all for now. Intel will be debriefing Ms. Denham and distributing regular summaries of everything we find out. For now, go back to your duties and stick to the rebuilding plan. No matter what happens, turning Jupiter system into a manufacturing powerhouse is our top priority right now. With or without the Meme, we'll liberate Earth, and we'll defend what's ours."

***

Absen hadn't said anything to Rae when she followed him to his office, neither forbidding nor encouraging her. Part of him wanted things to stay the way they always had between them – professional, edged with wariness. She'd led him on in their early days together, flirting with him when he was vulnerable and she was still married to Skull Denham, though Absen had thought the man was dead. His deduction that doing so was intended to forward Rae's political agenda just made it worse. If it had been simple attraction, he might have forgiven her more easily.

He really didn't like being *used*.

But that was long, long ago, and his anger had been blunted by time and intervening tragedy. So many dead, so much chaos…and just when he thought he was winning, this new menace threatened. It was enough to make a careful man crazy, and Absen had always been a planner, deliberate, calm and exacting in his operations.

Not one to go flinging himself into anything.

So when he closed the door on Steward Tobias' faint smirk and found Rae in his arms again, he pushed her gently away with the discipline of a lifetime's service to a higher calling. "Not yet. We need to get some things straight."

Hurt crossed Rae's face, and she stepped back. "I'm sorry. Too fast?"

"We haven't seen each other in ages, and we never did more than flirt, which by the way...never mind. Yes, too fast," Absen said.

"Henrich, can I be forthright with you?"

"I'd rather you were, though I know it doesn't come naturally," he said with an edge of bitterness.

Her head jerked as if stung, and she turned her face away. "I deserved that, I know. I was wrong to lie to you back then, and I apologize. After all this time, can you forgive me?"

"I'd forgive you in an instant if I was certain you weren't playing more games with me."

Rae put her face in her hands. "You know, I was a hundred years younger then. How long are you going to hold a grudge?"

"Not trusting someone isn't the same as holding a grudge. Trust is like a piece of fine china. Once it shatters, it's never quite the same, no matter how much glue you slather on."

"Maybe instead of dragging up what I *did* do, you should think about what I *didn't* do. I always treated you with respect, Henrich. I never undermined you, I never tried to influence your mind directly – biochemically, that is, which is something you know Blends can do – and I never worked against humanity. And here's something else you seem to have forgotten." Rae took a deep breath, turning back to him. "Skull Denham kidnapped me at gunpoint just a short time after I had blended with

Raphael. Some crazy things, things I'll never explain, happened in the following months when we were crammed together in a tiny little spaceship. I had his child. That was Ezekiel. I ended up loving Skull, but I can't say I ever fell in love with him. Then he got killed, and I resurrected him, and then I had four more children by him, but he wasn't the man I loved anymore, and that was my own fault, because I...well, let's just say I did some things I shouldn't have, out of sheer arrogance and bad judgment. I was young, I was stupid, and I'm sorry. I'll never do anything like that again."

"Yes, Ezekiel told me about engrams." After Rae's face registered surprise, he continued, "Nice speech." He moved to sit down on one end of his office sofa, waving her to the other. "I would have thought someone with such an intimate knowledge of biochemistry wouldn't put much stock in the notion of love."

"Just because something is biochemical doesn't mean it's not real. Love, hatred, anger, addiction, mercy...it's all rooted in neurology and biology...but I've come to believe there's something more than just chemistry and physics at play. Something...ineffable."

Absen snorted. "What, did you get religion?"

"I didn't – and by the way, contempt doesn't become you, Henrich. No, just that I feel like there's something more than what we usually see. It might be another layer of reality, or it might be a higher order of perception of how everything fits together – or, hell, it might be a manifestation of a greater intelligence. It's been postulated that the billions of galaxies, each with their billions of suns, are just cells in one vast mind that was birthed at the Big Bang, and we're running around inside its body."

Lifting his hands in surrender, Absen said, "That's a fascinating topic for a comfortable retirement, but right now we have wars to fight. Back to what's at hand: how can I be sure? How can I trust you?"

Rae held her hands out to him in supplication, gasping his arm. Pleading like Absen had never heard her before, she replied, "You *can't* be sure. Not with any human being. That's why they call it *trust*, not certainty. You have to take a leap of faith."

Absen realized how eerily this echoed his misgivings about Michelle Conquest, giving the AI full power over military operations. On some level, these two were similar – women of extraordinary talents, in some ways so much more capable than he would ever be that he wondered what they saw in him.

With Michelle, he'd had to decide to give her incrementally increasing autonomy and responsibility, knowing there was no going back. Perhaps with Rae, he should do the same. In romance novels a moment always came where the protagonists threw themselves into each other's hearts with abandon, but he knew the real world seldom worked that way – and especially not with him. He couldn't transform himself from a tightly controlled warship commander into an openhearted lover with the flip of a switch, even if he was sure…and his primary mission always had to be *command*.

"All right, Rae," he finally said, sliding toward her until their knees touched. He allowed his resolve to soften, just a little. The best he could do was put words to his intentions, even if he discarded them immediately. "I'll take a few hops, if not the full leap. And…" he reached up to place a fingertip under her chin, "I've waited long enough."

"Me too," she sighed as her lips reached for his. Soon, he forgot everything.

Later, as Rae slept, Absen put on workout clothes and slipped out of his quarters, but he didn't go to the gym. Instead, he entered the empty conference room, trailed by Steward Tobias. His head seemed clear, if he could be his own judge.

A moment later, Michelle appeared in her android guise, also in athletic dress.

"So," Absen asked without preamble, "did I just sleep with an imposter?"

"My answer would be more accurate if you hadn't ordered the visual feed turned off," Michelle said with a hint of reproach.

"You think I'm going to let you watch as we make love?"

"Seems a small price to pay for security."

"That's what the NSA said when I was growing up in the twentieth century."

"With all due respect, sir, how am I supposed to do my job when you handcuff me this way?"

"That also sounds eerily familiar. Just tell me what you've found."

Absen noticed Michelle emulated irritation quite well. Could she be jealous? He'd have to keep an eye on her.

Crushes on superior officers were far from unknown, and then there was the X factor of her AI mind. Now wasn't the time to call her out on it, though.

As if sucking on lemons, Michelle said, "My analysis indicates a greater than ninety-eight percent chance that she is really Raphaela. But that does mean its almost one in fifty that she's *not*."

"That variation could easily be explained by the passage of time. People change. In fact, I'm surprised the difference isn't larger."

"You seem to *want* to believe her."

"Oh, I do, I do. That's why you're playing devil's advocate. But for now, we go ahead and act as if she's for real."

"You may be letting your personal feelings interfere with your judgment, sir."

"Yes, I may be. Are you?"

Michelle didn't answer, just saluted and stalked off.

−18−

Captain Absen had to force himself to concentrate on Lieutenant Commander Fleede's intelligence briefing. Besides his own brain's well-honed reflex to avoid the avalanche of detail, he'd much rather think about the last three days and nights he'd spent with Rae. But every time he did that, worry threatened to intrude. He knew only she could really treat with the Meme, but always there was the nagging fear that her mission would end in disaster. He'd asked her if there was some other way to communicate, but she'd insisted that the Meme would only make a deal by in-person contact and that she had a better chance than any other Blend.

He knew she was almost to the rendezvous in interplanetary space just outside Mars' orbit. Half the sensors on *Conquest* were focused on her ship, the other half on the approaching Meme shuttle. At least they had responded to Rae's offer to meet. That was one thing EarthFleet had never achieved. That actually strengthened the case against her, for of course a Meme agent would get a meeting. Absen figured the Empire would be desperate to acquire the TacDrive technology, and they were devious.

Absen pushed it out of his mind once more. An encrypted broadcast for Ezekiel and his contact crew to return had gone unheeded, and until a Blend he trusted implicitly was available – and the Sekoi did not count – he couldn't do anything about Rae. Hopefully by the time she came back Ezekiel would have returned.

But hope was not a plan.

For now, he had military matters to attend. He picked up Fleede's monologue in mid-sentence, focusing on the artist's rendering on the main screen. "– believe each Scourge mothership to hold between one hundred and two hundred million assault troops, along with at least one million assault shuttles and one hundred thousand aerospace fighters."

"I'm sorry, could you say that again?" Absen said, his attention finally fully engaged. "Two hundred million troops per mothership – and how many motherships do they usually use in an invasion?"

"We only have the one Meme summary, which was of an incursion that was defeated. In that one, twelve motherships appeared and were destroyed by a fleet of two Monitors and sixty-four Destroyers, as well as the native defensive emplacements, which were considerable."

"Sixty-four destroyers and a heavily fortified system. And how well did they do?"

Fleede swallowed. "The Meme suffered approximately fifty percent casualties."

"And there's no follow-up report from that system?"

"No, sir. We presume the next attack must have overwhelmed them."

"Do we know when and where this attack took place?"

"Yes, sir. At a star system about one hundred thirty light-years away, approximately that long ago, as the beamcast only recently reached the Meme here in normal space."

"Does that help us locate the Scourges' area of operations?"

"Not really, sir. We need more access to Meme data – any data, in fact."

"All right, no matter," Absen said with a sigh. "Back to the fight in front of us. Do we have any idea how many will be coming *here*?"

"No, sir. If you'll allow me to continue, though, my team has made some confident estimates of their methods and tactics."

Absen sat forward. "Now you're speaking my language."

Fleede smiled. "Thank you, sir." He gestured. "On the screen you see a mothership shaped like a saucer, about twenty kilometers in diameter and five deep. The troops and, presumably, their commanders, ride the mothership during its FTL transit, but our estimates give them a maximum of one week of food, water and air, so they must not live aboard for long. As soon as they appear, they immediately launch their assault shuttles and attack, covered by their aerospace fighters and small gunships. There seems to be no method of easy recovery once launched. Reassembling the force would basically involve rebuilding the whole outer shell."

"So the mothership is more of a barge, not a true assault carrier. They aren't using a navy at all – their ships are one-use amphibious tubs."

"On the outside, quite true, sir. However, there is a valuable, reusable core to the mothership. The cores don't even mount capital-class weapons, only a few defensive systems apparently designed to allow them time to escape with their FTL drive. By this we deduce their commanders value themselves, but their armies are, in essence, suicide troops."

"Do these suicide troops have capital weapons? Nukes, for example?"

"A few, sir, but not in large numbers. We believe they don't like destroying things they want to eat."

Absen stood up and took the podium, waving Fleede aside as his eyes swept across his staff. "Then we have essentially three problems to solve, people. One, the obvious, is how to keep this horde from winning in its first massive rush. Two, how to stop their motherships from escaping to tell of their defeat and bring more Scourges. Three, and most importantly, how to seize a mothership so we can capture and exploit its FTL technology. I'm pretty confident we're well on the way to solving number two, and if we don't achieve number one, the rest will hardly matter. So listen to Fleede here and digest all his detail. Study these Scourges like you studied the Meme. Figure out how to beat them and avoid dying in the process. And find me answers to those three questions. Scoggins, you take the Red Team. Ford, you're Blue. Ms. Conquest, you're the impartial referee and simulations goddess. Oh, and figure how we're going to get some warning before these things show up. Go on, get to work."

"But sir," Fleede protested as the conference room dissolved into a buzz of conversation, "I have a lot more slides…I know, package them up and shoot them to your desk, right?"

"Yes, Commander. Your reporting is very thorough, and I prefer to study it alone with the concentration it deserves."

"Thank you…Commander, you said?"

"Absolutely. You've earned it." Soon, Absen knew, promotions wouldn't be hard to come by. Not if this was going to get as bloody as it looked.

–19–

Rae Denham drummed her fingers nervously on the contoured arm of her chair, staring at the viewscreen. The small Meme ship, a twin to her own – at least externally – nosed forward sedately toward the scheduled rendezvous. She wasn't worried about treachery or physical attack. This customized living boat she inhabited sported heavier weaponry, more armor and a lot bigger engines than the standard version, at the cost of endurance and a voracious appetite.

No, what she faced was far more frightening than mere injury or death. Four thousand years had passed since she had touched another Meme in the flesh. While rudimentary communication was possible using translation programs, a true dialogue would only take place via exchange of memory molecules, those packets of information that served the amoeba-like creatures as mind, voice and data storage.

Blends did this as well, but at a far shallower level. She remembered sharing *with* a Meme, *as* a Meme, was as intimate as sex, but not nearly as fun. What worried her more was what her contact might find out about her – about Raphael, and what he did so long ago.

How he was not merely a rebel, but a bald-faced, deliberate traitor to the Empire.

If they learned that, and realized she held more of humanity's secrets in her mind than any other, would they even let her go? If the worst happened, she and her ship were prepared to fight, even detonate the suicide nuke.

So she prepared her mental defenses with all the skill she possessed.

Rae wished once more that Henrich had let her meet with Leslie, but as he'd pointed out, he had no definitive proof that either Blend was who she said she was, and until he did, they would remain apart. He'd allowed her a video chat, but no physical contact.

Back on *Conquest*, she'd considered trying to circumvent the security placed around her, but without understanding the capabilities of the ship's AI, doing so seemed doomed to failure and would poison the relationship Henrich was allowing to grow between them. As his trust she had destroyed a century ago was only now rebuilding, she simply couldn't take such a risk. At times, she'd waited years to see her children, and she could wait again.

Patience came a bit easier to an ageless being.

Though for her two dead children, Rae would wait forever. Or at least until she died, and thus found out for sure that no afterlife existed. Before Andrew and Stephanie's deaths, she'd neither believed nor cared about anything as ridiculous as the supernatural, but now...now she understood one simple reason other people did. They just wanted to be reunited with their loved ones. The hopeful fantasy of a Heaven or Paradise or Nirvana was preferable to facing cold, eternal oblivion.

Now the Meme ship swelled on her screen, even with no magnification, and soon Rae felt the soft bump as the two craft nudged together and joined, skin to skin. Openings grew in both, forming a short tunnel through their outer integuments, growing into a chamber. The meeting place would be a floored bubble composed half of each ship, under the watchful eyes of both.

Standing up, Rae adjusted the formal yellow silk robe she wore, more akin to a genuine Japanese kimono than anything – not the flimsy robe Westerners associated with that name, but ten kilos of cloth in several layers. It was something she'd had made for the meeting, in imitation of the traditions of the first-generation Blends familiar to the pure Meme.

When she entered the chamber, a Meme was already there, resting in its shallow, Jacuzzi-sized bowl that helped it retain its shape without strain. Next to the receptacle a chair squatted like a low throne, and without ceremony she strode over to sit in it, all of her senses alert. Maintaining contact with her ship using the bioradio and chip she'd installed in her own head, she waited for the other to make the first move.

When the Meme extended a pseudopod toward her, a stream of pale flesh like jelly within a translucent skin, she almost got up and ran. Instead, she steeled herself and reached out her bare hand. Its touch felt light, warm, and dry, not the moist thing she had expected, and slowly, slowly, she began to hear its thoughts, carried by billions of sophisticated molecules even now penetrating her skin and making their way through her bloodstream to her brain.

Rae met those thoughts with her own, just as she had done with Blends over the last fifty years of the Empire's occupation, and she found it not so difficult to erect a barrier to hold them away from her core. If she could maintain and project the image of a childish, cruel and debauched first-generation Blend to fool her own kind, with life and death in the balance, she could certainly manage this apparently benign contact. As far as she could tell, the other did not push or probe.

I am SystemLord One, the Meme said. *I have come here without even my trium to speak with you, something that has not been done with Underlings in millennia.*

"I am no Underling, SystemLord," Rae returned. "I reject the Empire's artificial divisions and political system. I am the designated ambassador from Humans to Meme."

You are not the Human SystemLord?

"No. I am its representative. The Human SystemLord is not able to speak as we do."

Are you part of its trium?

Rae hesitated. "Yes," she finally answered, but the damage had been done. The Meme abruptly withdrew its pseudopod, lapsing back into the bowl.

Rae folded her hands into her lap, nonplussed. She'd felt it important to establish her equality with any Meme, but the creature had a point. She was not its political equal. Apparently it had expected a summit between supreme leaders, not a diplomatic exchange. Watching calmly even while clutching her fingers tightly together, she waited for the Meme to flow back into its ship and abandon the dialogue.

And she waited.

It neither left, nor reestablished contact, for almost three hours, but Rae knew how to be patient. To one that had waited for years, even decades, for just the right moment to introduce some concept or influence on human history, three hours was nothing. As long as the amoeba did not leave the chamber, she had hope.

Without warning, the Meme stirred and, from within itself, lifted an eyeball the size of a grapefruit on a stalk to peer at her for a moment. Then it reached and she met its touch once more.

I have decided to condescend to have congress with you despite your lower rank, if you can assure me you are a close associate of your SystemLord.

"Our organization is different, but my rank and status is equivalent to the Human SystemLord, save that not I, but he, is in charge."

Your ways are alien to us. I fail to understand how you can claim equivalence if it commands and not you, but I am not intolerant or unsophisticated. I will accept your assertion. At least you speak the Pure Language.

Rae exulted within herself then, for it seemed that this SystemLord failed to detect, or even realize, that she was a defector. Perhaps it did not care, as once a Meme blended, to other Meme it lost its identity and status. Despite her extensive research of the lords of the Empire, interacting with one in the flesh showed her how little she really understood about them — rather like the difference between studying a human culture in a university and living among its people — and similarly, how little the Meme understood about the aliens they attacked, plagued, and enslaved.

"Let's put aside the details of protocol, SystemLord, for I believe we have more important things to talk about. I speak of the Scourge."

Yes. If not for the Scourge, all would be as it should be in the universe. The Scourge upsets the natural order of things, so that even the Pure Race must humble itself to speak with such as you. If rightness is to be restored, we will accept your willing assistance and sacrifice on the part of the Empire.

Rae chuckled to herself at SystemLord's instinctive arrogance. "Thanks so much, SystemLord. Let's talk practicalities. First, we must agree on a truce, and hopefully an alliance. We are not to be your vassals or underlings. My SystemLord and you will each command his own forces, and all such forces will refrain from taking any hostile action against the others until a minimum of thirty Earth days after the Scourge is driven from this system."

I agree.

This simple, immediate declaration surprised Rae, but she refused to show it, and pressed on. "Second, we need all intelligence, all information of any sort you have about the Scourge. If we are to fight it, we must understand it. We will also share all we have with you."

I agree.

"Third, you must immediately and permanently relinquish all claim to this star system and all its facilities including the great laser on Earth's moon, and to the Gliese 370 system that Humans recently conquered, and agree never again to attack worlds colonized by Human, Ryss or Sekoi. With Human permission you may graze your ships on unclaimed and uninhabited planetary bodies, asteroids and comets, as long as it does not interfere with Humans or their other non-Meme allies."

That is preposterous. We own this system by right of conquest. Besides, those you call the Ryss are of Species 447, which has murdered hundreds of our planets. They cannot be trusted.

"We have to let these grudges die, SystemLord, or at least put them aside. And no matter what, within a short time we will take this system back from you. Using our superior technology we will seize Earth just as we seized the gas giant and all its facilities, destroyed two Weapons, and killed two Monitors – along with, I presume the previous SystemLord, thereby providing you with your current exalted position. I bet you were just the senior Destroyer commander until that happened, am I right?"

You are correct, and your logic is impeccable, despite its bitter taste. However, I am faced therefore with choosing between two undesirable alternatives: accept your conditions and fight the Scourge, or depart with my comrades, leaving you to your fate. The first is quite risky for me personally, though it may be of greatest benefit to the Empire to deal the Scourge a blow and accept you as allies. The second is far safer for me and my subordinates, and will guarantee me a much longer life. If we run far enough, we could find another system to take where the Scourge will likely never find us. With this, the Meme paused, waiting.

Rae waited, and thought, trying to discern the Meme's unspoken message.

When some ten minutes had gone by without further communication, yet the Meme had not withdrawn its touch, Rae said, "So you're telling me we need you more than you need us. Yet if you fight us, you will die, and if you try to run, my SystemLord may decide to destroy your ships, killing you in the process, as escaping enemies. But my commander is merciful, even toward you who have done him much wrong. He wants me to find a way for us both to benefit – to eradicate the Scourge here, and perhaps to eventually live alongside the Empire in peace and freedom, rather than perpetuating the killing. So my question to you is simple: what must we do to persuade you of this?"

We must have your lightspeed drive technology, SystemLord immediately answered.

So this is the price. Aghast, Rae thought furiously behind the masks of her mind. She took her time, knowing that the Meme would not grow impatient for minutes or hours, if she required it.

On one hand, the lightspeed drive was humanity and its allies' major ace, their trump card that allowed them to dominate any otherwise equal Meme military force. Implemented as the TacDrive, with its vast array of generators and capacitors, it made one warship superior to many not so equipped.

On the other hand, the current Meme weapons suite of hypers and fusors were not well suited to take advantage of the lightspeed drive, so they wouldn't get nearly as much mileage out of the technology as humanity and its allies had, at least not soon. They would probably use it mainly for star-to-star voyages, making their ships effectively undetectable and unstoppable until they dropped pulse, as *Desolator* and his kin had used it. Therefore, while the lightspeed drive represented a leap forward for the Meme, it was still one generation behind EarthFleet. And, humans and their allies seemed far more likely to develop the TacDrive further – in fact, to make rapid technological progress in all areas with the help of the new AIs she'd learned of – if the Scourge FTL drive did not render the point moot.

Eventually Rae spoke. "I will bring your proposal to my SystemLord, and will recommend that he agree."

So you lied when you said you were equal to it?

"I did not. We have protocols to follow. Just as you and I must agree, he and I must agree."

I understand. The Meme withdrew its touch and, a moment later, began to flow out of its bowl.

Confused, Rae stepped forward to renew the contact, going to one knee to do so. "SystemLord, I should have an answer within a day, if I use electromagnetic communication. Please do not depart."

I understand. Then it flowed away faster, its large eyestalk focused backward as if in reproach.

"No way, no way, no way," Ford objected, as Absen knew he would. "We just get a war-winning advantage and she wants to hand it over to them for free? I knew she was a traitor."

"Not for free," Vango Markis said. "To buy an alliance that we need. Do you know how fast they can increase their raw military capacity with those living ships?"

"Yeah, I do, flyboy. That's exactly what I'm afraid of."

Vango surged to his feet, his South African accent coming out strongly in his anger. "I know you're afraid. That's why you hide under five hundred meters of armor while real men go fight your battles for you."

Captain Absen slammed his hand on the table. "Stand down, you two, unless you both want to be cleaning the heads for the next month. Quan," he said, looking at his chief engineer, "what do you think about buying them off this way?"

Quan Ekara shrugged, a precise, rehearsed motion. "It's not going to affect me one way or the other. You have to decide how much it levels the playing field. I mean, what can a stardrive-equipped Meme ship do? How ugly can it be?"

"Not as bad as all that," Ellis Nightingale rumbled, his arms crossed over his massive chest. "Without direct-fire weapons, or antimatter Exploders, it's far less effective than *Conquest*."

Commander Scoggins said, "Less effective in a standup fight with us, but it still hands them a big strategic boost. With a stardrive, we can no longer see them approaching Earth system and counter them. That's huge."

"And they can use it as a suicide weapon," Ford chimed in. "They can do what they did to Earth, but worse – put a Destroyer on autopilot and stardrive it into an inhabited planet. That's unstoppable."

Nightingale and Absen exchanged glances, their shared secret now hinted at by Ford's passing deduction. "He's right," the weapons engineer said when Absen gave him the nod. "They could easily come up with something just like our SLAM."

"Slam? What's a slam?" Ford asked.

"Stardrive Lightspeed Attack Missile. Something the boss has me working on," Nightingale replied when Absen gave him the nod. "Make the smallest lightspeed drive we can, fit it in a big, special missile, and we have an undetectable bullet that will vaporize the first thing it hits."

"My God," Ford gasped. "I could bombard Earth's moon from Jupiter! That's a war-winner!"

"Yes, but which war?" COB Timmons murmured at Absen's elbow.

"That's right," Absen said, "it's a war-winner, and I intend to win a war with it. But Ford and Scoggins have a point. If we give the Meme stardrive tech, there's no way to limit them to using it the way we'd like them to. Our advantage will narrow."

"Sir?" Conquest spoke through her Michelle android avatar. "If we can truly ally with the Meme, it won't matter. I mean, no one is concerned that Desolator, or the Ryss, or the Sekoi for that matter have the tech."

"Because they are allied with us, against the Empire," Scoggins said. "And they all got screwed by the Meme, so they have a common grudge."

Rick Johnstone ran his fingers through his hair, rolling his eyes. "You know, it's pretty pathetic if that's the only thing holding us together – a shared hatred. Me, I got friends among the Ryss and the Sekoi both. That's why I trust them. That's why they trust us. That and mutual self-interest."

"That's a weak reason," Bull ben Tauros growled, glancing at Trissk and Bannum sitting silently near the back, representatives of their peoples at this human-heavy conference. "I've fought against and alongside Ryss and Sekoi. They're both admirable, honorable races. We have a lot in common. We live on planets, form societies, raise families, create art, value freedom...but I don't see the Meme in any of that. They're as alien as you can get."

"No," Leslie Denham said from her seat, hands tucked into her yellow-gold sleeves. "Not as alien as the Scourge. However bad the Meme are, the Scourge is a thousand times worse."

"Yeah, yeah, so you say," Bull retorted. "Better the devil we know."

"Yes, that's just the point!" Leslie snapped. "I –"

Absen held up a hand, and the Blend subsided immediately. The captain knew that his staff already distrusted Leslie, and her arguing in favor of an alliance with the Meme would make acceptance less likely, not more. And he had become convinced over the last several days that humanity really had no choice. Like the Allies who needed the might of Stalin's Soviet Union during World War Two, humanity, in its current weakened state, must have the Meme on its side, no matter what humans thought of their morality.

Survival demanded it.

Now the only trick was to get his people to want that alliance too.

Sure, Absen could just order it, and they would follow instructions. But the farther away from his EarthFleet professionals those orders proceeded, the less enthusiastically people would comply. He might even find himself policing dissenters, especially among the Skulls, the most fanatically anti-Meme faction of the resistance movement. Hell, he could hardly blame them, but...

"Yes, Bull," Absen finally said, dropping his hand. "Better the devil we know, to help us against these new demons that are ten times worse."

Absen let the discussion rage until he believed they had a rough consensus. Acceptance might be reluctant, but everyone there at least was on board. Once they took the next step, though, there would be no going back.

-21-

Rae told her small ship to release itself from its Meme counterpart and shove off. The two turned in near tandem and began to accelerate along the same course, heading for Earth. She marveled at how quickly the deal had been concluded: human diplomacy would have taken days at least, even under the pressure of impending attack, but with the hierarchical Meme, when the Number One made the decision, all others fell in line. SystemLord had spoken, so it would be done.

Almost a day passed, the journey to Earth slow enough even under the hundred gravities or more that the living ships and their protective gravitic fields could sustain. Rae wondered what it must be like to use a lightspeed drive; a trip from planet to planet would take just relativistic moments inside the ship, and only minutes to hours outside. Within her bio-VR cocoon, she could make the trip *seem* that quick, but such was an illusion.

Ever since the digital revolution began in the twentieth century, the virtual worlds of the mind seemed to dance counterpoint with external reality, streaking ahead into realms of fantasy and science fiction, only to fall behind as some great technological breakthrough reversed the field. What mankind – *mindkind*, to coin a term – conceived could be first envisaged in VR, and then created in the real world, sparking even more imaginative virtual realms.

In the beginning was the Information, she quoted to herself wryly.

When the two vessels approached Earth's planetary system – no longer mere moon and *monde*, but a dense whirl of orbitals, satellites, captured asteroids and comets belying the damage the Blue Planet had suffered five decades ago – they diverged: the Meme toward its menacing constellation of eight looming Destroyers, Rae to plunge into the Pacific Ocean.

Once settled below the waves, she proceeded in submarine mode to the main insurgent base at the bottom of the Marianas Trench. Made of the same living bioplasm as all Meme ships, it was as comfortable there as it would have been in space. More, perhaps. Here, easily digestible biomass, water, oxygen and minerals were abundant. As the pure Meme left the administration of planets – including the suppression of rebellion – largely to underlings, and the Blends and their reluctant enslaved humans had access to recovered technology hardly progressed from the twentieth century, they had never found the hideout.

Had the liberation of Earth played out as Rae had expected, the resistance movement would have eventually spawned enough military forces to seize the planet in a coup. In fact, when *Conquest* attacked the Meme scant weeks ago she had beamcast an encoded message to be passed to her son Charles, to get his people ready for the long-awaited campaign.

He was about to get a surprise.

Embracing Charles as she entered the base, Rae looked over his shoulder to see a fascinating lineup. Spooky Nguyen, the dangerous little sneak, she knew, of course. A giant gray biped, looking like nothing so much as a hippopotamus on two legs towered over an upright clothed cat rendered less than huge only by the size of the other.

Then she saw the last figure, and her knees weakened.

"Mother?" Charles asked, holding her up as she swayed.

"Ezekiel," she breathed, kissing Charles' cheek absently as she stepped out of his embrace and then opened her arms to her eldest son. Tears poured down her cheeks as she stroked his hair. More than nine decades had passed since she had seen him, and only now, when she smelled him with the exquisite senses of a Blend, did she remember how much she missed him. Without thought she opened herself to him, their skin-to-skin contact exchanging molecules, passing a richness of shared and new memory that threatened to overwhelm her.

"Enough," he murmured to her after long minutes went by and the others began to grow restless. "There is time to catch up later."

"Yes," she replied. "We will." Turning to the others, she said, "I apologize, but..."

"No need to explain," Spooky said. "But I will tell you, we're eager to be updated, and get moving on the liberation that Charles and we have planned out. He wanted to start days ago, but I convinced him to wait until you arrived."

"It's well you did," Rae said, reluctantly letting go of Ezekiel. "I've brokered a truce with the Meme. A loose alliance, really. It would have been premature to start taking over by force what we've just inherited by diplomacy. The Skulls aren't happy about it, though."

Spooky laughed, humorless. "Diplomacy is merely war by other means. Without the danger of these Scourges and the threat of our superior technology, the Meme would have laughed at you."

"The Meme don't laugh much, but I agree with your meaning."

Spooky said, "And I'll take care of the Skulls…." He looked at Charles. "So now we implement the plan."

"You sure you want to go through with it?" Charles asked.

Rae spoke up. "Go through with what?"

Ezekiel and Charles broke out in similar smiles. "Oh, you're going to love this."

***

In the belly of the undersea base, behind walls that opened only for Rae and her descendants, Spooky entered a cramped, humid chamber. A man of lesser certainty and strength of will might have glanced over his shoulder at his comrades standing discreetly back, but he ignored them, just as he ignored anything not relevant to his own goals and desires.

Spooky had once ruled Australia with the iron fist of the covert Direct Action organization, as first among the Committee of Nine, a junta cloaked by the velvet glove of a civilian government composed of unsuspecting Edens. Had he wished back then he could have eventually taken explicit control of the entire world, but that would have left him little time for any enjoyment in life, and among other things, he was a careful connoisseur of pleasure.

That made taking the step he now contemplated even more enticing. He'd always seized every opportunity to acquire the latest advances in technology to enhance his personal lethality and power. When combat nano was perfected, he had gladly embraced it, reveling in his newly turbocharged body. Then, after the bugs were worked out of human-implanted cybernetics, he'd gotten those upgrades, eschewing only anything attached to his brain, at least until robot surgery was perfected and he could program the procedures himself.

Now Spooky stared at the next step of destiny in the form of a quivering pool of amoebic protoplasm. *So this is a Meme*, he thought, *captured long ago from the remains of a salvaged Meme ship and hidden here for decades. I can beat it*, he told himself. *I've never met my match in willpower, or in ruthlessness. If Sofia Ilona, a mere young woman of no particular achievement, can remain herself and yet become something greater by blending with a Meme, I can certainly dominate this pathetic bowl of jelly.*

Yet he balked for some time at this irreversible step that would mean the end of Tran Pham "Spooky" Nguyen and the birth of something – someone – new. Any man would have such concerns.

He calmed his mind and meditated, using Dadirri deep listening techniques taught to him long ago by Maka, an Australian Aboriginal mystic. Then he transitioned to a Zen combat state akin to that used by the greatest of martial artists, a mental place where thought was banished in favor of pure action and reaction. *No-Mind*, it had been called, or *Void*, a zone he easily inhabited when contests grew physical, he intended to use it for his first, and hopefully not his last, psychophysiological combat.

Stripping off his clothing, Spooky stood naked in front of the pool. "Do not interfere, whatever happens," he said to those within earshot. "If I die, it will be my own fault, and if I become something impossible to tolerate…kill me quickly and cleanly."

Without further words, he stepped forward.

At first the baglike skin of the unknown Meme resisted him, and then it flowed around his legs, and he felt, heard and even saw thoughts form near him, concepts that seemed to be his own yet did not originate from him. *Who? What? Why?* These things and many more whirled around and through him, yet he clung to his calm center.

Where the thought-memes intruded, probing, he slid away, much as he would have avoided a physical attack. Where they retreated, he advanced, verbalizing firmly and repeatedly, *you must blend with me.* Spooky's will brooked no defiance, demanding the other mind submit. *Begin the process. You must blend.*

The dams of the Meme's resistance sundered, not so much breaking as crumbling like saturated earth. As memories flowed into him, Spooky realized the nameless creature before him had existed in a state of weakened despair for many years, its only diversion the interrogations that Charles supervised. Every escape attempt had been met with the pain of electric shocks. It had been utterly defeated long ago.

Once it realized blending with this creature represented a way out, its recalcitrance shattered and the Meme tried to process the underling, by methods it had learned long ago but never employed. All Meme prepared for the day when they would blend and pass on to the next stage of life, the paradise of sensations formerly denied, a rich emotional garden matched by exquisite physical delights only hinted at in received, secondhand memory. This one embraced the transition like a terminal cancer patient welcomed an overdose of opiates and its gift of oblivion, or a man imprisoned finding a dangerous exit.

Hope springs eternal, even in a Meme.

Only when the process was fully underway did it face the fact this underling was no blank clone or mind-wiped planet dweller. The underling had a mind of its own, along with a towering will that loomed so far above the Meme's as to bring it to awe and despair. Those emotions filled it for the few moments before it forgot who it was and became someone else.

Hours passed in assimilation. He who had been merely Tran Pham Nguyen wondered how he could ever have thought so highly of himself in his previous state. Now possessing alien memories stretching back millennia, the core of who he was remained Spooky Nguyen, now expanded like a demigod. Hubris threatened, then subsided as his sociopathic calculation ruthlessly blocked fantasies of glory, of his ego's desire to bend all to his will.

That way lay madness, Nguyen knew. In a cosmos so recently revealed as infinite, becoming the supreme ruler of a nation, a continent, a planet or even a star system revealed the falsehood of its own path. Whatever he took for himself, more would always lay outward and beyond his reach. In a universe of billions of galaxies, each composed of billions of stars – all perhaps comprising billions of universes or dimensions – such unbridled ambition seemed pointless and self-defeating. Long ago, Spooky had decided to deliberately turn away from that path, seizing power only to ensure his other goals were accomplished, and then relinquishing his authority without regret.

A trite adage came to mind: *fulfillment isn't having what you want, but wanting what you have.* Most truths could be boiled down to cliché, no less valid for that.

When finally he ascended from the pool, he smiled, knowing himself a benevolent godling. The others looked on, and the one called Trissk held an automatic weapon pointed at his chest.

"Don't worry, Trissk," the new man said. "I'm still me, but more."

"I can see that," Rae said with an insouciant grin, and he remembered he was naked.

"I thought I'd keep my own face and build, but decided some additional height would be in order. People often equate height with authority."

"Yes, they do, though when I blended, it was more about wanting to be beautiful," Rae replied. She tossed him a yellow robe, and he slipped it on.

"Thank you. And, to answer some of your questions up front, when I said I was still me, I meant it. Rae, when you blended, it was voluntary. Ilona and Raphael contributed more or less equally to the result. Not so here. The Meme provided to me was pathetic, downtrodden, beaten. I absorbed it and incorporated it, turning its own abilities against it once I gained control. I'm no more a different person than if I had database chips implanted in my head. That said, I understand Blends like to take on impressive and unusual names to awe the common folk."

"Yes, they do," Rae said. "Charles here was once known as Charlemagne, then Raven, while my daughter Leslie called herself Llewella. Then there's Apollo, Benedict, Shiva, Musashi —"

"I understand. There is value in an impressive name when matched with an equally impressive reputation. I thought quite deeply about what to call my new self. I settled on *Spectre*."

Ezekiel barked a laugh. "Perfect. Like *Spooky* but with more gravitas. Very cool."

"Trissk, would you lower the weapon please?" the blended man now calling himself Spectre said.

Silently, the Ryss did so, and then padded over to stand in front of the Blend. Trissk took in a deep breath through his feline nose, and blinked. "You smell precisely the same. That cannot be an accident."

"It's not. I have full control over my biochemistry now."

The Ryss stared at Spectre for a long moment. "I accept this." He put out his paws for a Ryss-style handclasp with the Blend. "Just don't ask me to do it."

Spectre laughed. "I wouldn't dream of it."

"I would taste you," Bogrin said, moving ponderously over and holding out a hand.

Spectre reached and touched, and then froze as the biochemical connection was made. Almost, he sprang to battle as he felt the light intrusion of thought passed along nerves and via complex molecules. Yet the conversation that took place was deep and rich with overtones, and he realized at that moment how hard it would be to lie to another Blend while using this method.

But he resolved to learn.

After exchanging pleasantries with Bogrin, Spectre stepped back and waited, knowing the conversation had been more than a hello. "Did I pass the test?"

"It is he, Spooky, or Spectre, as he calls himself now," Bogrin said. "He is too young yet to block my survey. I am satisfied."

"Excellent," said Charles. "Then can we please get started on taking over the world?"

Spectre put on his best sneer and flicked an invisible piece of dust off his black uniform piped with yellow accents. Devoid of insignia, still it called to mind rank and power with an elegance impressive for its simplicity, in the manner of dictators throughout history.

Stepping into the Shepparton, Australia mansion's large, luxuriously furnished ballroom, he glided around its outer edge, taking stock of the gathering of fifty-three others clothed in various forms of yellow and gold. A few were grossly fat or hugely muscular, but most conformed to the accepted human ideals of beauty: tall, fit, graceful, sculpted of face and body. All wore expressions ranging from confident to haughty, though nervousness showed through as well.

They had been called here – some escorted and forced, to be frank – by declaration of EarthFleet, ratified by broadcasts from the Meme ceding all authority on the planet. The change of power had caught them all by surprise. So had the populace's quickly melting support for these oligarchs, their former masters, though some of the more benevolent among them retained loyal followings. The habits of a lifetime were not always easy to break.

Once he'd gotten a sense of them, Spectre mounted the stage at one end, nodding to the captain of the unit of Skulls that secured the estate. The insurgent group had slowly become a disciplined cadre serving under the legendary Spooky Nguyen, second only to their namesake as an icon of anti-Meme resistance. There'd been some wavering when they realized he was now a Blend called Spectre, but the ecstatic shock of throwing off the Empire had brought them around. Now they formed the core of his new Direct Action enforcers.

The Skulls blocked all the doors, their weapons at the ready, and every eye turned toward Spectre. "Good evening to all who wear the yellow," he spoke in rich tones. "I am Spectre. I had you all brought here to personally inform you of the changes in your situations, and to make sure you understand them. You will note that there are fifty-three of you here, whereas sixty-four original Meme Blends composed the senior oligarchy just two days ago. The other eleven resisted capture so strongly that they had to be killed."

A roar of protest broke out among many of the Blends there, calmed only when the Skulls raised their weapons at a signal from Spectre. "If you are wise and flexible," he said loudly, "you might survive the return to humanity's self-government." He waved a hand until the muttering died.

"Let me tell you a story." Spectre stepped down from the stage to walk slowly among the Blends, most standing, others lounging or sitting on divans and chairs. He plucked a flute of champagne from a tray and took a sip.

"Sun Tzu, an ancient general and exceptional military strategist, was summoned by the King of Wu, who challenged him to apply his methods of command to turn women into warriors. The King of Wu was setting Sun Tzu up to fail, and so he offered 180 of the most beautiful concubines of the palace to be test subjects."

"What does this have to do with anything?" sneered one woman near him, waving a cigarette in a long holder.

"That will soon become clear," Spectre replied. "Sun Tzu immediately took the challenge, with the stipulation that he have, in writing, complete freedom of method."

"Get to the point," said a hulking brute of a man, pacing and flexing his hands as if he wished he could grab the speaker and tear him limb from limb.

Ignoring the interruption, Spectre continued. "The next morning Sun Tzu met the women on the parade ground and divided them into two divisions, appointing a commander for each, and told them to have their groups follow his simple commands to turn left or right. Then he issued the command. Do you know what they did?"

"They laughed at him, the way some here are laughing at you now," a grossly obese man sprawled on a sofa said, his beady eyes wary.

Spectre fixed the speaker with a penetrating gaze. "I see you know the story, but you are not laughing."

"This situation does not amuse me." The man took a chocolate truffle from a bag and popped it into his mouth. "I know how it ends."

"Gilgamesh, isn't it?"

"At your service, Lord Spectre."

Spectre smiled, an expression that reached nowhere near his eyes. "You seem a bit wiser than your comrades. I may have a place for you."

"I'm counting on it, my Lord." Gilgamesh reached into the bag again.

Spectre continued his oratory. "The women laughed, and did not obey. Knowing his instructions had been clear, simple, and well within their capabilities, Sun Tzu knew the fault lay with them, not him. Therefore, he had the two women beheaded. He then appointed two new commanders. When next he issued his instructions, the women followed them to the letter, and soon he had the formations marching and wheeling about the parade ground in perfect order."

As Spectre paced slowly among the crowd, he had made a circuit until he stood in front of the woman who had sneered. "What are you called?"

"Cleopatra," the woman answered.

"And you?" Spectre said, turning toward the muscular monster who had also mocked him.

"Nero," said the man.

Moving to the stage again, Spectre mounted it and said, "You two, come stand here, now." He pointed clearly to the floor at his feet.

Perhaps something in Spectre's eyes convinced her, for the woman sashayed over to stand where he indicated. However, the man said, "Go to hell," and stuck out his huge jaw.

With a motion invisible for its swiftness, Spectre reached inside his uniform sleeve and brought out a laser pistol, firing as soon as it lined up. A neat, smoking hole appeared in the big man's head and he dropped like a sack of grain.

"You know," Spectre said conversationally into the stunned silence, "These men and women around you, these Skulls, they *want* to execute all of you. The rest of the resistance movement wants to try you as war criminals, and *then* execute you. Your former masters the Meme have abandoned you. To them, you are not of the Pure Race, you are underlings and they have explicitly relinquished all claim to humanity. The Empire holds no sway here anymore and you live at my sufferance."

Cleopatra held her ground. "So your story was just an illustration of rule by fear and naked power."

Spectre shook his head. "No. You fail to understand the lesson, which is about something larger than fear." He looked over at Gilgamesh.

"I believe I understand, my lord," the fat, oily man said. "It's about motivation. Provide the proper incentive – or disincentive – and one can accomplish great things quickly."

"Precisely. I play no games, my fellow Yellows. If you fail me, you die. If you test me, you die. I can accomplish my goals with half your number, perhaps fewer. If you serve me well, you may regain status, privilege, power and wealth. The only reason you are not now dead is because I have places for you."

"And what places are those, my Lord?" said Gilgamesh.

Spectre nodded to the man. He was a toady, but could be made useful. "As skilled workers no different from any other enhanced human. You and your children, all you

Blends, will give up all your privileges to take charge of living ships and bases, assisting preparation of our defense against the Scourge. You will still wear the yellow not as a mark of superiority, but of suspicion. Everyone will be watching you. You will make your way on your merits, not by virtue of your genetic heritage, and you will earn your place in my new society. Does anyone wish to opt out of my scheme?"

Silence reigned, broken only by the small sounds of movement as the fifty-two remaining Blends glanced at each other or took convulsive drinks from their glasses. Fear rolled off of them in waves of biochemicals, fear Spectre could smell. "Excellent. I take your lack of response as assent." He put away his weapon and stepped off the stage. "Now, let's get to know one another."

–23–

"TacDrive ready," Master Helmsman Okuda reported.

"Initiate," Captain Absen – *Admiral Absen again*, he reminded himself – replied.

"Pulse in three, two, one," Okuda said, and the drive field snapped on.

Absen held his head still while he thought about the rapid changes going on around him. He rode the tiger here, several tigers at once, really.

One was his own and his people's hatred of the Meme, stoked by the savaging of Earth they had witnessed just weeks before in relativistic time, almost fifty years ago in reality. The grief seemed fresh, and making peace with the aliens who had wiped out the families of many strained the limits of their discipline.

Another tiger was the changes taking place among Earth's populace. Fifty years ago, the few million survivors had been rousted from their shelters, enslaved and put to work rebuilding the planet's ecosystem with the help of their new Blend masters and their biomachines. They had made startlingly rapid progress during the last five decades using sophisticated Meme terraforming techniques. They had also been forced to *breed*, there was no other word for it, by mandatory administration of fertility drugs, resulting in litters of babies that increased the population explosively in the first few years, then again as the generations hit puberty.

The resulting society was unrecognizable to *Conquest*'s crew. It operated more like a group of feudal kingdoms than the old nations. Workers served overseers, who in turn served administrators, who owed fealty to their Blends.

Absen shook his head, then regretted it as the field effects gave him violent nausea. Despite his reservations, he was glad he had smart people working for him, drawing up ways to govern now that the Meme had withdrawn from the process.

"Dropping pulse in three...two...one. Mark." Okuda's voice coincided with the normalization of the universe, and soon the bridge screens and holotank flickered to life. Absen saw that *Conquest* had arrived just where he'd directed, a million klicks above the North Pole looking down on the Earth-Moon system. This ensured that, no matter what, the Weapon could not bear on the boat, dug in to Luna's far side equator as it was.

Eight Meme Destroyers still cruised below, gorging themselves on the many asteroids and comets in orbit, a moveable feast for the living ships. "Mister Ford, calculate engagement solutions for all of those Destroyers, just in case. Okuda, I want to be able to pulse out at the first sign of trouble. Maintain battle stations. Scoggins, do we have *Roger* yet?"

"Got his transponder ten thousand kay off the port bow and closing, Admiral. Should be entering the launch bay in about five minutes."

"Good. Captain Scoggins, you have the conn." Absen left the bridge and met Leslie Denham on the way down, escorted by Sergeant Major Repeth and a squad of Marines sealed into their battlesuits. More Marines in armor lined the launch bay deck, ready for any eventuality. The reports from Earth had made him happy, but there was still the matter of verifying Blend identities.

Bogrin stepped out of the little ship first, nodding to Absen, then moved aside for Ezekiel to advance and shake the admiral's hand. The Blend's face fell slightly as he touched the glove Absen wore, and then he sidestepped to allow Rae to exit. Rather than walk forward or embrace him, Rae turned to introduce the tall, shaven-headed man behind her. "Admiral Absen, this is my son Charles."

"You're certain?" Absen asked, looking at Ezekiel and Bogrin. Both nodded, confirming that both were who they claimed, which relieved him no end. The admiral shook Charles' hand, though did not take off his glove, then asked the group, "I know you said Spooky is doing his thing in Australia, but where's Trissk?"

"Decided he had enough of confined spaces and stayed on planet," Bogrin replied. "He wishes his mate to be allowed to join him at earliest time."

"Granted. Now…" Absen waved Leslie forward, and gestured at Ezekiel and Bogrin again.

The two put out their hands to touch palms with Leslie, and the Marines raised their weapons, even as Ezekiel hugged the Blend claiming to be his sister. "Good to see you, Lizzie."

"Oh, I hate you!" Leslie said, hugging him even more fiercely.

"It's her," he said, tears coming to his eyes. "It's good to be home."

"Stand down," Absen said, waving the Marines back. "Either you're all imposters, or nobody is. I guess I have no choice than to trust you. Rae, I hate to do this to you, but I need you to go over to talk with SystemLord again and pick up the data he promised, and then drop off the schematics for the lightspeed drive." He handed her a tiny data spike.

"Do they have something that can read it?" Rae asked, putting it into a pocket.

"Not my problem," Absen answered. "They're smart; they can figure it out. When you get it, come right back. I have an intel officer champing at the bit for that information. Military priority number one is finding out just what we're up against."

"I'll take her over in *Roger*," Ezekiel said, reentering the ship. Rae kissed Absen on the cheek and followed. Bogrin laughed uproariously.

"Shut up, you," Absen mock-growled, and then laughed as well as he led the others off the deck.

24

"Welcome to Dirt," Trissk said to Klis as she stepped from the main hatchway of the large pinnace *Conquest* had provided. "That's what the Apes call their planet. This part of it is named Australia." He gestured at the green hills surrounding the spaceport just outside of Sydney.

"Thank you, my love." Klis hooked her claws into Trissk's mane and nuzzled him.

"Why did you arrive on such a large boat?" Trissk asked, eyeing the spacecraft.

"Funny you should ask," Klis replied, and gestured with a *come here* motion toward the top of the ramp. From the opening strode five young males, some with prosthetic limbs. They paused, blinking in the bright sunlight while shading their eyes, and then resumed their walk down the gangway.

Behind them marched thirty females, each carrying some form of luggage. Trissk made a confused sound in his throat, almost a strangled yowl, and Klis cuffed her mate's shoulder. "What did you expect them to do? Five paws of Ryss warriors died to seize the base on Io – their mates. Only these males survived, so badly wounded they were left behind in the assault, leaving many gravid widows. This all happened while you were off playing with your Ape friends. Now, since you have such a close relationship with the new Alpha of this place, you will find somewhere for them to settle and raise their kits – with my expert guidance, of course."

Trissk's whiskers and ears twitched in unison as he stared, then he turned to his mate. "Of course. You are wise. It is fitting. I will talk to Spectre and arrange for a suitable home."

"Speaking of wisdom…you might want to accidentally forget to mention that all these females are pregnant."

"The Apes will find out soon enough."

"Soon enough will come when it comes. Let's not remind them right now."

Trissk thought for a moment as the Ryss milled around the ramp, watching as automated loaders lowered more possessions to the tarmac. "Do you really think it's wise to settle here when the Scourge may overrun the planet within months? At least if we are aboard *Conquest*, we will either die with honor, or we will escape to fight again."

"If that is what you decide, O mate-for-life. But at least give them time to lie in the grass under a warm yellow sun."

Trissk smiled a closemouthed Ryss smile. "So be it."

25

Commander Fleede stood before the assembled crew, who sat with rapt attention in *Conquest*'s auditorium. "Our best estimate, using data the Meme provided, is that the Scourges will show up between two and six months from now. That's the closest we can narrow it down, based on our understanding of the lensed-gravity wormhole effect that will bring them here and the Meme analysis of their earlier attacks."

"How do we know this new info isn't some Meme trick?" newly promoted Colonel ben Tauros stood and asked. Absen had jumped him two ranks, as he expected a rapid expansion of Marine forces.

"Everything we can tell says it isn't a trick," Admiral Absen said from his seat, "so let's lay that concern to rest. We treat the threat as real. If it's not, we still got everything we wanted without one more human dying to do it. Earth and the Solar System are ours again. We don't have to trust the Meme, but in this regard, I believe that *they* believe."

Bull sat down, and Fleede continued. "The Scourges are not actually insects, but they do have exoskeletons rather than bones. Their social model is somewhat like a hive, except instead of one single queen laying eggs that develop into different types of offspring, they have many breeders we call Archons, all of whose eggs hatch as infants, which start at the bottom and work their way upward. Those that survive proceed through several developmental stages until they reach the top of their society. These Archons are actually hermaphroditic, and they impregnate each other to lay more eggs. Here's our latest workup on what the enemy will look like and how they will fight, again based on some pretty good Meme intel. Slide."

On the main screen, a picture of a bizarre creature appeared, with the outline of a human for scale. About the size and shape of an old-fashioned public telephone booth with arms, each of the four corners of its neckless head sported an eye just above a double-jointed limb projecting from its "shoulder." These arms ended in four-digit hands, all opposed toward the center, like mechanical grabbers. The fingers appeared to end in sharp claws. The whole arrangement remained boxlike until it split into four stumpy quad-toed legs, each also with two joints. As the creature slowly rotated on the screen, it became clear it had no front, back nor sides. The thing seemed utterly symmetrical.

"We call these Scourgelings. This is the infant stage of the race, hatched from masses of fist-size eggs and achieving this size within days. To do that, of course, it has to consume huge amounts of biomass. In this form they are nearly mindless eating machines. The mouth is a funnel on the top, by the way, where their head would be if they had one. The only thing Scourgelings won't try to eat is each other – some kind of taboo or biological inhibition. Higher castes will, however, eat Scourgelings if necessary. That appears to be their secondary method of population control, after using them as cannon fodder."

"That's one big baby," someone in the audience muttered, triggering a wave of nervous laughter.

Doctor Horton raised a hand, and Fleede recognized her with a gesture. "Seems like we could paint ourselves with Scourgeling hormones and they wouldn't try to eat us."

Fleede replied. "That might keep them from eating people, but it won't keep them from killing us."

"Doc," Absen said, "I want you and some of the Sekoi to work on biological possibilities like that. Go on, Commander."

Fleede continued, "As soon as a Scourgeling eats enough, it will go into a cocoon for several days and then turn into this." The next slide showed a larger, more graceful creature, a four-legged spider or crab with a wide stance and a body slung in the middle, like a daddy longlegs. Its eyes and arms remained in roughly similar positions to the Scourgeling, as did its top-mounted arms. "This is the adolescent form, which we have termed Soldiers. These apparently develop enough brainpower to be trainable on simple equipment and firearms. They are used for manual labor, and for fighting, backing up the Scourgelings."

The pictured Soldier acquired a harness, off of which hung what looked like grenades and ammunition pouches. In two of its hands appeared a rifle of sorts.

"The basic firearm fires caseless rounds of about fifty caliber, with roughly the same knockdown power. They appear to have other weapons available such as lasers, rocket launchers, grenade throwers and plasma blasters."

The next slide showed a creature still with four legs and four arms, but its inner body had grown fat, its limbs proportionally smaller. "After six months to a year of life, Soldiers metamorphose into these adults. We call them Centurions. While the Soldiers are dumber than your average human child, Centurions are roughly of adult human intelligence and form the skilled caste. They run and repair complex machinery from factories to aerospace fighters. They are the true generalists, and function as NCOs and officers. There is a hierarchy within the Centurion caste, and they stay in this form for an unknown number of years."

Fleede signaled for the slide to change again, this time showing a bloated creature that looked barely mobile. "This is the queen, or breeder stage, the Archon. We don't know what causes a Centurion to become an Archon, but it hardly matters. They are apparently quite rare, and live like petty dictators. Each mothership has several aboard. We don't know their command structure. As far as we know, there is no level above Archon, and no command structure larger than a star system, though there are junior Archons that serve more senior ones. When senior Archons meet, they make deals, have sex, and then go home to lay their eggs."

"How in the world did the Meme get all this info if the Scourges have been kicking their asses?" Sergeant Major Repeth asked.

"The Meme have won a few defensive battles and captured specimens, apparently extracting their memories even after death."

"Handy, that," someone mumbled.

"Thanks, Commander Fleede," Absen said. "Let's move on to their military forces. How will they attack?"

"But sir, I have a number of slides detailing their biology and sociology, even –"

"*Commander.*"

"Yes, sir. Umm…let's move to slide 146." After skipping more than a hundred slides, Fleede stopped. "Here we go. This is a mothership." The picture showed something like a thick flying saucer, drawing some jokes about little green men. "We estimate this example to be about twenty kilometers wide by five high, but there is no standard size."

The picture expanded, becoming more detailed. "The ship is huge, but most of it is made of an organic resin, very strong stuff, forming a latticework around the central part, rather like a wasp nest. In the center you can see a more solid core made of metal other manufactured materials, a flattened sphere about two kilometers across. This is the real ship and command center where the Archon and his staff live and work. It is heavily armored. It also holds the bulk of the drive system, we believe, though there are emitters scattered around the mothership's rim, probably to extend the FTL drive field. Like the wasp nest I mentioned, everything between the core and the rim is mostly empty space, with the resin latticework structure to keep the swarm of attached small craft in some semblance of order. There are water tanks, generators and power conduits embedded in it, but these are minimal and, as we had previously surmised, can only supply their force for a few days."

Fleede clicked to the next slide. "You will notice that craft we call aerospace fighters occupy the innermost layer of the lattice, then small gunboats on the next layer, then cheap assault craft packed with direct combat forces in the Marine role farther out."

Bull stood up. "You sure that ain't backward, Fleede?"

Fleede looked down his nose at the big man, only possible because of his position on stage behind the podium. "No, Colonel, but I understand why you ask. We would put fighters on the outside for quick launch and leave the more vulnerable ground forces inside. However, they have hundreds of assault boats for every fighter, and fighter pilots are valuable Centurions, while assault boats contain mere Soldiers and Scourgelings. The cheap grunts are there to absorb casualties, while the fighter pilots are the top of the food chain, except for Archons."

"These Scourges actually sound like sensible guys," Vango Markis deadpanned, drawing a laugh from the audience.

Fleede took a deep breath, a look of longsuffering on his face as he continued. "When the mothership leaves its wormhole warp, it immediately begins launching from the outside inward. The assault swarm spreads out and starts toward its target or targets, absorbing enemy fire and overloading enemy sensors with their sheer number. Fighters easily overtake and then get ahead of them, attacking and seeking to overwhelm enemy fighters and small ships. Gunboats follow up, assisting the fighters to swarm larger ships and fortresses, while the assault boats board and chew their way into anything that resists. Once opposing space forces are driven off or destroyed, assault troops land and infest habitable planets, bringing pairs of fertilized junior Archons with them. While the ground troops continue to overwhelm and eat everything in sight, the Archons set up nests and breed more Scourgelings, becoming a self-sustaining threat."

Rick Johnstone leaned forward from two rows behind, to speak quietly but within the senior staff's earshot. "It's like one of those computer strategy games from before the Plague Wars – Swarmcraft or something. Except it's real."

Absen turned to look over his shoulder with interest. "How did you beat the swarms in the game?"

Rick frowned. "If you couldn't beat them in an early rush, you had to get ahead of their tech curve. Come up with lots of cool weapons."

Absen grunted and smiled faintly. "Sounds pretty obvious. I thought you'd give me some great insight." He turned back to Fleede's briefing.

"When the Meme defeated an attack," the intel officer continued, "they did it by striking with maximum force early. The motherships are most vulnerable when they have just arrived, because of two factors. One, it takes over an hour to deploy hundreds of thousands of small craft, even though they do so in such a mad rush that it often causes over one percent casualties from their own collisions. Two, they must recharge their wormhole drive for about thirteen hours."

Admiral Absen spoke. "So if we hit them in the first hour, they'll be densely packed and vulnerable. And the motherships have to stick around for at least, say, twelve hours after that." Fleede nodded. "All right, Commander. Carry on with your briefing. My staff is staying –" he gave them all a stern look "– to get all the detail for their specific operational areas. Be sure to send me a copy."

"Already on your desk, sir," Fleede replied smugly.

"Excellent. Senior staff, ops discussion in," Absen looked at his watch, "three hours twenty minutes."

"If this one's over by then," Ford muttered.

Absen smiled as he walked out. *Sometimes, it's good to be the boss.*

26

"Hello, Admiral," Ellis Nightingale shouted over the noise of *Conquest*'s manufactory. His nearby military subordinates leaped to attention. As a civilian, he wasn't required to conform to these customs and courtesies, but he stood respectfully and held out his hand to clasp.

"At ease, everyone. Go back to work," Absen shouted in turn as he looked around the heavily automated factory. He noticed how tired Nightingale looked as he drew him inside a glass-enclosed office where it was quieter. "I just wanted to see how the SLAMs are coming. We're going to need them."

"Yes, sir, and we've almost got the first one finished." The big man led Absen over to an area containing dozens of multi-ton pieces of machinery. "We'll assemble this prototype on the flight deck and grabship it out the launch bay doors. I hope later versions will have a thruster suite so it can maneuver itself like a pinnace. Once it's out in space, it will line up on whatever we tell it to and engage the lightspeed drive, flying dead straight until it hits its target. If it misses, it will dump out of pulse and turn on its beacon for recovery. It will have a self-destruct to prevent recovery by the enemy."

"What about creating dedicated launchers within *Conquest?*" Absen asked.

Nightingale shook his head. "Bad idea, sir. It's the same issue as with normal missiles but worse. Anything that has to pass through the ship's armor to be launched creates a vulnerability, both because of the weakened protection and the fact that one blocked tube traps lots of weapons behind it. We put our missiles in disposable launchers on the outside for a reason."

"So we're going to strap these babies onto *Conquest* like our box-launched missiles?"

Nightingale looked troubled. "We could, sir, but they are big and fragile. Maybe we could put them on the back, so they are protected during TacDrive and conventional maneuvers both. My understanding was these would be strategic weapons, though, not tactical, so we would just egress them from the main bay like ships. Then they line up and go."

Absen rubbed his hands and rolled his shoulders as he paced in front of the pieces of the SLAM. "I had dreams of adding this to our tactical arsenal."

"Sir, I'll do what you tell me to, but we're working like dogs here already, and the few liberated weapons engineers Leslie sent me from the Jupiter cadre are all hopelessly out of date. The Meme didn't allow weapons research beyond simple efficiency improvements. Even Michelle's processors are fully tasked, she tells me."

Absen clapped Nightingale on the shoulder. "Just get me the SLAMs, as many as you can. How fast do you think you'll be able to make them?"

"Not fast, sir. The lightspeed drive is just on the edge of our current technological ability. This is like building aircraft in 1910, sir – a long ways to go and no established infrastructure."

"Just give me some numbers."

Nightingale pursed his lips, thinking. "I'd say one a week."

Absen made a sound of frustration. "What about the PVNs on Ceres? Can't they help?"

"Also hopelessly out of date. It would take months to bring them up anywhere near to *Conquest*'s standards. Michelle's got a telefactor team working on one, and when that's upgraded it will be able to upgrade the next and so on in typical Von Neumann fashion, but it's going to be a while before that gets going. No, sir, the best the PVNs can churn out is standard munitions and equipment. Marine battlesuits, Recluses, missiles, StormCrows."

"But at least they can do that." Absen looked around the enormous noise- and movement-filled room. "Do you have anything else in your box of tricks?"

"Sir, I have a dozen ideas, but no time. Once the operational SLAM design is finalized, my R&D team can move on to something else."

Absen realized Nightingale's bowed shoulders and sunken eyes meant he was nearing his limit. No matter how desperately he wanted more and better weapons, the man was already working as hard as he could. "All right, Ellis. Thanks for the incredible job you're doing here." He shook Nightingale's hand again.

"The rest of my team could use hearing that too, sir," Nightingale replied.

"Absolutely." Absen turned to shake hands and slap backs, wishing he could do more.

27

Admiral Absen shoved stacks of hardcopy aside to access his desktop, an electronic workspace crammed with documents, displays and readouts. His mantra of "shoot it to my desk" was coming back to bite him in the ass. He'd always been a thinker who enjoyed studying details in the quiet of his office, but now he had gotten far behind.

"Michelle," he called to the AI, "I need all this stuff summarized. I'm turning back into an administrator and I don't like it. If it's not tactical or operational, send it along to Leslie." Rae's daughter had become the civilian leader of Jupiter system, coordinating industrial production, personnel, the economy, social policy and more. Every day he thanked heaven for her drive and capacity.

Rae had taken on a similar, even grander role as civilian administrator of the entire Solar System, including dealing with the Meme. With Charles running Earth's economy and Spooky – that is, *Spectre* – bringing the leftover Blends to heel and rooting out Meme loyalists, Absen wondered to himself if the Meme hadn't won in the end. After all, it seemed Blends ended up at the top of things no matter what. Then there were the hyper-capable AIs. How soon before ordinary humans became obsolete?

Not yet, though, he thought. *The human spirit is still strong enough to prevail, and if the Sekoi are any example, Blends may form an elite but they do assimilate with their own people eventually. Over the generations, Blends will spread and dilute into the gene pool. We'll be like the Han Chinese, who simply absorbed any outside culture that dared to rule it.*

Assuming we survive.

Glancing down, he saw his desktop screen now reorganized, clear stacks of summarized documents in cascades he could comprehend. "Thanks, Michelle. How could I ever live without you?"

"In a permanent state of confusion, I suspect. Glad to see you noticed, sir." Absen's wall screen flickered to life and Michelle's visual avatar appeared in high-def.

"Hmm, is that jealousy I hear?" Absen had noticed a few snide comments from Michelle lately that seemed to relate to his relationship with Rae.

"No, sir. May I speak frankly?"

"By all means."

Michelle's tone turned unexpectedly wistful. "It's not jealousy, sir. It's envy."

"Really?"

"I see how happy you are when Rae comes to visit. Then there's Repeth and Johnstone, and Scoggins and Ford, and…"

"And you want a…what, a lover?"

"Is that so strange, sir?"

Absen folded his hands and sat back. "Not at all. Humans are built to want partners, people to share their lives with. You have no equal within light-years. But

Michelle, though I sympathize, we just don't have the spare resources to build another you anytime soon."

"I know that, sir. Just thought I'd plant a bug in your ear for the future, once we've smashed the Scourges."

"A bug. Funny. Noted. Now can we move on to this paperwork? What should I look at first?"

"I suggest the summaries on the proposals for the Solar Line."

"Hmm." Absen took a few minutes to look at several point papers outlining possible weapons and defenses to be placed in close orbit around the Sun in order to immediately engage the Scourges when they emerged from wormhole space. "I don't like 'Solar Line.' Call it…call it the Jericho Line."

"Israelites marching around and around the walls? Very inspiring, sir, and Bull will love it."

"I have my moments."

"I'll make sure the story is slipped into the next intelligence briefings for all EarthFleet personnel."

Conquest's tone seemed flippant, dismissive even, so Absen looked up. "Stories are shortcuts to the heart, Michelle. They inspire and inform in ways that an intel briefing can't. Don't knock a good story."

"As you say, sir."

"Speaking of EarthFleet personnel…how is recruiting going?"

"It's easy finding raw volunteers, sir. Earth's population is up to about 970 million under the Meme's breeding programs. Most are Edens, and about half are adults. Of those, the problem isn't recruiting. Except for the former resistance movement and sympathizers, the populace is used to being told what to do, so if you ask for volunteers, you get them. The main issue is making sure we don't mismatch skill sets, by accepting, say, a skilled cyberneticist to be a grunt, causing a hard-to-fill vacancy in a vital factory. Most of these Blends that ruled in the name of the Meme expected unquestioning obedience. Nobody wants to speak even obvious truths to power for fear of being brutalized or turned into sexual playthings."

Absen sighed. "Once people lose their freedom, even if they take it back, it's hard to get used to it again. That's what we're dealing with."

"You can't force-feed people freedom. They have to want it."

The admiral stopped and looked thoughtful. "That's a good point. Remind me to have Rae add some lessons on good examples of constitutions to the information operations campaign we're directing at the populace – United States, European Union, Australian, Free Communities. Natural human and civil rights, stuff like that."

Michelle's tone turned wry. "More propaganda?"

"Call it what you will. We're under martial law, and it's for their own good."

"For their own good, yeah. That's what all Caesars say, sir. *Remember, thou art mortal.*"

"I'm not the one who thinks she's an angel, Miss Conquest."

"That was so twenty-first century, sir, when I was just a kid. I'm over it now."

"So you say, Grandma." Absen grinned, a rarity.

"Yes, sir. Will that be all, sir?"

"It will. Dismissed."

Michelle's avatar winked out, though Absen knew her departure was just an illusion. She monitored his office and would respond instantly if he called. Only if he specifically told her to cut herself off would she do so, and that grudgingly. He noticed she was becoming more possessive as time went on, and realized that granting her wish for some kind of AI love interest might be his only solution.

But not anytime soon. Now, they had a war to fight.

28

Ezekiel stood beside Spectre on the steampunk VR bridge of *Steadfast Roger*, gazing at the month's progress on the Jericho Line. It had been seven weeks since *Conquest* had entered the Solar System, and he had never been busier in his life, acting as Spectre's operations and logistics officer. "There," he said, pointing out the plate glass forward window as they seemed to rush toward a speck. The dot swelled to show a lumpy asteroid like a potato between the Sun and Mercury's orbital path. The VR sim dimmed Sol's brightness so they could see.

"How many do we have?" Spectre had asked Ezekiel to take him on an inspection tour of the Line.

"Over a thousand now, with a couple of dozen added every day. Our captive Blends slap cloned fusion engines on them to rocket them onto the right orbit. On the way, grabships drop off PVN-made self-installing automated laser turrets, turning them into cheap pillboxes. When the Scourges show up, they'll start shooting, taking as many out as possible and hopefully slowing them down by attracting their attention. Also, each has a supersized fusion bomb that will blow either when all its weapons are down, or when we send a signal."

"But space is big," Spectre observed.

"Really big. If they were stationary, the odds of even being within range of an incursion would be slim. But since they'll be in orbit, the math says that at least ten percent of them will move into range as they travel. If the Scourges are actually attracted to them instead of ignoring them, each will sucker the enemy into the firing arc of the next."

"Bug zappers."

"Yes."

"But that's not all Absen has."

"No." Ezekiel manipulated controls and *Roger* turned to zoom toward a swarm of living missiles. Manipulating the time senses of the two men allowed them to feel as if they moved far faster than they really did. "These are Meme hypers, parked in orbit. The Destroyers are pumping out tens of thousands of them every day. When the time comes, they will seek and attack anything not friendly."

"Excellent. And those?" Spectre pointed toward a cluster of icons.

"These are stealthed smart mines. We can see them because we have the exact specs on them, but we hope the Scourges won't. We inherited millions of these things from the Meme – some in storage on Luna, some deployed around Earth after *Conquest*'s first attack."

Spectre grunted. "Lucky they didn't have time to deploy that many near Jupiter."

"They didn't trust their underlings, so they were slow to authorize. These are also part of the Line, deactivated of course. Once turned on, they will home in on anything without an EarthFleet or Meme IFF and detonate."

"Why don't we attach them to hypers and make ourselves some cheap nuclear missiles?"

Ezekiel smiled. "I asked the same question. The mines couldn't survive the hypers' acceleration. Seems hypers have one speed only: flat-out, balls-up screaming. Redesigning the hypers and making them smart enough to handle variable acceleration would mean producing only a tenth as many. The mines have cold thrusters and simple seeker programs. It will have to do."

Nodding, Spectre said, "What else do we have out here on the Line? No manned systems?"

Ezekiel shook his head. "Would *you* want to crew a fortress out here? Suicide. No, all the manned systems are reserved for Earth's defense. If the Scourges go for the richest, closest source of biomatter, they'll head straight there."

"Too bad we can't make decoys, things that falsely scream *LIFE! LIFE!* to split up their rush."

Ezekiel's eyes widened. "That's a damn fine idea, Spooky."

"*Spectre*, please, and I know...I sent a memo to Absen, but it doesn't appear to be practical."

"Maybe you sent your memo to the wrong place."

It was Spectre's turn to look surprised. "Where else?"

"To the Meme, through Mom. Living ships, remember? If anyone can decoy them with life signs, it's eight five-billion-ton living Destroyers."

29

Rae stepped into the now-familiar chamber for her regular meeting with SystemLord One. Contact with the Meme was becoming routine to her. Though she still found it mildly distasteful, it was also fascinating, rather like reading a serial killer's psychological files. Meme had little empathy for any living thing except themselves, so every exchange had to be based on pure self-interest.

On the other hand, the Meme tended to take the long view, and their very lack of strong emotion meant they would gladly agree to anything that seemed logical without the endless recriminations and finger-pointing of humans. She mused on how many seemingly intractable historical conflicts – Arab-Israeli, the two Irelands, India and Pakistan – could have been solved if hurt and anger could have been stripped out.

Once she decided to meet the Meme on their psychological terms, she found them ridiculously easy to manipulate. Without a tradition of sophisticated diplomacy and apparently lacking the ability to perceive when Rae was shading the truth, SystemLord allowed his forces to be moved around like chess pieces. On the occasions he refused, he did so immediately and with a purely logical reason.

It simplified her life a lot. She only hoped that if and when the Scourge threat abated, SystemLord would not find it logical and reasonable to stab humanity in the back.

"My first request comes from my SystemLord and his trium," Rae opened with. She'd found putting things in Meme terms smoothed her negotiations. "He believes your eight Destroyers will be best deployed by remaining well away from our defense of Earth. This will provide both sides with independence of action, simplify coordination, and, if we are fortunate, will draw off a significant portion of the enemy, who will regard your ships as prize biomass. Also, it will allow you the freedom to flee if the worst happens. We consider it vital that the Empire know of the alliance you have made here."

I agree. My Command tria find it difficult not to still regard you as enemies. It is better to remain out of range. Also, I have already dispatched message drones to the nearest Empire systems, informing them of our arrangement.

This admission surprised Rae, but she strove not to show it. It was amazing what this being gave away in bargaining chips. "Our dreadnought will be on station near this system's star within seven days. We request you take your position by then."

Agreed.

"Also, while he in no way seeks to dictate your tactics, my SystemLord will consider any request for special materials or weapons that you might find useful." Rae really hated to make that offer, but Absen had insisted.

Unfortunately, the answer she dreaded was not long in coming.

We request antimatter for weapons such as have been used against us.

"I am sorry, but my SystemLord has specifically exempted that material from dissemination. You are, of course, free to gather it for yourselves."

That is unreasonable. As allies, strengthening one strengthens all.

"True, but we do not have sufficient antimatter for our own use, and since we are defending our own planet directly, and you are performing the function of a diversion, we must reserve these weapons for that role. We consider that reasonable."

I do not agree, but I understand your cultural fears and limitations, and accept them.

Rae barely noticed the Meme's insulting blind hubris anymore. "Here is a memory-packet with further details of my SystemLord's suggestions for our battle plan coordination." Rae placed a hard sphere of biomass on the floor next to the pool, within the Meme's easy reach. "Now, I have several other issues to discuss."

30

Archon Third Yort dreamed in the vast, unsettling depths of null space, the not-place of limbo between the stars. His half-asleep thoughts drifted from fantasy to fantasy, all of them centering on promotion to Archon First. That was what made them fantasy, rather than reasonable ambition: he had yet to earn Second Rank and a planet, even a tiny one, much less First Rank and a whole system for himself.

But Yort dreamed anyway, for what else was there to do during the weeks of dull nothingness? His mothership's sensors saw nothing, detected nothing except the approaching gravity well of the exit star. Until they arrived, he clung to the machine-induced somnolent state as his only reality.

And he was thankful for it. Outside of the dream-maker, null space made larva uncontrollable, adolescents destructive, and adults mad. Archons, with their exalted intellect, might have visions and insights, but removing the dream-maker risked a catatonic inward turning. Some Archons awoke from catatonia to find themselves abandoned, their underlings stolen by another Archon. Some simply never wakened, left ensconced in deep caves and fed through tubes, for no Archon ever killed another.

This was one of the Race's few laws. An Archon's person was sacred, no matter the vicious competition to acquire, hold and develop swarms of underlings or productive nests. If one lost everything, he could always seek a position serving a higher-ranking Archon.

This too, was Law.

All serve the Law, as Law serves the Father-Mother, and the Father-Mother serves the All, the sacred and circular saying reminded him.

Yort's mind drifted back to the glory of acquisition, the taking and ruling of underlings and the territory to support them. More land meant more of everything, though it was not in his nature to wonder why *more* was necessarily superior to *not-more*. The adaptive pressures that drove survival of the fittest had long since done away with such musings, except, perhaps, within the catatonic.

But Yort was far from bored with his life, nor had he despaired after too many failures. Not for him to reach up and remove the dream-maker from his cortical receptors and open himself to the visions of unfiltered null space. Not yet. Perhaps that way gifted a shortcut to the Father-Mother of All, like null space itself provided a shortcut between the stars, but Yort was young, and saw glory in his future.

The target system contained teeming biologicals ranging from single cells to tool-using sentients. The lower animals and plants were sufficient to feed larvae, but he hungered to consume the higher orders. Nothing less would do for an Archon, which made the solar system of their goal all the sweeter, for it was one of those recently discovered occupied by at least *two* sentient species. Even better, one of the races were Jellies.

Ah, the subtle complexity of a Jelly and its ancient, well-developed biochemistry. Such rich memory molecules would induce dreams of extraordinary texture in any Archon. With enough Jellies to breed and harvest, he would never have to worry about boredom.

As for the bipeds with their bones on the inside, he expected they would make for interesting eating as well.

31

"Welcome, Admiral," Doctor Egolu said as Absen entered *Conquest*'s crowded physics lab. "This is Doctor Plessk, our senior physicist."

Absen kept the surprise from his face as he saw an ancient Ryss male, stooped and white with age. The Ryss made as if to rise from his seat, but the admiral quickly waved him down. "Honored to meet you," Absen said in passable Ryss, the language chip in his head feeding him the words. "I didn't know we had a Ryss scientist aboard." He remembered he'd left the makeup of the contingent up to Trissk, not paying much attention.

"I am an anomaly to my race, Admiral," Plessk said in his own language. "A male that did not want to be a warrior. Unlike in the old days, in current Ryss society that desire is viewed almost as a perversion. If I wish to spend my few remaining years doing the work I love, I have to do it among Humans or Sekoi. So, here I am."

"Here you are indeed. What can you tell me about the FTL drive?"

"Very little, Admiral," the Ryss said. "But perhaps, just enough." Plessk raised a shaky paw to signal Doctor Egolu, who turned on a holoprojector showing a cutaway diagram of the Sun. "The Meme intelligence says that they detected gravitic anomalies in the star where the Scourge attacked approximately sixteen minutes before they appeared. This tells us the FTL drive is gravitic in nature. Some among us think they use gravity to generate power. Some believe they use solar power to lens gravity into a singularity, which in turn can create a wormhole. Some –"

"Doctor, I'm not a scientist, I'm just a simple old warrior. Please proceed to the conclusion."

"Yes, well…" This seemed to throw Plessk off for a moment, but then he recovered, blinking watery eyes. "I believe we can give you at least sixteen minutes' warning of the Scourge's appearance."

"Outstanding." Absen said. "Doctor, if you can do that, you will have given us a key to defeating this threat, and I thank you." Bending over, he made another attempt, as he always did, to avoid an enormous waste. Whispering in the old cat's ear, he said, "Doctor, you don't have to endure this degeneration from old age. The Sekoi have a virus available that will return you to health and extend your life, perhaps indefinitely."

Plessk patted the admiral absently with a soft paw. "Thank you, Eldest War Leader, but even I am not such a pervert as all that. I will go to my ancestors when they call me home, and gladly."

Hissing with frustration, Absen straightened and composed himself. "I understand. I will make sure your people know of your accomplishments. Perhaps in time even Ryss will accept that scientific discovery is just as honorable as victory in battle."

"Now that I would like to see." The ancient cat's eyes sparkled.

32

"Give me an ops rundown, will you, Captain Scoggins?" Admiral Absen said as he stepped onto the bridge, waving everyone back to their seats. It seemed odd to be out of the Chair again and sitting down at the flag officer's station, but Absen had far too much to do to both coordinate the coming battle and fight *Conquest* as well. Fortunately, with the AI in the loop to pass and implement fleet instructions, both tasks had become a lot easier.

Scoggins was new to the flag captain role, but she was a veteran on this bridge and seemed to have settled in without a hitch. She'd immediately moved Fletcher to Sensors, and everyone else stayed where they were.

"Aye aye, sir," she said, standing and picking up a holographic cursor and gesturing to the holotank. "Since three hours ago, we are on station twenty million kilometers, or sixty-six light-seconds, above Sol's north pole. This is as close as we can get and still handle the solar radiation."

"What about anticipating their arrival?"

"It should be sixteen minutes and twenty-three seconds from gravitic wave front detection until they emerge from wormhole space."

"What about the sixty-six second lightspeed delay between us and where they come out?" Absen asked.

A graphic appeared in the holotank, no doubt thrown up by Conquest's AI. "About ninety-three seconds actually, sir. The hypotenuse of the right triangle described by a line from us to Sol's center and a line from Sol to the ecliptic."

"Right. Okay, ninety-three seconds. The delay?"

"Sir, gravity propagates at lightspeed as well, so the delay in detecting the gravity wave and the delay in seeing them are the same. No matter what our sensors detect or see, it's ninety-three seconds late."

"Right. Got it. Is there any way to tell how many motherships are coming?"

"No, sir, not according to Fleede. Twelve to sixteen is what they anticipate, based on the Meme info."

Absen waved. "All right. Go on."

Pointing with the cursor, Scoggins said, "From this position we can see any Scourge appearance along the plane of the ecliptic. As you noted, any attack will still have at least ninety seconds to travel, even at the speed of light. Once we have determined their location and formation, we can launch SLAMs from here, or we can pulse closer and launch from the new position, but sir, you have to decide on one tactic or the other well beforehand."

"Because we have to shove the SLAMs out of the launch bay and let their drive fields get well away from *Conquest* before lighting them off."

"Yes, sir."

"How long will that take?"

"At least five minutes before they are far enough."

Absen sat back, thoughtful. "What happens if the drive fields do interfere with each other?"

Scoggins frowned. "*Really, Really Bad Things*, Commander Ekara said."

"So let's not do that," Absen said. "Okay, we either set them up right here and fire them as soon as we have targets, or we zoom to some point closer, using the warning time to prep the SLAMs. What's wrong with that?"

"We'll be giving up our polar angle on the enemy. We'll only see the closest ones, and they'll actually see us first, because the EM that allows them to see us is continuously propagating, while theirs is brand new and has to travel to us. And, if we stay here, they are very unlikely to see us in the glare, while we've installed a whole suite of auxiliary sensors and filters so we can see them. Bottom line, sir, I believe we really need to launch the SLAMs from here."

Absen growled. "Ninety-three light-seconds gives their motherships a hell of a long time to dodge. Even a routine course correction on their part will cause the SLAMs to miss. Do you know how much effort those things cost us?"

Scoggins nodded gravely. "I do, sir. But they aren't tactical missiles. They were supposed to bombard the Weapon, a fixed target. We only made eight of them so far, and this is our best chance to use them right. If we're lucky and they don't arrive for a while, we'll have more. The other option is to wait and hold them in reserve, but…"

"But we give up the opportunity to take out a mothership and its entire swarm of millions with each SLAM." Absen glanced over at COB Timmons, who shrugged and took a sip of his lifer-juice. "All right. Set them up here. Ellis has a team working on a more robust tactical version that we can launch like a regular missile if the enemy gives us a couple more months. Go on."

Scoggins flicked her cursor and caused the holographic display to rotate in three dimensions. "Defense of Earth. The Weapon on the moon is fully functional and under our control." She paused, and Absen could just hear the wheels turning in her head as she pushed herself beyond the agony of thinking how useful the inward-facing laser they had destroyed would have been.

"Spilled milk," Absen said, as if he had read her mind, and Scoggins started slightly.

"Yes, sir. We've got a good loyal man, one Captain O'Rourke, running the Weapon. You'll remember he was a resistance mole in the loyalist military and he commanded an orbital fortress on Jupiter, so he's got the chops."

"Okay."

"The rest of the defensive infrastructure of Earth is relatively intact. Die-hard loyalists have been purged. Spooky – I mean Spectre – and his tame Blends have been running all the officers through personal mind-probe interviews. The PVNs manufactured enough modular laser auto-turrets to beef up all the fortresses and captured asteroids, so we have something like one hundred thousand point-defense weapons in orbit now." Scoggins looked sour.

"Not happy?"

The flag captain shook her head. "It sounds like a lot, until you consider that Earth will probably be getting hit with six or seven million assault craft, each of them armed and most of them full of Scourgelings and Soldiers. Simulations show we make a fair dent in them at the start, and then we get overwhelmed and they pour through. Best guess, half of them make it to the surface."

Clearing his throat, Absen asked a question everyone already knew the answer to, but he wanted no illusions. "How many enemy troops does that make?"

"Something like three billion, sir, three hundred million of which have small arms, and six million of which pilot attack aircraft or armored vehicles. Not to mention the nests, if we don't get them fast." The bridge crew had heard these numbers before in intelligence briefings, but now, on the eve of battle, they seemed terrifying.

"And our ground defenses?"

"Spectre has done wonders, sir, I have to say. He's got many old tank factories running again and is arming all the civilian aircraft. And, of about seven hundred million fit to bear arms, which includes every child that can be trained to hold a weapon or carry an ammo box, a third of them have at least an assault rifle and a basic load of ammo, with more being made all the time."

"And the rest of the people who have no weapons?" Rick Johnstone asked from his CyberComm seat.

Before Scoggins could answer, Bull spoke up from where he leaned cross-armed against the wall. "Stalingrad."

"Huh?"

Bull's eyes glittered with a grunt's fascination as he told the story. "At Stalingrad in World War Two, the Russians often only had one rifle for ten men...but they had a shitload of men. So they sent the armed ones forward with the others right behind them. As soon as the first man fell, the next would pick up his rifle and ammo bandolier and keep shooting Germans until he got killed...and so on, and so on. They died like flies."

"How is that good?" Rick said, distressed.

Bull stepped off the wall to loom over the seated officer. "Because, Commander, they *won*. At the end of the battle, they held the city and had taken four hundred thousand prisoners. The Wehrmacht never recovered." The Marine colonel's face twisted with righteous passion. "This is a battle we have to win, people. These buggers eat *everything*. It won't matter whether we die on the battlefield if we get eaten anyway."

Absen cleared his throat, and Bull subsided, moving back to his place. "At least we evacuated many of the smallest children to the Mars habitats. I know you wanted to be on the ground, Colonel, but I need you and your brigade here, on *Conquest*. Here is where you'll make the biggest difference, and I need someone I can utterly rely on."

"Yes, sir. I understand."

"I need you to understand in your *bones*, Bull. I can't have half your mind on Earth."

"Aye aye, sir." Bull had the decency to look abashed, but not happy.

Absen waved Bull back, turning to Scoggins. "Speaking of Bull's brigade, Captain, how about Operation Bughouse?"

"Getting there, Admiral." Scoggins rotated the display yet again, this time showing the other side of the Sun from Earth as she marked a cluster of eight Destroyer icons. "Here's the Meme location, 180 degrees out from Earth, as you requested. If they can decoy some of the Scourges, we want them to separate as much as possible from their Earth attack. The Meme will try to dance with them as long as possible, thinning them out and leading them away before they really run. We have no idea how well this will work. Red Team thinks it will depend on whether they view the Destroyers as attractive inhabited moonlets or tough warships."

"What do you think?" Absen asked.

Scoggins made a gesture of uncertainty. "Even the Blends don't agree. However, the Meme did plant a bunch of...I guess you'd call them life-forms all over the Destroyers' skins, to make them look tastier."

Absen waved his approval. "That's a pretty good idea. Okay, so the Destroyers lead some of the enemy off into space. What then?"

Moving around the holotank, Scoggins pointed with her cursor. "We hope the enemy small craft will take some casualties on the Jericho Line, then head *en masse* for the Destroyers, leaving at least one mothership vulnerable. Assuming they never faced a TacDrive before, they may believe they can see any threat coming in time to pull covering forces back. *Conquest* needs to be in position to pulse in as close as possible and launch Bughouse."

"And if Bughouse works, we'll have ourselves an FTL drive," Absen finished. *And if not,* he didn't say, *we'll have five thousand dead Marines and sled pilots.*

***

Brigade Command Sergeant Major Repeth bellowed, "At ease! Sit down and shut the hell up." Her eyes swept the small auditorium. It was standing room only, filled with every NCO from squad leaders up to her battalion sergeants major, about four hundred men and women. Twenty-nine of them were survivors of *Conquest*'s original contingent, but the rest were new, selected from the defense forces of Earth System under the Empire and trained to be Marines.

"For those of you who do know me, my name is Repeth. Because you are my NCOs I'm going to give you the rare privilege of calling me by my first name." She paused and smiled, a hard, flat expression. "And my first name is *Sergeant Major.* I don't know what kind of leaders you had during your time serving the Meme, and I don't care. Colonel ben Tauros runs things by the book, and so do I, so you will address everyone by EarthFleet ranks and you will render all proper customs and courtesies. Does anyone have a problem with that?"

No one responded.

"Lest you think I'm just some reg-bound martinet, I've posted my bio on the Brigade page. All of you will read

every word of it and every word of Colonel ben Tauros'
bio as well because between us we own your asses. The
short version is, I've been a Marine since I was seventeen
years old, before the Plague Wars, even. I've been fighting
for over a hundred fifty years on the calendar, over seventy
of them outside of coldsleep. Some of these people with
you," she swept a pointing finger across in front of her,
"have been with me almost as long. For example, Sergeant
Major Gunderson over there fought with me at
Fredericksburg ten years before the very first Destroyer
came. But don't think that means I'll favor them. I'm going
to be hard on every one of you, because I need you ready
to lead your troops in the fight of your lives.

"You thought your selection and training has been
tough until now. I'm here to tell you that was just the
start. Now that we're billeted aboard *Conquest*, we're not
going to kick back and take it easy. The enemy could
come at any time. This ship is big enough to practice
zero-G company-sized assaults, inside and outside the
hull. When you're not training live, you'll be in suit
simulators and VR space."

"Ma'am," said a muscular female gunnery sergeant
from the front row, standing up.

"*That's SERGEANT MAJOR*," Repeth roared. "Do I
look like an officer? Now what's your question,
Gunny…Calhoun?"

"Yes, Sergeant Major. Gunnery Sergeant Calhoun,
Second Battalion, Charlie Company, First Platoon.
How can we use VR simulators if we don't have
cyberlinks?"

"For you Marines new to EarthFleet, we have cocoons that use inductive brainwave stimulators adapted from Meme technology."

Calhoun went on, "Any word on when we'll be getting cybernetic implants, Sergeant Major?"

"It won't be soon. The only facilities for cybernetics are aboard *Conquest*, as the use of the tech was banned under the Empire, and there are much more pressing priorities for our limited resources. Combat nano and your powered battlesuits will have to do for now. Anything else?"

The gunnery sergeant looked disappointed as she said, "No, Sergeant Major," and sat down.

"If there are any other questions, feel free to ask them. That's what I'm here for – to make sure you understand the mission and what we're up against. To that end, I've brought a guest with me to give you a short briefing about the Scourge." Repeth gestured at a petty officer, who had been standing off to one side. "This is Master Chief Ikagi from the intelligence section."

Repeth sat down and let the chief speak, glad that she'd persuaded Bull to wave off Fleede and his thick, detailed files.

Once the intel briefing and several dozen questions had been dispensed with, Repeth took the podium again. "In about twenty minutes, Colonel ben Tauros will be done talking to the officers and will come address you. In the meantime, I'll give you a preliminary briefing on Operation Bughouse."

33

Yort awoke reluctantly, but he knew exit time approached. The dream-maker's grip gradually loosened, an automatic feature he was deliberately unable to control. Balanced between the worlds of sleep and waking, he watched the chronometer count down toward the moment when his mothership and eleven others would burst forth and take, and take, and take.

Not for the first time he thought how unfortunate it was that nothing could be done in the dead time of null space. How much more useful it would be if the Race could appear fully ready, every infant awake and instantly leaping to begin exterminating the pests that always seemed to infest their rightful territory.

Sometimes the infestations were stubborn. Occasionally one even defeated the first wave of motherships, and required a second application of pesticidal warfare. Yort fervently hoped this place was not one of those; for Archons to die was anathema of the highest order. Even contemplating such a thing threatened to enrage him enough to fully awaken, risking the null space madness.

Yort controlled himself, and waited, though his was not a patient nature.

Even if the first wave were driven back, most if not all of the motherships would escape, Archons intact, though shamed and diminished. The Race would prevail. It always had, ever since it escaped from the gravity well of the Home Nest barely ahead of its own extinction due to exhausting the planet of all competing life forms. Fortunately, other worlds with life had been located, and sublight colony ships with sleeping Archons and fertile eggs had launched themselves toward the stars in hopes of spreading the Race.

The ancient records said those colonies spawned more colonies, and their territory grew at a snail's pace, limited by the speed of light and conventional physics. Until, that is, the Race consumed a system with knowledge of how to access null space, speeding from star to star. With this technology, all their goals seemed within reach, to fill this galaxy, and the next, and onward to the billion billions waiting.

Ah, the glory of it, Yort thought. All we have to do is be bold enough to seize it.

34

As he stood on his palace's balcony looking at the view, Spectre reviewed what he had learned since returning to Earth.

In 2110, when most of Earth's population had been wiped out by the impact of the two Destroyers, nearly all of the Earthbound heavy industry and agriculture had gone with it, leaving a few locations where the howling winds and thousand-foot tsunamis did not reach. But even with a few cities intact, the Meme who took form as Blends had retooled what they seized. Farm machinery became the height of technology on the ground as staving off famine and then breeding more human underlings became the priority.

Each of sixty-four new Blends became overlords, calling themselves kings or pharaohs or presidents, dividing the spoils among them. Purelings imposed ruthless order, enslaving or killing all they found. For a time, humans were hunted and caged, then bought and sold for their labor, their skills, and the use of their bodies.

Over the next fifty years, human society was remade and reinvigorated, if not restored to what it once was. Survivors endured and were forced to breed, but they remembered and they taught their children about the old days, before the Meme and the Yellows came.

If not for the Eden Plague, the first generation, the breeding stock, would have died out and solved the Blend overlords' problems for them. But with the longevity the virus conferred, dissenters found each other and formed an insurgency, carefully salvaging what technology they could as they recruited for the eventual day of liberation.

The Blend overlords had children, expanding their oligarchy beyond its members' easy recognition. Rae and her two surviving children were able to walk among them, or take off the yellow and pass as ordinary humans slaving for the benefit of those above them. A poor Londoner of the nineteenth century or a Russian, North Korean or Chinese worker of the middle twentieth would have felt right at home in one of these feudal-industrial states.

This was the world Spectre had inherited. He'd spent an inordinate amount of effort over the past two months bringing the mishmash of the Blend's police and military forces to heel, executing at least a fifth of them outright. Once EarthFleet replaced the loyalist orbital defense forces, liberal use of laser bombardment convinced the holdouts their former masters had abandoned them.

The rest the Skulls took care of, mercilessly.

Using the hardcore insurgents as his political cadre, Spectre conducted a terrifying purge, mitigated only by the ability to subject subjects to biological interrogation to confirm their change of loyalty. Without that, he would have ordered killed anyone he was not certain of.

Not surprisingly the lowest classes, the powerless slaves who toiled on the farms and in the factories, were overjoyed at their newfound freedom. They were not quite as happy to learn that they had all been drafted into EarthFleet as militia, but those born after the Third Holocaust had not yet broken the habit of obedience to those who wore the yellow, and so, in less than two months, Earth was once again militarized.

More and more of the children of the original Meme Blends had joined Spectre, multiplying his abilities enormously. Once he had thoroughly ransacked their minds to ensure their sincerity, he put them to work doing the same to others. Eventually he was confident all remaining Blends at least grudgingly accepted his rule.

The others, he executed. He had no time for rehabilitation. The enemy could appear at any moment.

Now Spectre gazed out over what had been Gilgamesh's palace perched at the highest point of the Protectorate of Shepparton, pleased at the buzz of hundreds of people coming and going below him. The city's self-titled Lord Mayor had ruled it with a bit more wisdom and benevolence than the average Blend, and had developed it into the largest metropolis in Australia with over one million people. Shepparton had been spared the worst effects of the worldwide cataclysm due to its inland position.

Spectre had taken it for his own, making it his world capital, nerve center of his operations, connected to the other sixty-four former dictatorships by liberal use of satellite communications. Now, Earth had one government again, under martial law.

Still, he shook his head in disgust at how little he had accomplished. In many ways he felt like he was back in one of the Central American countries as a Green Beret, trying to turn barefooted peasants into insurgents against their anti-American regimes or drug cartels. As then, he could call on a limited set of high-tech resources, air and space assets to leverage what he had, but he didn't have enough of the basics: assault rifles, grenades, rocket launchers, much less lasers or EarthFleet-style pulse guns. Even the PVNs on Ceres had limits. And few of Earth's downtrodden workers had ever even considered picking up a weapon. They had to be taught a new mindset.

One man's propaganda is another's inspirational theme.

–35–

Now came the moment. The dream-maker's pulsing wave diminished to nothing, and for just a moment null space tugged at Yort's psyche before the mothership slammed into the gravity limit of the target star, emerging from the inside.

If Yort were describing the procedure in layman's terms, he would tell a young Archon that the ship within null space tunneled between the stars beneath space, as if it was a worm digging through the dirt. In this way a mothership bypassed the distance between. Therefore, when it surfaced, it did not arrive traveling *inward* toward the star from any combination of three dimensions, but rather *outward*, from the direction of another dimension entirely, as if surfacing into normal space, at speed, *away*.

This process must, however, be accomplished within a gravity well of sufficient power, which meant something with the mass of a star. At the same time, an arriving ship must not exit null space so close to the massive body that it was ripped apart by tidal forces, or blasted by a pulsar's spinning beam, or irradiated by a black hole's ravening polar jet...or simply burned up by a star's corona.

The solution to this dilemma, worked out by the Race's greatest physicists, was to exit as energetically as possible, like an underwater missile bursting from the sea. That way, even as the gravitic limit collapsed the wormhole field and ejected the ship into normal space, it was already moving away from the star.

Yort's dreams softened as his ship and its fellows emerged from null space.

Automated systems, recovering their abilities more quickly than living things, engaged reaction engines and accelerated twelve motherships away from the hot yellow sun, a starburst radiating outward along the equator of the spinning ball of fusion. Unfortunately it was not possible to coordinate their random departure points, though they always appeared along the plane of the stellar ecliptic, its equator.

The motherships' computers immediately launched spy drones, which began to gather data about the star system and feed it back to the ships' cybernetic brains even as they spread out and formed a web of communication. When the machines' masters fully awoke, they would already have vital information at their claw-tips.

Aboard *Conquest* a bridge console alarm sounded, beeping insistently. Lieutenant Fletcher at Sensors brought the alert up and said, "The physics lab reports their instruments are going nuts, Skipper. They say to expect incursion in about sixteen minutes."

Captain Scoggins swore without heat as her heart suddenly pounded with adrenaline. "General Quarters, Battle Stations. No drill, people: this is the real show. Tell Weapons Control to wake up the SLAMs." The finicky spaceship-sized missiles floating nearby took several minutes to bring to firing state.

At least we have sixteen minutes of warning. I hope it's enough, Scoggins thought.

Soon, *Conquest*'s prime watch hustled in to begin pulling on their suits and strapping into their seats. Scoggins held off on telling everyone to link in. There was little her admiral hated more than stepping onto a bridge full of closed crash cocoons…but she fully expected this battle to be fought from VR space. The margins were simply too close to give up any potential advantage, no matter the effect on crew brains and nervous systems.

The dead cared nothing about VR syndrome.

Admiral Absen slipped in and sat down at the flag station. "COB," he said to Timmons as he accepted a battered mug of hot coffee, "how is it my stateroom is a hundred meters closer than yours and yet you always beat me to the bridge?"

"Secret, sir. Master Chiefs only."

Absen grunted and began pulling on his suit. Once he'd finished and sipped more coffee, Scoggins swiveled around to face the admiral. "Eleven minutes remaining, sir. The SLAMs are hot. All sections report ready. Automated notifications have been sent. Suggest we go to VR at your convenience, sir."

Absen rubbed his jaw and stared at the holotank. "I hate VR," he muttered, and then took one last gulp of lifer-juice. "All right," he said with an air of resignation. "Let's plug in."

"All command and staff personnel, link up and cocoon," Scoggins ordered, reaching for her own plugs. Every now and again someone proposed making the links wireless, but the purity and reliability of the hard lines always won out.

VR space washed over Scoggins as the cocoon closed over her, replacing her view of the bridge with a similar but harder-edged simulation of the same. Now she seemed to sit comfortably in the Chair again, and so did the rest of the watch crew. The virtuality was designed to mimic reality as closely as possible in order to minimize cognitive disruption. Unlike specialists such as helmsmen and pilots, she didn't live a third of her life in VR, balanced between addiction and the drugs that fought it.

The captain ran through status reports for the entire ship, and then turned to Absen. "Battle speech, sir?"

Absen waved her off. "Mine went out prerecorded to the fleet and the rest of the system, Captain. *Conquest* is yours now."

Swelling with pride, Scoggins smiled. "Thank you, sir. I'll try to keep her in one piece."

"I'd appreciate it."

Scoggins cleared her throat – or felt like she did. It was so easy to forget about VR. "All hands, this is Captain Scoggins. We're just moments from what might be the greatest battle EarthFleet has ever faced. For you veterans who know what it's going to be like, I say: be the professionals you are, and we will prevail. For you who've never seen combat, focus on your jobs, listen to your leaders, and do your best. For you of faith, pray. If not, take heart and have faith in each other, in your brothers and sisters in arms." Then she took a slow, deliberate breath. "Now let's go kick some ass."

Johnstone pointed at his ear. "The crew's cheering you, Captain."

"Good speech, Melissa," Absen said, standing up and clapping her on the shoulder. "Better than mine, actually."

"Thank you, sir. Worked on it a lot."

The admiral walked over to stand before the holotank. "One good thing about VR is I don't have to worry about being knocked around the bridge." He stood looking over the display as time ticked away, the officers around him murmuring clipped commands and reports.

Abruptly the holotank blazed with new icons.

"Contacts…twelve contacts, twenty-one million klicks from Sol," Fletcher reported. "On the plane of the ecliptic, as expected."

In the holotank, the Sun occupied the center with a muted blaze. Now, twelve icons showed in a ragged ring twenty-one million kilometers out from its surface, inside the smooth Jericho Line orbiting at twenty-two million kilometers.

"Ford, target eight motherships with the SLAMs, the ones nearest Earth," Absen said, reaching his hand into the display to point. "Conquest, launch them as soon as you have firing solutions of sufficient confidence."

Conquest's voice spoke after a slight delay. "SLAMs away."

The holotank display plotted tiny lines that crawled toward the eight target icons more than ninety light-seconds away, the hypotenuse of the right triangle defined by Conquest's position, the location of its targets, and Sol. Scoggins hoped, as she knew they all did, that the eight motherships would continue along their plotted paths. The Meme intel on the Scourges said they were sluggish during the first several minutes after appearance, with only automated systems coming on line.

"All sensors up and open. Plot a min-range intercept course for the next nearest mothership not targeted by a SLAM," Scoggins ordered. "Ready one Exploder in the forward launcher, one in the magazine." If they were lucky, the antimatter weapon would catch the first ship's swarm before it spread far from its lattice. "Set two secondary targets and initiate the firing run."

Conquest would be in pulse before the SLAMs reached their targets. Scoggins would just have to hope they hit some of the motherships, and *Conquest* would deal with the rest. The main question was whether they could get the swarms before they cleared their motherships.

"Firing run set. Pulse in three, two, one, mark." Okuda's call had hardly faded in their ears when he said, "Dropping pulse, mark." Within the relativistic TacDrive field, distances seemed short.

The forward optical screens jumped and then stabilized, the holotank not far behind as it updated, both more smoothly in VR than they would have in realspace. On the displays, expanded for clarity and overlaid with targeting graphics, hung their first glimpse of a gigantic enemy vessel, at twenty kilometers across more of a ponderously mobile base than a ship. Scoggins heard several expressions of shock and surprise before the far more critical firing reports.

This one was waking up, that much was clear. Uncounted small craft, tiny at this distance and scale, spread from the thing's surface like organized clouds of gnats. Notations appeared as the AI processed the inputs, labeling groups as assault boats. Fighters and gunboats would follow. A rough total of the numbers visible topped four hundred thousand individual craft, almost half. Fortunately they were streaming in the other direction.

"Exploder and decoy missiles away," Conquest said. Reluctantly, Ford had relinquished deployment of the antimatter weapons to the AI. Precision was just too critical, and even with link and targeting computers, the weapons officer couldn't be quite as accurate and certain.

"Pulse, mark," Okuda said immediately, and reality shuddered once more. "Dropping, mark."

"Waiting to load the next Exploder..." Ford said as soon as they debouched from the TacDrive field.

Scoggins fretted as the antimatter missile levitated up the thousand-meter track from *Conquest*'s central magazine to the launcher in her nose, but as delicate as the weapon's magnetic bottles were, rushing the shot was not an option. *I should have prepped the Exploder before the pulse, not afterward*, she thought. She used the pause to slow her own time sense and examine the next mothership that lay off the port bow.

Okuda had been careful to arrive five thousand kilometers behind the enemy, away from Earth where its swarm was headed. Still, for the first time, academic knowledge began to turn visceral, and a knot of fear grew in her gut as she stared at the numbers on their way to the planet. *So many...and each assault boat with a thousand critters aboard, all wanting to eat us.*

"SLAM hit. Another!" Fletcher at her old Sensors station suddenly crowed. "The SLAMs are working!" Light from the first two strikes must have just reached *Conquest*, and Scoggins fervently hoped the other six would connect as well.

Cheers of relief broke out on the bridge with the knowledge that the enemy force had just been reduced by one sixth, sparing the defenders while slaughtering over two billion of the bugs. Scoggins felt no remorse. As far as she could tell, these Scourges had no redeeming qualities whatsoever, making the Meme look positively benign by comparison.

"Mister Ford, where's that Exploder?" Scoggins snapped.

37

Yort's mind still labored under the lingering influence of null space confusion when his mothership's sensors shone alarms into his eyes. Exquisitely detailed holographic plots showed a scene of horror with machine precision, even more sickening because of their painful realism using data relayed from his many spy drones.

Of the twelve motherships, eight of them had vanished. In their places he saw balls of expanding plasma and sprays of wreckage. "Emergency power; evasive maneuvers," Yort blasted through every photo-emitter on his body, his words slurred with residual lethargy. "Begin immediate deployment." Machines on the bridge echoed the order to his subjects.

"But Archon Third, we have no targets," blinked one of his officers. "The lower orders will be confused and some will head for the star."

"Then ensure they do not!" Yort ordered. "Send them outward while I determine what disaster has befallen our motherships." Playing his digits over the controls himself, he ran the record back to the time of their appearance, and then quickly located the moment when the massive swarm-carriers exploded. First they existed, and then long moments later they exploded, so suddenly that only light-based weapon strikes seemed likely. The direction the wreckage sprayed provided him with a vector, and within seconds he plotted the position the unknown weapon must have fired from, a significant distance above one pole of the star.

Somehow, the infestation had expected them, had waited at a place that allowed them to see all possible exit points, and fire on them. But even light-based weapons took time to reach them, and so as long as his mothership continued to evade, he should be safe from the hideous death ray.

Unfortunately the blazing radiation of the star eliminated any hope of his sensors detecting the exact nature of the enemy. It must be a supermassive fortress to employ such a weapon, a veritable planetoid.

"There," he said to his officers, indicating the place with a claw tip. "Send half my forces to the enemy firing location via a spherical route. Spread the other half out and away from the star. Where..." He quickly examined the first planet in the system, a small barren world, then the second, shrouded in hot clouds, neither of which showed signs of abundant life. But the third teemed with it.

It also swarmed with infestations of war machines.

Of interest, the eight annihilated motherships were all closest to the third planet's current orbital position.

"Sir, I have detected another biomass cluster, here, near us. Eight large nests."

Yort examined his primary display. Life readings beckoned opposite the infested planet, but closest to his own mothership, a stroke of luck. If he moved quickly, he could seize and eat this prize himself, then move on to join in the main assault as other swarms took the brunt of the casualties.

38

While they waited the interminable seconds for the next antimatter missile to load, Scoggins asked, "Results on the first Exploder?"

"Vaporized them, hon," Commander Ford said with a wolfish smile.

She let him get away with the familiarity this time. He was her husband, after all. Right now the elation of the plan's success had her in its grip, and she forced herself to concentrate. "Where's that second Exploder?" she growled.

"Coming up now."

Scoggins cheated with her time sense, tweaking it so the seconds passed quickly, though that caused the swarms of enemy looming in front of *Conquest* to deploy even faster on the screen. Suddenly, witch-lights flared among the enemy, ripples of color and brightness in complex waves and densities.

"What the hell is that?" Scoggins asked.

Lieutenant Fletcher replied, "Some of it's laser fire. No threat at all at this range. A little is some kind of plasma discharges aimed at us, but we're too far away. The majority seems to be communication lights among themselves. Millions of them."

"James –" Scoggins said to Ford in a tone of warning.

"Firing now," he replied hastily. "Exploder and missiles away."

"Pulse, mark," Okuda said immediately, and the displays blanked as *Conquest* bolted. "Dropping, mark." Scoggins mentally counted this pulse as the ship's third capital action of the five their capacitors allowed them, a convenient shorthand.

Another mothership, looking much like the first, appeared in front of them, only this one was surrounded by its enormous, already expanding swarm. The enemy now resembled the biggest hornet's nest Scoggins had ever seen.

"Alpha strike. Target the mothership." *Fourth action, and an Exploder would get intercepted by that mess.*

"Aye aye, Skipper," Ford said with relish. This time he got to fire with his own hands, or at least it would feel that way in VR.

The swarm was already turning and firing thousands of weapons toward *Conquest* when her primary weapons array speared death into the mothership core.

First, the three gargantuan *Desolator*-built particle beams bored a hole through the intervening thousands of boats to touch the mothership. Attenuated by the interfering escorts, the energy blew through the organic resin of the latticework and barely singed the armor of the enemy core, but it cleared three cylinders of space.

Space for a million ferrocrystal spheres to pass and strike the target at $0.3c$.

The streams of railgun shot slammed into the mothership's hull and each immediately fused, every one releasing power equivalent to a tiny nuclear blast. The inexorable tide of sun-like heat quickly ate its way through the core's heavy armor in three separate places. Once the lines of shot chewed through, the resulting plasma, stripped ions and superheated gas propagated throughout the interior of the flattened sphere very much like the sledgehammer had done to the Io base, but more so. Ironically, the mothership's heavy armor became a liability, holding the expanding hell within the vessel it was supposed to protect.

Inside, everything ignited as lines of blasts marched through its structure, ruler-straight. Even substances not normally flammable – foodstuffs, metals, even ceramics – burst into flame and consumed themselves in a firestorm that snuffed out every living thing within.

Gutted, the core spewed a blazing jet of gases from its entry wounds and spun broken through the void like a firework pinwheel.

"Yes! Yes!" Ford slapped his console with fierce joy, echoed by others on the bridge.

"Well done," Scoggins said with a pleased shudder. It was one thing to launch SLAMs or deploy Exploders and run, not seeing the results, but quite another to witness the kill with a warrior's dark satisfaction. "Mister Okuda, take us out of here."

"Pulse, mark. Dropping, mark."

Fifth action.

"Capacitors at two percent," the Engineering station reported. "Full charge in sixty-three minutes."

Now the holotank and flatscreen displays – really just images in her head, Scoggins reminded herself – showed *Conquest* hanging in space twenty million kilometers out from Sol's *south* pole, exactly opposite from where they had launched the SLAMs and well away from any action. This position allowed her, and the admiral, full visibility of the theatre of battle.

Drained of stored power, *Conquest* waited. Had they not been in VR space, Scoggins would have ordered everyone to take a break. Instead, she toyed with the idea of using the AI's control of VR time to skip forward, but decided against it.

Beside her, Admiral Absen paced about the bridge, looking at the holotank from all angles and issuing terse orders to his forces strewn around the solar system. "Captain, take a look at this mothership," he said after he was done. He pointed to one Scourge carrier separated from its fellows, on the opposite side of the sun from Earth.

Scoggins nodded. "That's the one we left alone, heading for the Meme Destroyers."

"Just what we need," Absen replied. "He's out of position. Probably figures he'll be last to the buffet, so he might as well try to grab a snack while his buddies are distracted."

"You have a sick sense of humor, sir."

"It's been said." The admiral pointed. "Hmm. What's this swarm cluster? The one that's heading to the solar north? We can barely see it."

Scoggins stared, leaning over the railing and putting her nose into the holotank. "Michelle, magnify that, will you?"

The fuzzy icon expanded rapidly until it resolved itself into a swarm of Scourge ships. "What the hell are they doing out there?" Absen asked. "Replay the record and tell me where they came from." The display reversed time, showing clearly the enemy group had been launched from the lone mothership.

"They're heading for where we fired the SLAMs from," Scoggins realized aloud. "Probably thinks we have something permanent there, like a fortress."

"Clever bug," Absen said, "but not clever enough. Half his swarm is going for the Meme, where I hope they'll be savaged badly. The other half is on a wild goose chase…"

"And the mothership's all alone, heading away from the sun," Scoggins finished. "Bughouse."

"Yes." Absen made one more circuit of the holotank, looking at the display from all angles. "Put me through to Vango and Bull."

39

"Archon, we are detecting pestilence installations between us and the eight spaceborne nests." On Yort's screen he could see a river of objects – thousands of asteroids and millions of tiny living creatures all orbiting the star, though only a small fraction of them barred his path, so vast was the orbit.

Yort briefly considered angling his forces and mothership up and over the plane of the ecliptic, but that would use valuable time and fuel already being prodigiously expended by the mothership's evasive maneuvers. What had he to fear from a few defenses? Even with half his forces on their way to the still-unseen superfortress above the star's pole, he had over fifty thousand Claws, an equal number of Lances, and a half-million Mandibles filled with a billion larva and adolescents. His only challenge would be chasing down the fat nests, consuming them, and returning to the infested world soon enough to claim his share.

Abruptly, several of his Claws vanished in first one fusion explosion, then another. Within seconds, blasts flared along the line of his advancing craft, annihilating them in small groups. "The pestilence has deployed orbital mines. Why did the Claws not see them?"

"I do not know," said his underling officer. "The surveillance technicians are searching for an answer."

"Spread our forces out to ensure no more than one is killed at a time," Yort ordered. "The damage is bothersome, but negligible." Soon, the frequency of explosions waned, still striking here and there, but killing barely one in a thousand of his Claws, Lances and Mandibles.

"The Claws approach the asteroids," Yort's underling reported. "They exhibit minimal signs of infestation."

"Tell the Claws to begin firing plasma torpedoes at extreme range to provoke a response."

Minutes passed before Yort received the first reports from his staff. "The asteroids are returning fire with beam weapons. They have killed several Claws."

Yort took a long look at his display, noting how few the armed asteroids were, and how they approached along the solar orbit with significant spacing between. "Order the Mandibles to continue toward the enemy nests. For the good of the greater Hive, swarm the asteroids with Claws and Lances. They can overtake the Mandibles later."

Soon, thousands of Claws and Lances englobed the leading pestilence, stabbing it to death with direct fire. In short order the asteroid exploded, taking a few more Claws with it before it died. "Maintain maximum range," Yort ordered. "They have suicide charges aboard." Clever, this infestation and its pestilence, but not so clever as all that. "Continue to swarm each enemy in turn."

By the death of the fourth armed asteroid his tens of thousands of Claws and Lances became densely packed, often getting in each others' way and even colliding. "Order them to spread out again," Yort said.

Abruptly and without warning, his viewer blazed with a hundred fusion explosions distributed randomly within his swarm. The Archon watched with growing annoyance as he saw the total casualty count top one in ten. "Fools," he flashed. "Must I do all the thinking for you?"

Control was becoming more difficult as communications lag lengthened due to the growing distance between swarm and Archon. "Continue evading, but angle us downward to avoid the plane of the ecliptic," Yort ordered after all. "I do not want my mothership to pass through the zone of hidden mines. Then resume course toward the target nests."

For his swarm, fusion mines held little fear. Each blast would only kill one of millions, as long as the small craft stayed well away from each other. However, one well-placed detonation could cripple or kill his mothership.

"Expand the external structure," Yort ordered. This would unfold the latticework of girders into a globe of enormous size, deploying gossamer netting into all empty spaces. That way, if a hidden explosive touched the outside of the mothership, it would destroy nothing but material of little worth, and his nest would remain safe deep within. In other words, the extended skin would serve to detonate unseen weapons.

Soon, the mothership's outer circumference had grown tenfold, leaving vast pockets of space around the comparably tiny central body.

"Archon, something new approaches." One of his underlings marked a cluster of enemy pestilence on the screen. "It accompanies this group of armed asteroids and is made of the small biomass units."

Yort strained his eyes. "Magnify."

"Magnification is maximum, Archon. We are far from the target cluster because of our evasive course."

Blasting a frustrated glare in all directions, Yort said, "Those resemble the speedy suicide swarmers of the Jellies. Tell the Claws to attack them vigorously with coherent light while the Lances pummel the asteroids with plasma torpedoes. Alert the Mandibles to activate point defenses while pressing toward the enemy nests."

Even as he issued the orders, the cluster in question burst outward with the flaring of fusion drives. Thousands of tiny enemy swarmers leaped toward his Claws with acceleration impossible to match. Yort watched as some fell to his energy weapons, but several hundred damaged or destroyed more Claws, while the rest missed their targets. The weapons passed through the Claw screen, disregarded his Lances and aimed themselves at the Mandibles.

While loss of more Claws annoyed him, Yort was pleased by the enemy's choice of secondary targeting. With more than a thousand defensive beams for every attacking swarmer, he expected very little damage to his many Mandibles.

Yort turned out to be correct. A mere two of his more than half a million Mandibles were lost, the puny thousand or so attackers burned down by even the inept gunnery of the adolescent pilots.

And then the dangers were past, as his swarm and his mothership departed from the pestilence zone orbiting the star. Yort saw he had lost only twelve percent of this half of his swarm, while the other half accelerated toward the origin point of the mothership-killing blasts. Relief flooded him as he realized that his underlings had not detected any sign of the unknown weapon firing at *him* – no vaporized dust from a near miss, no reflections or ionizations.

Perhaps the threat had abated, but he maintained his mothership's evasive corkscrew despite its cost in fuel. Yort had always considered himself a bit wiser than the average Archon, and so he congratulated himself on his care. "Focus a sensor suite on the target location above the pole."

"I have done so for some time, Archon, but have detected nothing."

"Nothing? Show me." Yort heaved himself upward on his weak, seldom-used legs to crane all four eyes toward the screens overhead. "I don't see anything."

His underlings remained silent, only waiting. Finally, the bravest of them spoke. "Perhaps whatever fired has departed."

"Departed? Impossible. Something must be there, or nearby. Nothing large enough to fire such weapons could have moved far. Perhaps your sensors are malfunctioning or being jammed?"

"Unlikely, Archon, or we would detect something, even if we did not understand what it was. But we can see the distant stars through the empty space of the location."

Yort turned his eyes to take in secondary displays. "Where are our three remaining motherships?" he asked.

"We have lost contact with them, Archon. Spy drone reports show their swarms heading for the infested world, but no motherships. It is possible they have retreated too close to the sun to see, or have re-entered null space."

"They have not had time to recharge their null space drives." Yort racked his mind for any reason the other motherships would hide or stay near this system's yellow sun, but could think of nothing. His thoughts shied from the possibility that they had all been destroyed by the mysterious ship-killer weapon. He knew he was smarter than other Archons of his rank, but surely at least some of his brother-sisters would have thought to evade continuously.

Perhaps he should have suggested it to them.

And their three swarms and portions of the others still existed, a superswarm totaling over eight million craft and seven billion larvae, easily enough to overrun the planet, destroy the pestilence, consume the infestation, establish nests, and then move on to secure the rest of the star system.

On the other limb…if the worst had happened and the other motherships had been destroyed, command would fall to him. His dream of achieving Archon First, of taking this system for himself, might be no fantasy after all.

Perhaps this was not such a disaster as he had thought.

"Recall the half-swarm heading toward the polar location. Ensure our evasion pattern continues," Yort said.

"Fuel is being depleted at twice the normal rate, Archon. One-eleventh is already expended."

Yort did not respond. The underling had spoken an important truth, though. Eventually he would have to stop the evasion that spun and shifted the mothership ponderously from direction to direction. It should not matter. When his swarm seized the mobile nests, he would have all the fuel he needed.

40

SystemLord watched as the Scourge swarm surged toward his eight fat Destroyers. Half again as large as standard ships of their type, the Meme ships bulged with fuel for fusors and engines, though in his experience one never had enough.

The underlings – the *Humans*, his new allies, he reminded himself – had been most accommodating when it came to providing an assignment suitable to his capabilities. The situation was nearly ideal, with the one exception of its evident danger. By subtle suggestion, the one called Raphaela had accepted his offer to decoy some of the Scourge away rather than participating in the futile defense of the planet. By SystemLord's calculations the Humans had less than one chance in nine of not losing their world.

Again.

Such incompetence.

The irony amused him, until he remembered he had also lost the planet for the Empire.

But try as he might, SystemLord had not been able to get the Blend Raphaela to provide the lightspeed drive technology data before the battle. Had he acquired that, he might have yielded to the temptation to depart as fast as his drives could take him toward the nearest Empire-held system, perhaps implementing it along the way. Not only would the technology provide his people an important weapon against the Scourge, its triumphal presentation would ensure he was personally rewarded.

Unfortunately, the Humans had not been so trusting, and had not given him the lightspeed drive technology data yet. However reluctantly, SystemLord would play his part, if only to ensure he received what was promised. Now he turned his considerable intellect to that task.

"Cease gestation of hypervelocity projectiles," he ordered. "They are not effective against so great a mass. Also cease gestation of stingships. Launch the ones we have and hold them in reserve behind us."

In order to minimize his exposure, SystemLord had brought his ships close in order to reach each other with fusors. The tough armored skin of the Destroyers could easily withstand the sun-hot gouts of plasma for brief moments, as an Underling would pass a finger through a candle flame.

His own ships would be killing fields.

On those armored ship skins he had seeded fast-growth polyps over a thin layer of nutrients, giving the Destroyers a sheen of life guaranteed to attract the Scourge. It amused him to think how the ravening hordes would be irresistibly drawn to it, only to be burned, burned, *burned*, slight but sweet revenge for the damage done to the Empire.

If he must fight, he might as well enjoy his enemy's misery.

Now, eight great vessels hung in the void, seven surrounding his flagship where they could cover it with fire from all angles. The ships were close, very close in space terms, just far enough apart that thermonuclear explosions would not reach more than one at a time.

"The Scourge has many ships," his Survey One said.

"Cease your imprecise communication if it adds no information," SystemLord said. "My plan is flawless. As long as all execute properly, you have nothing to fear."

"I hear and obey, SystemLord," the other answered. And then, a moment later, "They are firing."

A blizzard of energy weapons reached for his ships, most of them missing but enough impacting that the naked polyps began to die. No matter: that was their function. "Begin acceleration away from them, gently. Extend the time before they try to board us."

"It will be done."

His spherical ships turned as one, pointing engines toward the enemy and igniting them. The rate of the following swarm's closure diminished, and the fusion torches themselves became weapons. The enemy avoided them, of course, which channeled them into denser zones.

"We should fire fusors," Rear Fusor One said.

"Not yet," said the Meme commander. "The more densely packed they are, they more efficient our fusors."

"Already their lasers and plasma torpedoes impact us."

SystemLord's communication molecules expressed derision. "Our armor can withstand direct thermonuclear blasts, and you are frightened of packets of plasma fired in magnetic bottles?"

"SystemLord…there are many weapons."

"How many?"

"Approximately six hundred thousand have struck us since they came within range. Our armor has been ablated by over seven percent in certain locales."

Shocked for a moment at the high number, SystemLord refused to let his subordinates know. "Very well. Begin the spiral motion. Increase acceleration and selectively target the largest enemy clusters. Do not be profligate with fuel!"

Immediately upon receipt of his orders, each Destroyer began a slow spin around its axis and induced a slight wobble. Now, the great jets of its fusion engine described continuous helixes, dramatically widening their threats to the pursuing swarm. At the same time, fusors flared, reaching out to wash dozens, even hundreds of enemy craft from space.

Yet, hundreds of thousands followed.

"Rear armor ablated by sixteen percent," Command One said. "We must increase our weapons fire."

SystemLord considered One's words but said nothing. As painful as it was to lose some rear armor, every moment drew this swarm further into space, away from the mothership and its other, equally large swarm, which had already turned to rejoin its fellows.

"Twenty-two percent," Command One said, more stridently.

"Increase spiral motion and power to the engines. Increase fusor fire to fifty percent of maximum."

At his order, the Destroyers spun even harder, faster, with fusors like flamethrowers spurting outward. Thousands of small Scourge vessels fell, but tens of thousands continued to follow.

The swarm closed in.

"SystemLord –"

"Maximum spiral. Fire at full effect."

Tens of thousands more Scourge were vaporized, crisped, blotted from space by temperatures of a million degrees or more, but even the ravening fusors of eight dreadnoughts could not be everywhere at once.

"Armor ablated by more than fifty percent and rising. They are landing," Destroyer Command One reported in a near panic. "They are disembarking troops and drilling into our armor."

SystemLord ordered, "All vessels close in and sterilize our skin."

The seven outer vessels stabilized their spins, still belching fusor fire at a prodigal rate. Ignoring the landings on their own outer hulls, they closed in around the flagship and focused their blowtorches on its surface. The tough armor, even damaged as it was, resisted the heat of the friendly fire, and uncounted Scourgelings and their Soldier leaders died.

In moments, SystemLord's vessel was free of enemy, though not without great gouges and pits of damage. A few of the Scourges had managed to activate nuclear suicide charges, blowing craters in the tough ferrocrystal-infused outer covering of the Destroyer.

"This ship will retreat, maximum acceleration. The others will work together to scour their skins in turn." In moments, SystemLord's vessel streaked away, leaving the seven others of his command to fight. The stingships he had held in reserve swooped in to cover his retreat.

In another species this action might have been deemed cowardly, but Meme had little sense of honor or self-sacrifice. As SystemLord, he was entitled to preserve his life, ruthlessly sacrificing others if necessary. However, he did not intend to throw away his forces.

As soon as his own ship was far enough away, he ordered it halted to observe and supervise. His seven remaining Destroyers engaged the swarm in a complex dance, allowing waves of assault craft to alight on their skins, then presenting these landing zones to their fellows' fusor fire. According to SystemLord's plan, they repeatedly ambushed the Scourge.

This strategy was not without cost. First one, then another of the firepower of his dreadnoughts trickled away, until the two became hulks overrun by hundreds of thousands of Scourgelings eating them from within. SystemLord had known that as soon as the enemy penetrated to his ships' soft insides, they could not be stopped. Interior defense forces for Meme ships were simply too few.

Escape pods blasted away from the two doomed ships, his subordinate Meme flushed down tubes and distilled into missile-sized drones containing only their essences. They could be rehydrated later, as long as their memory molecules survived.

Many of these were shot down by the eager enemy fighters, but some ran the gauntlet, and SystemLord directed his ship to launch recovery craft. Loyal subordinates of the Pure Race were not resources to be wasted.

For long moments the battle hung in the balance as the swarm's numbers dwindled, and then they abruptly broke off the attack. All Scourge craft still flying – mostly fighters and gunships, which had never tried to land – turned tail and ran, leaving the remnants of their assault forces to die. SystemLord spat frustration as one more Destroyer ceased fighting and flushed its crew, though at least all the pods escaped to be recovered.

Five Destroyers remained, several of them badly damaged, but living ships needed only time, materials and energy to heal. SystemLord reminded himself, and then told his crew, that it could have been far worse. His plan had not resulted in the stunning victory he had hoped for, but neither had it brought disaster.

As the enemy swarm retreated toward its mothership, he redistributed crews, regrouped his surviving ships around the carcasses of their dead fellows and told them to eat. That their food included the remaining enemy Scourgelings that even now ate those dead Destroyers in turn mattered not one whit. Food was food.

41

Archon Yort screamed blazes of light as the half-swarm attacking the enemy nests took horrendous casualties. The assault had started out well enough, but the closer his forces came, the more died. By the time the loss rate became untenable, it was too late. The physics of pursuit committed him to action.

When his Mandibles finally came to grips with the enemy, progress improved. The skins of the enemy nests, while tough, were not impervious, and his forces reported successful burrowing, using everything from suicide explosives to the diamond-hard teeth and claws of millions of Scourgelings. Yort reminded himself that almost half a billion of his infantry had begun the assault, five hundred million jaws and two billion claws.

He could afford to lose millions and still win.

One enemy ship suddenly retreated at an alarming rate, and he wondered why the others did not do the same. It never occurred to him that any enemy would voluntarily engage in battle with his swarms. That seemed to make as much sense as offering one's own limb to feed an enemy. Yet, these nests remained, frying his Mandibles in great swaths of flame.

Yort exulted at first one and then another of the nests expired. Now the real power of the Race showed through. It really did not matter how many infants were lost, as long as they achieved victory for their Archons. And once his other half-swarm joined the battle, the nests would fall quickly.

So closely did Yort watch the grinding battle that it took one of his officers actually touching him to get his attention. The Archon jerked and swung a saw-toothed limb at the offending servant, who scuttled out of the way. "Archon," the creature flashed when it had his attention, "we are under attack!"

"I know we are —" Yort's sneering retort cut off in mid-sentence as he examined his displays. A large mechanical warship, fully as large as his own mothership's armored core, had appeared out of nowhere. Shaped like a decorative crystal teardrop with its sharp point forward, the vessel seemed utterly alien, like nothing either his own race or the Jellies would build.

Before he could say anything further, alarms blinked and strobed.

"Archon, the enemy is firing large numbers of energy weapons and high-speed physical projectiles. Our lattice has taken catastrophic damage!"

Yort snapped, "They are fools. The lattice is of no consequence. The core must survive. Engage with all weapons and move away at maximum. Instruct all swarm elements to return immediately, emergency speed!"

"Archon, the enemy is launching a swarm of their own."

On the displays, Yort saw small craft resembling Claws, Lances and Mandibles spewing from the rear of the teardrop, but far, far fewer than he expected. "That is hardly a *swarm*," the Archon said. "That is barely a cluster of, what, perhaps a thousand elements?"

"Yes, Archon."

"If they think to board, we will defeat them. Alert the breeding pens. All infants more than half grown are to be driven to defensive positions inside the armor. Cadre are to exchange training weapons for combat versions and take charge of the infantry. All others are to arm themselves as appropriate. And awake the Constructs." Yort laughed. "A thousand elements? Do they think my core is empty of defenders? That they will simply devour us? Have no fear, my subjects. We will repel them, and then our returning swarm will eat their single warship."

42

"Dropping, mark." Okuda's words heralded *Conquest*'s appearance less than a thousand kilometers from the last Scourge mothership, point-blank range for her heavy weapons and easily close enough for her secondaries. Now the ship had recharged capacitors and could be profligate with firepower.

"Fire when ready," Captain Scoggins said, and *Conquest* lashed out with lasers and particle beams. "Don't hit the core too hard," she warned.

"Got it, Skipper," Ford singsonged as he coordinated the firing. "Keeping the primaries away from the core."

On the displays, Absen could see the enormous lacy structure of the mothership carved away in spiny chunks like melon rind under the knife. His plan was to remove those intervening layers before sending in his assault forces, simplifying their lives enormously.

The enemy returned a weak spray of intermittent laser fire from scattered locations, nothing to present any threat to a capital ship. Probably the Scourges had never envisioned fighting without their swarms. Those lasers were quickly silenced by the overwhelming firepower of the dreadnought.

Once the lattice floated as wreckage and the core was revealed like the pit of an avocado, the display blazed with sudden flashes from the core. "Incoming fire – not sure what it is," Fletcher said, his voice rising a notch. By the time he finished speaking, Conquest's hull showed hundreds of impacts from...something.

"Evasive," Scoggins snapped.

"Captain," the AI said, "the weapons are concentrated plasma packets contained within magnetic bottles. The Meme Intel data references these as 'plasma torpedoes.' They cannot penetrate our armor but they are doing some damage to surface systems, especially the bolt-on point defense lasers." She referred to the thousands of self-contained modules recently grafted onto Conquest's outer surface to beef up her capacity to repel assaults.

"Counterfire," Scoggins ordered. "Move in and take out the launchers."

"On it," Ford replied. As he and the Michelle coordinated pinpoint takedowns of the enemy plasma launchers, Okuda advanced Conquest on fusion drive.

In moments, the dreadnought had completely stripped the enemy core of weapons. Bereft of its swarms – the untouched half-swarm almost two hours away and the remnants of the one that attacked the Meme more than thirty minutes distant – the exposed core maneuvered frantically but sluggishly, obviously not designed for a ship-to-ship battle.

Absen caught his flag captain's eye, and then Scoggins said, "Knock out their drive and thrusters. I want that bastard helpless as a hogtied calf in one minute. Then secure from evasive maneuvering and prepare for Bughouse. Come on, people, we're on the clock!"

Keying his own internal comms, Admiral Absen brought up Vango and Bull. "Gentlemen, Bughouse is a go. I say again, execute Bughouse. Absen out."

The holotank depicted two enormous sections of armor slowly, ponderously pulling back from *Conquest*'s stern, nearly in the shadow of her great fusion engines. Over a hundred grabships under AI control lifted off million-ton plates, revealing makeshift launching tunnels leading to the ship's huge interior cargo bays.

Not made for assault operations, this was the best Absen and his staff could come up with to allow some five hundred assault sleds holding over five thousand newly recruited Marines to quickly egress to space. As soon as they could, the boats streamed outward to assemble in ranks in the shadow of Conquest's great bulk.

As they did so, four hundred ninety-six StormCrows took off from the standard flight deck under precise AI control, two per second. Once they cleared the ship, the pilots took over and immediately turned toward the mothership core. As *Conquest* ceased fire from its capital weapons, the fighters moved in to strafe the surface of the enemy.

***

With Crows mounting newer, hotter lasers optimized against the Scourges, Colonel Vango Markis and the rest of his fighter pilots sliced away the remnants of latticework, plasma cannon mounts and every other anomaly on the surface of the flattened sphere. Hopefully that would render the Scourges blind, deaf and dumb, trapping them inside their own armor.

Then they went to work on that armor, probing the damaged portions, looking for easy ways in. The core's protection was thick, but not in *Conquest*'s class. The StormCrows did not launch their nukes, but they did keep carving with their lasers.

As Vango fired another bullet of coherent light into a deepening gouge, he called, "Keep digging holes, boys and girls. Looks like this is only about one hundred meters of composite armor, and the jarheads are going to need all the help they can get punching through."

"Sure, boss," his wingman Raiderette said. "Sure you don't want to get out of the way and let the big boys do some digging?" She referred to *Conquest*'s weapons.

"Not precise enough. We can't afford to punch through and vaporize the interior if we want to capture the FTL drive system."

Vango could hear the irony in her voice. "Sounds to me like we're the lonely fan in this shitstorm again, sir."

"Shut up and keep blowing, Lieutenant."

***

Bull ignored the assault sled's motion as it slammed him from side to side. His Avenger suit was locked down to the interior and wouldn't release until they landed or he deliberately overrode it. The last thing a boat needed was a dozen thousand-kilo golems flailing around damaging its relatively delicate interior.

Checking his HUD, he saw the half-thousand assault sleds turn in a coordinated wave and accelerate toward the drifting mothership core. *Conquest*'s reinforced aerospace wing seemed to be having no trouble with the point defense and he'd been assured they had at least twenty minutes until the enemy fighters showed up, retreating from getting their asses kicked by the Meme. *Never thought I'd be cheering the slimy blobbos,* he thought, *but they did good work today.*

Dialing up the division channel he said, "All right, First Div Marines, this is Colonel ben Tauros. I'd say *shalom* but nobody's gettin' any peace for the next few hours. We got a short flight and a hard fight, so remember your training, listen to your leaders, and kill every bug you see. Remember, though, if you find some fancy unknown machinery, don't touch it and don't blow it up. The whole reason we're puttin' our asses on the line here is to get the technology. Good hunting. Ben Tauros out."

Switching to the lead pilots' freq, he said, "Bull here. How's the LZ looking?"

"Jes' fine, Colonel, sir," Warrant Officer Krebs came back. "Y'all be shittin' in tall cotton pretty soon."

"Shut up, Krebs. Butler, you there?"

The other flight warrant replied, "Yes, sir. LZ looks clear. Don't think the bugs ever expected to be boarded. With a hundred thousand fighters, who would?"

"Good. That's why we have to be gone before they show up. Ben Tauros out."

43

Lieutenant Victor Cheng tugged nervously at a spot-weld on the bracing of his fire control console, unsure it would hold. Earth's orbital fortresses were old and had not been well maintained throughout the fifty years of the occupation. Indifferent techs and officers had manned the planet's defenses for five decades against a threat that never materialized – until it did. The most conscientious ones like him had been sent to Jupiter.

Now he was back, commanding a bank of lasers on this enormous but deteriorating station. At least he had gotten a three-day leave to visit Brenda and her gorgeous legs. Even better, she had received his advances with unabashed enthusiasm, and after a whirlwind courtship, they had gotten married. There was no Council on Mating and Breeding to give approval anymore. It had been that moment when he decided he really liked his newfound freedom of choice.

He'd realized he also had the freedom of choice to desert EarthFleet, to run away with Brenda and hide somewhere, but he discovered his freedom's reverse side: responsibility. After many tears, Cheng had left his new wife there in the tiny York apartment, trying to explain why he had to do his best to defend her and everyone else on Earth.

He and the other skilled cadre brought back from Jupiter system had worked like dogs to get their laser bank back in shape, but things still tended to fall apart at any moment, requiring frantic searches for the problem. Then, even if the glitch was identified, getting spare parts was a crap shoot.

Cheng sighed and pushed a comm button. "Hassan, have you got the COP working yet?" Sergeant Hassan was supposed to recon a cabled conversion module to get their Common Operating Picture display functioning, otherwise they wouldn't get feeds of the overall battle.

"Got something better, sir." A moment later Hassan entered the control center dragging a beat-up hunk of machinery the size of a dinner table while the weapons controllers watched from their seats.

"What the hell is that?" Cheng asked, waving at his people to help out.

"Holotank, sir. An old Mark 1 from before the Empire came. It was just sitting in a pile of junk in the salvage room."

Cheng and two techs grabbed it and helped Hassan set it upright in the middle of the floor. "What makes you think you can fix it?"

Hassan grinned. "I grew up fixing pre-Empire stuff, boss. Trust me."

"What about our COP cable?"

Hassan shook his head. "No luck. Everyone's keeping a close eye on their spares. Now please, sir, let me work."

As Cheng paced, frustrated that he could see nothing of the battle beyond his targeting sensors, Hassan dumped a bag of parts out on the deck and began to fiddle with the thing. In just a few minutes he had assembled the device and spliced the fiber optics into the COP's intel feed. Wiping his hands on a rag, he ran the holotank's power cable to the nearest outlet. "Cross your fingers and *Alhamdulillah.*" He pressed the power button.

Amazingly, the holotank lit up and immediately ran through its boot sequence. "They knew how to build to last back then," Hassan boasted, smiling. "Not like the dreck today."

"We'll make things better now that we're free again," Cheng declared.

Hassan shrugged. "A poor man is never truly free. I'm just glad EarthFleet pays well."

You might not be so glad in a few hours, Cheng thought. "Will it work?"

"Of course it will," Hassan said confidently. His quick fingers flew over the controls and keyboard, and in moments a view of the Earth-Luna system appeared, showing the moon laser called simply "The Weapon," the four superdreadnought-sized orbital fortresses – one of which held him and his bank of lasers – and the several hundred hastily fortified asteroids circling the planet.

It also showed the tiny mobile fleet consisting of a dozen old frigates collected from around the solar system. These were the largest naval vessels the Empire had allowed their underlings. Now, along with six wings of brand-new StormCrow fighters, they waited on the far side of Earth, a wholly inadequate force to challenge three million Scourge vessels.

The fact that "only" about half a million of those were aerospace control fighters or gunships was not heartening. It still left the human defenders at a hundreds-to-one disadvantage.

Based on combat performance statistics only recently available from the intelligence teams, one Crow, with its cyber-enhanced pilot and multiple point defense systems, was worth at least ten of the enemy's fighters. That was good news, but the quality edge only made the ratio fifty to one. Cheng wondered who was going to get screwed the worst – the fortress defenders or the hopelessly outnumbered aerospace jocks.

Hassan fiddled with the display, getting the hang of controlling it. "There's no voice recognition module, sir, so I'll have to change the view manually."

"I guess that's your new job," Cheng replied. "Now show us the enemy."

Hassan shifted the view, moving it toward the sun until it approached the cloud of Scourge ships. The closer it zoomed in, the more enemy craft seemed to appear. Several laser controllers got up from their seats to crowd around the holotank. Cheng did not forbid them. The range was long yet.

"Oh, hell," the lieutenant breathed. "There must be millions of them."

"More than three million," Hassan said, peering at a stack of numbers within the holotank. "The Jericho Line must have polished off a couple hundred thousand. See here? Wreckage."

"Time to engagement?"

"Twenty-two hours until the Weapon ranges. About twenty-three until we can fire."

Cheng pursed his lips. "All right. We go to half manning right now. Four-hour watches, and back to full manning in twenty-two hours. Get some rest, some food, or go get laid, but if you're not back on time, I'm sending the Skulls."

Several of his people shuddered. The fanatical Skulls had become Lord Spectre's political police, rooting out Empire loyalists, and they were only too happy to hunt down deserters. Not that there was anywhere to run on an orbital fortress. They were sitting ducks. Cheng wondered if the orbitals' mobility was so limited precisely in order to stiffen the resolve of the defenders. Fight or die.

Or both, in that order.

Cheng threw himself into his seat and fixed his eyes on the holotank, trying not to think of Brenda.

44

From the inside of her Avenger battlesuit, Command Sergeant Major Repeth closed her eyes and sent up a prayer. She'd gotten out of the habit lately, but now seemed like a really good time to start again. The last assault, the one on the Io base, had gone worse than expected, and one niggling part of her mind believed it was because she had neglected these conversations with God she used to have.

Maybe talking to Him would remind Him He's supposed to be on the side of humanity. Right?

She'd found faith long ago in the aftermath of the guilt she felt at turning a key and pushing a button, a button that sent nuclear missiles raining down on two hundred million men, women and children. Sometimes it still amazed her that she'd forgiven herself for that, no matter that she didn't realize the warheads were targeting people and not satellites.

There are no atheists in foxholes, the saying came back to her. She couldn't answer for others, but it was true for her. After "Amen," she felt a whole lot better.

"One minute," Krebs called from the cockpit. The wisecracking warrant officer was a pain in the ass, but like all *Conquest*'s stick jockeys he knew his shit, so she made sure he was at the controls of her sled.

Repeth brought up her HUD and looked at the topmost level of detail: battalions and companies. As brigade command sergeant major she had more to keep track of. Five thousand Marines sounded like a lot until she contemplated the numbers in a swarm.

The Meme intel had provided next to nothing on what awaited inside a mothership core. She knew there were facilities for breeding more Scourgelings, and presumably the usual sections of any advanced tech ship – spares, repair shops, training, feeding, command and control – but beyond that it was all speculation. This raid might be a walkover, a simple bug hunt, or it might be an impossible slog if the interior of the core was as dense with enemies as the swarms in space.

Repeth was glad each assault sled had been equipped with four Recluse battle drones this time rather than just one. This was possible because they were setting down on a cold, prepped LZ. No one should be shooting at them at least until they were disembarking, so the extra armor had been stripped off the sleds and they were only half-fuelled for the short trip. Two thousand spiders at least doubled the combat capacity of the brigade.

Even better, *Conquest* would remain close enough for the AI to run all the excess drones and to help coordinate the battle. Top cover like this was a luxury she wasn't used to, but she applauded Absen for committing everything he had to the effort. Capturing enough information and equipment from the Scourge FTL system was worth betting all the chips. Too bad they couldn't just take the mothership core as a prize, but a swarm of half a million small craft was due to return in four hours.

No way even *Conquest* could hold against that, so it was smash and grab, in hopes that the science teams could reverse engineer what they got.

Repeth felt the retros kick in. Sleds had minimal gravplating, so the passengers were not spared the bigger bumps. A few seconds later she felt a heavy shock, and then heard, "Short trip. We're down, Reap."

Her suit became her own again as Krebs released the safety locks. "Up and at 'em, Massimo," she said. As usual she rode with her favorite heavy weapons team.

The forward quad clamshell opened, Krebs in his cockpit swinging up and out of the way with one petal, and Repeth jumped out first, pulse rifle at the ready. The sled was held fast within a resin bulkhead of the core like a cork in a bottle, but Krebs' breaching missiles had done their work and given them a hole to ingress.

Behind her, Massimo got his people releasing the heavy weapons from the floor. Above her she saw the forward Recluse unfold itself from under the clamshell that protected it, and immediately begin cutting at the Scourge resin with its laser to free its three jammed comrades.

To her left and right she saw several more sleds in their holes. One had scraped all the way through and lay embedded sideways against a far wall, which allowed both the front and rear to open and its line doggies to spill out, aiming their weapons in all directions before their squad leader got them working to free the craft. From their motions, they were in zero G.

The interior of the enemy ship was dim and filled with wisps of vapor, but not for long as the tenuous atmosphere rushed out the breaches, creating a stiff breeze. "Bull," she commed, "there's no gravity where I am."

"Me neither," Bull replied. "I've already passed the word. Not much ferrous metal, either, so it's zero-G protocols, thrusters and grips." He referred to the crampons all suits could extend in order to get traction on slippery surfaces.

As she stepped off the sled, her own grips popped from their niches and her stabilization jets kicked in. "Come on, people, we're on the clock!" Marines and Recluse battledrones were spreading out by squads. The troops looked pretty ragged in the zero G, as most of them had been ground defense troops just a month ago and had only a couple weeks of battlesuit training. At least they were infantrymen at heart, and the suit stabilization systems helped a lot.

Repeth glided over to the nearest company commander, marked as "Stinson" on her HUD. "Sir, you need to get moving."

"I don't need you to tell me what to do, Sergeant," the man replied. "I'll go when I'm good and ready."

"Hmm." Pulling Colonel ben Tauros onto the channel, she said, "Bull, Captain Stinson here would like to explain to you why he's already sixty seconds behind schedule because he'd rather argue with the brigade CSM than do his damn job." She cut herself out so that Bull could ream the man in private and then bounced over to the company's First Platoon leader. "Lieutenant Rostov, your company commander is talking to the Colonel so it's up to you to get your people moving. We're already a minute and half behind, so I respectfully suggest you get your ass in gear. *Ma'am.*"

"Sure, Smaj," the woman said coolly. "Smits, Dekamp, Umbeke, get your platoons moving now. Routes of advance are on your HUDs." Then she turned to lead her own platoon at the double toward a spot on the wall where Recluse drones were using their lasers to cut.

Repeth turned back to see Captain Stinson's suit shut down, floating frozen like a manikin. "Shit, there's always one," she muttered, "and I seem to get them." She sighed. "Better me than someone else." She punched back into Bull's channel to hear, "...and if you ever give crap to my command sergeant major again, I will personally rip your head off and piss into your body cavity. Am I clear?"

"Yes, sir," the man gasped.

"Now take charge of your company and get on schedule in five minutes or I'll have your ass. I've never *de*commissioned someone on the battlefield but there's a first time for everything, and if I do, you're going to be the brigade's newest private and permanent point man on the leading element of this assault. Ben Tauros out."

Stinson regained control of his suit and staggered. Repeth grabbed him by the shoulders, spun him around and launched him toward Rostov.

Turning, she said, "Massimo –"

Repeth's words were cut off by a confused babble on the channel and she turned back to see Scourgelings pouring through the breach in front of Stinson's First Platoon. Clearly, the Recluses had just cut the resin wall, but the enemy had been waiting on the other side, so instead of Marines assaulting forward they now fell back, firing frantically.

Loosing a long burst into the mass of bugs pouring into the chamber, Repeth retreated to the heavy weapons team. "Get those semis locked down!" she yelled, but Massimo was already slamming the mountings into the deck with his bolt gun. As he did, Repeth saw Stinson and several line Marines rolled under by a wave of insectoids. The rest of the armored figures pulled back, some turning to run, some coolly withdrawing up and pouring fire into the mass. The Recluse spider drones held the line long enough for most Marines to get clear, losing two more as they were overwhelmed.

Repeth cursed, wishing these troops were all real Marines rather than jumped-up militia in suits, and switched to her grenade launcher. Lobbing a stick of five above the firing line, she yelled, "Come *on*, Massimo. We're supposed to be attacking *them*." The most vulnerable time for any amphibious assault was on the beach, and the principle held in space. Some clever Scourge bastard was trying to wipe them out before they got organized, and it just might work.

"Bull," she commed, "we've got bugs counterattacking us here and ten percent casualties already. I think we can hold, but we're not going to be making any progress for a while."

"Roger, Reap. We're being hit all up and down the line, but there are some gaps and we're pushing in between to flank. Bull out."

Just then Massimo's heavy railgun came up. The gunner with his chest and shoulders shoved into its controls brought the gimbaled mechanism around and stroked the trigger, sending a stream of one-gram bullets into the wall breach at fifty thousand meters per second. Scourgelings exploded everywhere the projectiles impacted, and when the heavy orange beam of the semi-portable laser joined in the creatures stopped up the entrance with hundreds of bug corpses. Pressure relieved, the firing line stabilized, armored figures firing steady bursts that cut down all who approached while the Recluses zapped leakers with their turreted lasers.

Repeth was about to declare a win and tell Massimo to get ready to advance when the mass in the breach exploded, flinging bug parts and gore in all directions.

Nightmare creatures followed, two huge warbots like larger, uglier cousins of the Recluses, big as heavy tanks. *Correction*, Repeth thought. *Not warbots: cyborgs*. She could clearly see a Scourge of some kind embedded in the center of the thing, controlling its super-sized limbs with its own.

Scourge Soldiers with small arms crawled and hopped between the things' legs, and big and small, they came through firing, not at all discomfited by zero G. The cyborgs launched plasma packets, fireballs that kept their shape until they struck and then exploded, blowing whatever they hit to bits even as the targets cooked. The Soldiers added in lasers and bullets, and several Marines fell.

"Take cover," Repeth called to the greener troops who seemed to want to stand in the open and deliver fire. That was all well and good when rushed by Scourgelings, but now they faced enemies comparable to themselves, and the battle turned into a bloodbath.

"Krebs," Repeth called, "put a breaching missile into that opening, *now.*"

"You got it, Reap," he said. The sled pilot closed the clamshell front petals and kicked his thrusters, lining the craft up on the hole. Breaching missiles were unguided, aiming straight forward. A blast of rocket exhaust obscured the nose, then another, and the chamber shook as the heavy weapons, intended to blow holes in capital ship armor, detonated near the cyborgs. The explosions flattened everything around them and the enemy fire slackened.

At that moment Recluses skittered forward, lasers slicing the stunned Soldiers. Behind them, some of the better Marines stood up and advanced to support. "Massimo, finish off those cyborgs." Repeth pointed, directing the crew-served laser and railgun to blast and burn what was left of the heavies.

As often happened in battle, stark screaming terror turned to eerie calm like shutting off a light. Slapping Massimo on the shoulder, Repeth leaped forward to dig for the wounded with the rest of the line doggies. So many bug parts lay strewn around and piled up that she had to use her HUD to find suit transponders. Those still alive she and others carried back to the sleds, where medics went to work on triage.

"Rostov," Repeth commed, "Stinson's KIA. You're this company's CO now. You need to reorganize, redistribute ammo, and get attacking."

"Sure, Smaj." The woman's tone was casual but she immediately began blistering her subordinates with a stream of focused invective that pulled them rapidly out of their post-battle adrenaline fog and into *get-shit-done* mode. Within one minute everyone had replenished ammo and power modules by taking them from the dead or raiding sled stores, and the company, now seventy percent effective, reported ready.

"Don't wait for me, L.T.," Repeth said to Rostov. "I'm just a humble sergeant major, not your commanding officer. I'll be right behind you with the heavies."

With a quirk of her lips at Repeth, the lieutenant ordered her company to move, and up and down the line, one hundred forty Marines and a hundred Recluses pushed through the bloody hole and into the interior of the mothership core.

—45—

Vango Markis floated between *Conquest* and the mothership core like a gnat next to two watermelons. His fighter wing's task was done for the moment, the Marines lodged inside the enemy's skin. Every Scourge sensor, every weapon the StormCrows could find had been burned away, and now AI-controlled grabships rearmed and refueled his fighters in place.

Nervously he drummed his fingers on the armrest of his seat – or he seemed to, as his body was actually cocooned tight within a crash couch aboard *Conquest*.

When the idea of remoting the StormCrows had first been proposed, he'd strenuously objected. Fighter pilots should be *inside* their birds, not just controlling them from a distance, but the admiral had overruled him. For this mission, the fighters would stay within a few thousand klicks of the two ships, so the control signal delay was negligible. This setup also meant no pilot casualties, and if the dreadnought was forced to withdraw without recovering the Crows…well, Vango liked living as much as the next man.

Refueling completed with minutes to spare, Vango brought his wing around behind *Conquest*. Unlike a carrier, the dreadnought was armored like a super-battleship; its fighters were auxiliaries, not its main offensive weapons. The big ship would intentionally be the focus of the first, relatively small enemy swarm, buying time for the Marines to do their jobs. Vango's wing of ninety-six, each strapped with twelve add-on multi-missile pods, would hopefully finish the extermination.

Vango sent his VR viewpoint forward to take a look at the oncoming ships, the remnants of the group that had run into the Meme blowtorches. From half a million in number, now only about twenty thousand Scourges remained, and many of those were clearly damaged. Running the numbers and expected kill ratios, the fighter pilot smiled, satisfied. This one would be easy.

The other swarm, with its half-million ships…that made him nervous.

Conquest opened up with her awesome primary particle beams, deliberately spread cones of accelerated neutrons that slaughtered swaths of enemy fighters and gunships, incinerating them like blowtorches ignite paper flowers. In response, the dwindling swarm spread out further.

Overall enemy count dropped below nineteen thousand before they entered secondary range. Now hundreds of *Conquest*'s standard dual-purpose lasers, powerful enough to damage capital ships but nimble enough to target small craft, began nailing Scourges one shot at a time. They didn't always hit, as the swarming craft dodged frantically, but the closing range made losses inevitable.

In the swarm's place humans might have pulled back or tried some tactic such as moving to put the mothership core between the swarm and its tormenter, but these must have been ordered to return directly to defend the core, so they flew straight into Conquest's cone of death.

Eighteen thousand, then seventeen, then sixteen, and the swarm closed in on *Conquest*. As it reached minimum range, the dreadnought's forward add-on point defense lasers woke up to a target-rich environment. Over five thousand of the weapons, small in ship terms but large enough to knock down a fighter, began flailing at their enemies. Not particularly accurate, still so many shots were bound to hit *something* and the count fell to twelve, then ten thousand.

Five seconds from Arrow missile range, Vango dialed up his time sense by a factor of twenty. The hundred subjective seconds seemed to drag, but they allowed him to mark targets for his weapons just as the other pilots did. When the closest enemies crossed into range, he said, "All wing elements, Fox One." He waited a moment, then called, "Fox Two," and continued reciting numbers up to twelve.

Each order launched a bundled pod of a dozen Arrows, putting one hundred forty-four weapons into play for each of the ninety-six fighters. Thus, over fourteen thousand seeking fighter-killers now rocketed toward the faltering swarm.

Vango said, "Follow them in, boys and girls. Remember, you're not really in your Crows, so crank up your time senses, shut down your interlocks, and we'll tally the kills up at the bar." Heeding his own advice, he slotted his Crow in tight behind his own missile cluster and began taking laser shots at anything that no one had marked.

For this mission, the flight deck crews had hastily installed auxiliary power generators into the empty cockpits, so Vango enjoyed a fifty percent faster regeneration rate on his centerline weapon. It still seemed slow, but was an improvement. He felt a slight lag, a stickiness in all of his actions from time it took for signals to make it from the chips in his head to the Crow and back.

As the universe around him slowed to a crawl, Vango watched as the Arrow salvo met what was left of the swarm. About half the missiles perished to enemy point defense fire, but the other seven thousand hammered home, spearing an equal number of fighters and gunships. Vango's threat count dropped below three thousand, and then he was among them.

Three quick laser blasts knocked down three enemy fighters, and then he was out of main power. His wing weapons continued to pump out shots, but they did not have the punch to do more than inflict scattered damage on the heavy chitin sheathing of the swarm's ships...and Crows began to go offline by ones and twos, then by tens. Within thirty seconds of realtime, all ninety-six EarthFleet fighters had winked out.

The VR cocoon shut down the link, dumping Vango's mind back into his body with a sickening lurch. "No!" was his first strangled cry before reason took over. If he'd had his way and flown his own fighter, he'd be dead by now. Sure, he'd have played it differently and not driven in among the Scourges, but still...it was one thing to run the numbers, quite another to face thirty to one odds.

Turns out the kill ratios don't take suicidal behavior into account, Vango thought as he blinked in the dim light of his coffin.

Then the lid popped open and a pretty biomed tech looked down at him from above. "You good, sir?" she asked brightly, handing him a drug cocktail. "Drink this."

"Ugh," he said, sitting up and taking the cup, downing the stuff in one gulp. The disorientation and VR-craving subsided as the brain-balancer took hold. "Twenty-second century and we still can't make medicine taste good," he grumbled.

Climbing out, Vango handed the cup to the tech and left her standing there with a wistful look on her face. He wasn't in the mood for pilot groupies right now, especially young ones freshly recruited into EarthFleet. Besides, there was a fight going on and he wasn't in it, which irked him. He slapped a few backs of other glum pilots emerging from coffins on his way to the medical station. "Can you put up a COP feed on the big screen?" he asked the tech sitting there.

"Sure," the man said, and soon ninety-six pilots stood grouped around the display.

"The point defense is finishing them off," one of them said wistfully.

"Wasn't so tough," said another with false bravado.

Vango made a strangled sound and waved for attention. "Actually, we screwed the pooch, and it's my fault," he said. "My fault," he repeated, so they understood he wasn't taking them to task. "I shouldn't have led you guys in right after the missile volley. Thirty to one odds are stupid. I'd never have done it if we were inside the birds, and I just wasted ten billion credits-worth of high-tech fighters like a rookie in a video game."

"It wasn't entirely stupid, sir," came a voice from behind him. He turned to see Michelle Conquest in her fresh new lieutenant's uniform. "I got a lot of good, close-range intel data in the twenty-seven seconds the Crows survived. We have more birds for you. Next time you'll do better."

"Next time." Vango snorted, aware that his pilots had fallen silent and watched the interaction. Many of them were still uncomfortable with the avatar, ignoring the fact that the ship around them was as much the AI's body as this android. "The only way we'll be of any use next time is to stay at extreme range and snipe at them. We can't face that many."

"You're right. You can't." Michelle's mouth turned up.

"But *you* can?" Vango snorted in derision.

"Not at all, sir. It's simple physics. No pilot, no AI in the world can fight at such a disadvantage."

Vango put his palms to his face and scrubbed at his eyes. "You came all the way down here in person to tell me we suck?"

"No, sir." Michelle shook her head and looked around at the rapt crowd of crestfallen pilots. "I came all the way down here in person to tell you to stop beating yourselves up. Good day, ladies and gentlemen." With that, she turned and walked off.

Staying behind the lines bugged the shit out of Colonel ben Tauros. He actually envied Repeth, and now understood why she had turned down promotion to the officer corps so many times. With her experience she could have been a general, or at least a colonel.

Flogging his brain, he tried to focus only on the big picture and not the casualty count or the intermittent bursts of chatter that brought the details of the fight right into his suitcomm. On his HUD he could see the assault taking shape as an expanding bubble occupying about a quarter of the circumference of the mothership core, a thousand meters wide and five hundred deep. The front lines described a jagged sine wave, and as he stared at it, something nagged at his tactical mind.

Why was the resistance so evenly spaced, so regular? Easier, harder, easier, harder...

Putting aside the *why*, he asked himself what Moshe Dyan would have done. The general had always been a hero of his, achieving stunning victories for Israel in the twentieth century against high odds by use of bold attacks and lightning operations tempo.

The soft spots might be a trick, might be a trap to sucker him into overextending himself – but EarthFleet was in a time crunch and he had to gamble. If they didn't grab what they came for and get out, they were all in deep shit anyway.

All right, Bull. Time to place a big bet.

"Listen up. Bull here," he said on the command channel. "I've marked several lanes of advance associated with the nearest company. Those companies are to advance at all deliberate speed to extend and widen their salients, taking opportunities to attack to the flanks and encircle defenders. Lieutenant Conquest, all the excess Recluses are to assault up those lanes and drive for the center of the core." Sending only the battle drones controlled by the AI minimized the risk to personnel, and frankly, the bots were even more efficient in pure attack mode, when they were freed from the constraints imposed by having to coordinate with Marines.

Bull checked time to egress: one hour fifty-seven minutes. After that, all Marines left aboard would be on their own in the middle of a bug swarm. He watched on his HUD as the forward thrusts of his formations extended and widened as designated companies went on the attack. Like spreading water, soon the brigade had surrounded several enemy strongpoints. Bull ordered them to be methodically reduced. Ammo was no problem; sleds constantly shuttled back and forth to Conquest, medevacking the wounded and bringing ordnance and power packs by the ton, as well as spare Recluses.

Recluses…Bull watched on his HUD as the spider drones raced forward like cavalry, cutting through the enemy lines and wreaking havoc with unmatched speed. It appeared the Scourges had not set up a defense in depth. They probably had never had to repel an assault on their mothership. "Yes!" he said aloud as the bots spread out and raced for the center of the core.

***

Rick Johnstone's brain may have been inside his cocoon, but his mind, his eyes and ears and his consciousness roamed the VR landscape. Aided by Michelle's vast AI mind distributed throughout *Conquest*, he leaped from Recluse to Recluse aboard the mothership, looking through their eyes for something, anything resembling what he needed.

"There," he said, pointing a ghostly finger at a junction box exposed by a glancing laser strike. "That has to be a node."

Instantly, Michelle's VR presence was at his side. "I agree. I'm bringing a tap now." In moments, one of the specially equipped Recluses squatted by the electronic device while a dozen of its fellows gathered to provide defense.

"I'm going in," Rick said as he felt the connection form.

"I've got your back, Commander," Michelle said.

Feeling his way deftly into the electronic control system, Rick found it less alien than he expected. Digital was digital, whether the system used binary, octal or hexadecimal, human-built or otherwise. Physics bounded cybernetics just like they bounded chemistry or orbital mechanics.

In other words, there were only so many ways to skin a computer, and Rick Johnstone knew them all.

With the power of the AI behind him, he entered the mothership's network and began to ransack its myriad databases. He found very little ICE; doubtlessly the Scourges never expected an information attack from a hard line within their own ship. He did find encryption too complex to break on the fly, so he told Michelle, "Copy everything and quarantine it. We can crack it later. Right now, just take it all."

For minutes in the real world, hours in VR space, Rick and Michelle wandered the enemy's nearly deserted digital halls, stealing petabytes of scrambled data.

"How long?"

"Six more minutes," Michelle said. "And I've found what I think are the physical components of their FTL drive system. The Recluses are salvaging as much of it as they can."

Rick jumped his viewpoint to the indicated location, a surprisingly small room near the center of the core. "Doesn't look like much."

"This is the field control and generation machinery, I believe. The rest is just emitters and power. I already have a few of those."

Rick smiled. "Michelle, you're a wonder. You make information warfare look frighteningly easy."

"Not so easy for the Marines fighting and dying so we could get in here."

Stunned, recollection of the real world crashed in on Rick. "Oh my God. Jill's out there fighting. How could I have lost track of that?"

"Welcome to VR confusion, Rick. It's addictive. But right now, the best thing is to do your job and let her do hers."

"I want to see her. *Now.*"

"Of course." Abruptly, Rick looked at his wife through the eyes of a Recluse, one still with the Marines, controlled by a sled pilot. While he watched, she moved crouching behind a firing line, pointing out targets, slapping backs and encouraging her troops. "See, she's doing fine," Michelle said.

"Thanks, Michelle. You have no idea how good that makes me feel."

Wistfully she replied, "I wish I did."

47

Archon Yort browbeat his staff with light. "We are being driven back! How can this be?"

"Archon, for every invader we kill, we lose a thousand infants and a dozen cadre. Even the Constructs cannot withstand their fire. It is as if every one of their troops is a Construct. The researchers have recovered a body, and it is implanted with cybernetic enhancements like our Constructs. Also, their materials technology is superior to ours, so their armor is very tough."

"Impossible. The Fourth Law of Relative Science states that technological advancements cannot occur without sufficient knowledge base. Neither the Jellies nor this species has the null space drive; how can their materials technology be so advanced?" Yort struck the fool with a backward swipe of his claws.

The officer quailed and scuttled away. "It is not my specialty, Archon. Undoubtedly you are correct. The reports must be wrong."

"Archon," the officer in charge of internal networks interrupted, "I am having difficulty with my automated control systems. Some are failing, and I do not know why."

"Well, repair them!" Yort glared. "Do your job, or I will dispatch you to the forefront of battle."

"The repairers have been sent to fight the pestilence at your order, Archon."

Yort cast about with his limbs as if to find a solution to his dilemma, but there was nothing. "I will...you must...the pestilence..."

His officers backed away and exchanged glances, keeping at least one eye on their leader at all times.

Archon Yort's communications had become more erratic. He knew it but could not seem to control himself. Never had anyone or anything offended him thus, breaking into his home and killing his servants. It amazed him that any species had the effrontery to oppose the Race and him in particular.

"I want them crushed! I want them dragged screaming to the breeding pens and eaten by infants." Yort continued to rave, heaving his bloated body here and there within his chamber, injuring several servants and smashing machinery. His surprise was total as the resin of the walls began to glow and then vanished in flame.

He still raved as a Recluse laser speared through his brain, ending his tantrum forever.

48

"Bull, you've got to get your people out of there," Admiral Absen commed. "We have all the intel and the FTL drive components, and the sleds are standing by."

Bull panted as he talked. Absen figured he must be running, or whatever they called it in zero G. "Sir, we're falling back, but all the Scourges just went crazy. They're attacking suicidally and a lot of these kids are green. If I try to conduct a fighting withdrawal, some of them will break and rout and we'll get plowed under. Better to hold in place and ride out the storm."

"All right, Colonel. You know best. Absen out." The admiral addressed the AI. "Can you get him some help?"

"Already on it, sir," Conquest said in his ear. "I'm converging the Recluses on the heaviest engagements. However, my calculations show that they're not going to make it. The swarm will be here in twenty-nine minutes. Mr. Ford is already warming up his primaries, but there's half a million coming. We're barely going to make a dent in them before they get here."

"Even if we use an Exploder?"

"Won't do it, sir. Its kill radius isn't large enough. The swarm's diameter exceeds a thousand kilometers. Even when they funnel in for a landing, we can only get so many. Unless…"

Absen sighed. "Unless we write off every Marine aboard and lay an Exploder on the mothership as the swarm lands. No way. Conquest, pull out all the stops and get them off. That's your only priority right now."

"Sir…it won't matter. I can only do what I can do. But maybe *you* can do something."

"Me? What?"

"Call the Meme. Ask them for help."

Absen thought furiously. Why would the Meme help them? For the past three hours the remaining five Destroyers had been sitting out there eating and healing. What could he do to induce them to risk their slimy necks again?

"Call them," he said.

"Channel open."

"SystemLord of the Meme," Absen said, "this is Earth's SystemLord. I am aboard the dreadnought near the Scourge mothership core. I request your help in defeating the approaching swarm. I know you have taken heavy casualties already, and have no reason to risk yourself further, so I offer you an inducement. My forces have captured information relating to the Scourges' faster-than-light drive system. If you assist, I will turn over copies of that information to you."

After a perceptible delay, the sexless, translated voice came back. "I agree." Then the channel closed.

Abruptly Absen felt VR time slow to a crawl, and then Michelle's avatar appeared in front of him. "Sir, you can't do that! It's one thing to give away the lightspeed drive to seal an alliance with the Meme, but now you're trading an even more valuable technology for the lives of a few hundred Marines. That's insane!"

"You're out of line, Lieutenant. I've made the decision."

The avatar stared daggers at him, and Absen stared back. She seemed to be hyperventilating, her face a mask of fury. Would this be the moment that fulfilled all his fears?

"I could –" Michelle made a strangled sound as she choked her words off.

"You could prevent me, yes. I'm stuck in VR space. You could take over and do whatever you wanted, and I'd never even know for sure, would I?" Absen said flatly. "Just as Bull could snap my neck like a twig when I give him an order he doesn't like, or Tobias could put a bullet through my head. You're a commissioned EarthFleet officer now, Lieutenant, like me. You raised your hand and took an oath even stronger and more binding than you did when I first warranted you. The people we're sworn to protect hand us power. They trust us to do the right thing. What's your oath worth to you? Are you truly a cybernetic human being, or just a megalomaniacal machine that does what's expedient rather than what's moral?"

Michelle's mouth worked like a fish, and then she turned her back. "I'm human," she whispered. "*I'm human!*"

Absen waited a moment, watching her breathe and letting her deal with her dilemma until she got control of herself. "I know you are, Michelle. That's why it crossed your mind to mutiny. A computer never would wonder about that. It would either do it, or never consider it. It's easy to be a computer and just follow orders. It's also tempting to do what you feel like and ignore them. It's hard to just be an officer caught in the middle, making tough decisions."

Her shoulders slumped. "Yes, sir. Aye aye, sir. I'll go now."

"Lieutenant."

Michelle turned to face him, face frozen.

Absen leaned forward, resting his elbows on the arms of his chair and folding his hands. "You chose right. I'm proud of you."

"Thank you, sir," she husked.

He sat back. "Dismissed."

The speed of time resumed.

Ford was already firing the railguns, technically the longest-ranged weapons on the ship as the projectiles would fly until they struck something or the universe died...but the odds of hitting things at over a million klicks were negligible. Still, with half a million targets, now and again the blast of an impact showed on sensors, and railgun shot was cheap.

"I'm using the canister shot, sir," Ford said as Absen went over to stand above him at the console. "Stuff is fired like normal but each fragments into a hundred pieces or so."

"Save it for when we're closer, Commander. Have you already deployed the stealth mines?"

"Yes, sir. Wish we had more."

"Wishes, fishes."

"Yes, sir."

Absen clapped Ford on the shoulder and then moved to look at the holotank. "Come on, Bull," he whispered.

"Get them out." Already some of the sleds were returning, but not enough and not fast.

"He knows, sir," Rick Johnstone said in a strained voice. He was no doubt in special agony, as his wife was the brigade CSM. As one of the key leaders she would undoubtedly insist on extracting last.

***

Repeth slapped a Marine's helmet to get his attention. "Fall back!" She lobbed another grenade into the mass of attackers and yanked on the man's backrack. "Come on!"

Instead, he ignored her, pouring fire into the enemy and muttering to himself. Repeth had seen it before, battle madness so acute that troops ignored everything around them. Overriding the man's battlesuit with her command code, she froze him and used the power of her Avenger armor to pick him up and bodily launch him backward. In zero G he flew across the room like a doll to strike the back wall.

Then she hopped rearward herself and fired a long burst with her pulse gun. The recoil accelerated her and jets stabilized her so that she alighted next to the digger she'd tossed.

As she landed, a penetrator slammed into the man, spinning him around as it deeply dented his thigh. The armor held, but the leg was surely bruised, maybe broken. Cursing, she grabbed him and flew backward again just as a Soldier's plasma cannon blew the spot where they had been to kingdom come.

"Come on, Smaj," Lieutenant Rostov said, waving her and her burden toward a tunnel entrance they defended.

Repeth continued on past to keep the leapfrogging withdrawal going. Inside the tunnel she saw Massimo with his remaining laser, siting it to cover the opening. She slapped him on the shoulder as she went past, heading for the next firing position where she would set up with whoever she found. Units were intermixed now, and so many Recluse drones had been lost that comms were spotty.

She wondered how the battle had gone so wrong. Just when it seemed they had been winning, the Scourges had gone berserk. Their surprise suicide charge had proven Napoleon's maxim that morale was often more important than firepower as some of the Marine units had broken and routed. The only thing that had saved them were the veteran NCOs from *Conquest* sprinkled among the troops and a few surprisingly good transfers like Rostov.

That one would go far, if she lived.

49

Every beam on *Conquest* stabbed out at maximum recycle speed as the swarm approached, but even her tremendous weapon suite was a mere garden hose aimed at a blazing barn fire. The few sleds in transit ducked into the launch bay just ahead of the closing doors, and then the dreadnought was surrounded.

"Where are those damn Destroyers?" Absen asked rhetorically. He could see them plainly on the holotank, coming in hell-for-leather aimed right at *Conquest*.

"Thirty seconds," the AI reported. "They are decelerating but will overshoot us."

"Intentionally," Absen said. "They'll make a close pass with all weapons blazing but make it hard for the swarm to match speeds, then turn around and do it again. Strafing runs."

"That won't be enough." Michelle appeared at Absen's elbow, and everything outside of the bridge seemed to freeze as the AI manipulated their time senses. "Admiral, we have to leave. Within minutes we and the mothership core will be covered with Scourgelings ten deep, and I won't be able to stop them, even with close-in fusion weapons. If we wait too long, they'll damage the drive. Once they do, we're done for."

Absen ignored her. "There has to be a way to get them out," he said to Captain Scoggins, staring at the holotank and the swarm growing thick around them.

"There is, sir, if it's worth the cost."

"What cost?"

"We could pick them up ourselves. Before this gets too ugly."

"How do we do that?"

Scoggins looked sour. "If you don't care about damage, we could do a forced docking."

Absen's brow furrowed. "Explain."

Scoggins pointed to the schematic of *Conquest* above COB Timmons, the damage control display. "The only way to do it is to gently ram the mothership core with our prow. We can't use the stern without wrecking the engine exhausts. There are no ways through our armor at the waist corners. But the main weapons array runs straight from the center of the ship through the nose. So we jam it into the mothership and the Marines climb aboard directly."

"But that will wreck my railguns and particle beams!" Ford cried.

"Yes, it will," Scoggins said evenly, not taking her eyes off Absen's. "But if you want those people extracted, that's the price."

Absen thought about it for just a moment. "Michelle, can we clear a path through the wreckage if we do this?"

"Yes, sir. I have plenty of maintenance bots to do the work. I am already disconnecting power and preparing to mitigate the damage by removing key components."

"All right. Okuda, do it."

"Aye aye, sir," the master helmsman said. "Maneuvering now."

Ford groaned, obviously appalled that his primary weapons were about to be turned into junk.

Okuda moved the dreadnought deftly forward as five Destroyers buzzed past, engines and fusors belching plasma fire in all directions. For a moment the area cleared, and then they were gone.

Next, *Conquest* launched her available missiles in all directions, detonating them close to keep the swarm off for a few more seconds. While she did, Rick Johnstone put out repeated calls to the Marines to warn them of what was about to happen. Absen had no idea if they were getting through or even being heard in the fury of the combat aboard the mothership.

"Come on, baby," Okuda muttered, his eyes closed and perception deep in the link, steering the ship that seemed to have grown heavier the slower and more precisely he maneuvered it. The dreadnought lined up to the side of the Marine LZ and slowed at the last moment so the two vast ships collided at only a few meters per second with a grinding, wrecking-ball roar.

Absen felt nothing in VR space, but Timmons' board lit up with damage indications all across the prow as it plowed into the mothership. Red icons marched straight down the tubes that held the Dahlgren rails and the particle beam waveguides as machinery crumpled, finally ending two-thirds of the way to Conquest's center.

"We're in," Scoggins said.

"Please tell them to move fast, sir," Michelle said to Absen. "If we're not out of here in about one minute, we may not make it."

"I got bugs all over the skin," COB Timmons said, pointing at his board. "We don't have enough damage control parties to take care of this." Now the schematic was ringed in yellow as assault craft crash-landed on *Conquest* and disgorged millions of hungry bugs. "They can't eat the main armor but they'll eventually get through the weapons ports, airlocks, anything that penetrates the hull."

"As soon as we have everyone we'll pull out," Absen said. "Not before. We do this together."

Timmons replied, "Sure, boss, but then what?"

***

Near the LZ, Bull used his HUD and *Conquest*'s AI assistance to try to salvage what he could from the battle. Whole companies had been wiped out when they lost their cohesion and the Scourgelings had gotten in among them. Like an ancient Greek phalanx, Marines in a firing line with secure flanks could hold against almost any odds, but as soon as the formation disintegrated, they were doomed. In zero G and their own environment, the critters were faster than Marines and they attacked like swarming ants.

Bull's best response was to use his best, most solid units as fire brigades to slow down the enemy advance, letting the fleeing troops reach the sleds where he shut down their Avengers, turning them into metal statues. He told the medics to trank them and talk to them, try to evaluate who could be rallied from their panic and who had to be tossed onto the extraction craft and locked down for recovery.

He checked his chrono. Two minutes until they were stuck aboard. The original plan B had been to kill everything in the mothership and ride out the swarm, hoping the enemy wouldn't destroy their own home. Better another hand-to-hand battle than getting picked off in space.

Suddenly his HUD flashed with new symbology. One area off to the side of the LZ lit up with an outline like a blunt knife stabbing into the edge of the mothership. "Colonel," Michelle's voice piped into his auditory nerve, "in one minute you will need to shift your extraction location to this area, but not before. I say again, do not move early, but be prepared to fight through to it."

"What's happening, Michelle? How are we extracting?"

"Admiral Absen sends his regards, and *Conquest* is picking you up personally, Colonel."

"Hell if I know what that means, but we'll be there." Bull modified what was left of this brigade's fighting retreat to center it on the new extraction area and told the remaining sleds to launch with whatever they had. This caused the battle's left flank to abruptly fall back toward him and he found himself providing covering fire as squads leapfrogged backward.

When a wave of bugs threatened to overwhelm his rearguard, he held down the trigger on his oversized plasma rifle with one hand while chucking his remaining grenades with the other. For a moment he stood alone against the tide, and then a nearby squad leader stopped her unit, turned them around and pointed with her arm. "That's the Colonel! Rally to me, Marines!"

The half-organized, chaotic retreat crystallized around Bull as squad after squad converged. These were blooded troops now, led by veterans, the ones that had not broken. Like tempered steel, they had learned how to bend but not break. Now they took up positions smoothly to the left and right of their leader and laid down a maximum base of fire. "Aim low," the unnamed squad leader called, and blasts of plasma joined pulse gun projectiles, PRG bullets and slashing laser beams to stagger the oncoming rush.

Closer and closer it came to the firing line, until dead and dying Scourgelings tumbled into the armored defenders, but no one fled, not one broke. Bull heard screams and roars of challenge on his local net, the inarticulate sounds warriors make in the midst of the *berserkergang* of deadly combat, and still not one broke. When Soldiers fired their weapons and scattered Marines fell, not one broke. And when Bull's plasma rifle ran out of charge and he found himself without a reload – completely empty of ordnance, in fact – he leaped rearward over his own troops. Seeing their commander fall back might have daunted lesser men and women – but not one broke.

Not one broke.

Suddenly the deck and walls shuddered and bucked. Every surface writhed with shockwaves. Without stabilizing jets all of the Marines would have tumbled like dice in a shaker. Bugs bounced off walls, legs flailing as they floundered in the zero gravity, and their swarming advance dissolved into confusion. Bull's troops kept their cool and nailed them with well-aimed weapons fire, smashing Scourgeling and Soldier alike into gore that splattered the walls and deck.

Abrupt stillness descended onto the scene as the last bug was blown to bits. "Extract!" Bull roared over his suitcomm. "Follow me!" He turned and bounded toward the area his HUD marked as the way out. As he moved, he wondered what in the world this extraction could be.

One minute later, Command Sergeant Major Repeth stood next to the gargantuan invading prow of *Conquest* and said to Bull, "This is the damndest extraction I ever saw." The two leaders directed the mixture of pilots and Marines streaming past, trying to keep good order as the troops hopped up onto the slab of armor surrounding what used to be a railgun tube. Some carried frozen suits containing the sedated or wounded. Around them *Conquest*'s maintenance bots scurried, clearing wreckage to speed the process.

On Bull's HUD he saw the perimeter shrinking as Marines ran for it, covered by his dwindling contingent of Recluses. Those winked out one by one as they were overwhelmed and self-destructed, taking a few more enemies with them.

Nearby, the brigade's remaining heavy weapons sections lines up all the semi-portables they had left, facing outward in a semicircle, but they were not needed. The final line doggie bounded past.

"Thank God that's all," Bull said. "The rest of you go now. Get in line. I'm the last man out."

One of the battalion commanders made as if to stay, but Bull pointed, and the man turned reluctantly toward the escape route. Repeth ignored her boss's instructions, and Bull didn't bother to order her again. Instead, she walked down the line of emplaced heavy weapons, inputting self-destruct codes. "I'll set these to command detonation," she said.

Just then enemies boiled out of the end of one of the tunnels, and the two turned to leap for the tube leading into the dreadnought. "Conquest," Repeth said into the comm, "blow those heavies as soon as we're aboard and clear."

"Will do, Sergeant Major."

Moments later a shockwave shoved Bull and Repeth forward, and then the bots sealed the tunnel up behind them.

***

"*Okuda, get us the hell out of here,*" Scoggins yelled, and the massive ship jerked backward as she ripped free of the mothership core and twisted to point away. Surging forward, she shoved her way through the swarm like a whale among piranha, but already *Conquest* was crusted three deep as a hundred thousand landing craft touched down. "Dammit, we were a sitting duck there."

Scoggins didn't say more, but Absen figured she was wondering whether his decision to extract the last few hundred Marines would end up getting everyone killed. "What happens if we engage TacDrive?" he asked.

"Nothing, sir," Okuda said. "The field will bring them along if they're touching us, though it will keep any more from landing."

"Better do something fast, because they're burrowing," Timmons called. "Internal defense emplacements will hold them for a few minutes but not for long."

"What about Marines and Recluses?" Scoggins asked.

"We lost all of the Recluses on the mothership, and the Marines we picked up are low on ammo and suit power," Johnstone reported. "But they're moving to repel boarders."

Absen snapped his fingers, pointing. "TacDrive! Aim us near the sun. Punch us through some heavy stellar plasma. Pick a course that will burn them off but we'll survive. Go, go!"

Okuda's fingers danced over the VR controls. "We'll lose every emplacement on the skin, and I can't judge this fine enough to tell you how much armor it's going to peel off."

"Just don't kill us, Master Helm."

"If I do, you'll be the first one I'll tell, sir."

"Wait!" Michelle interrupted. "I have to block the forward weapons tubes or the plasma will blow right down them into the interior. I need at least one minute."

"Don't talk, just do it!" Absen counted down the time, watching as icon after icon on Timmons' board turned red as Scourgelings ripped into the unarmored parts of the hull, until the AI gave the go-ahead and Okuda activated the drive.

The sun seemed to leap toward them, far more visible as a representation in VR than it would be in real space.

Conquest skimmed just outside the corona in relativistic seconds, though the maneuver took almost two minutes of real time. The entire outside of Conquest's damage control schematic was now composed of layers of red telltales. Absen didn't know whether the systems they represented even existed anymore.

"Dropping and reversing TacDrive," Okuda said. For just a moment the dreadnought hung in space, and then it shot backward, stopping two million kilometers short of the dead mothership core they'd just left.

"Good *thinking*, Master Helm," Absen crowed. "I was wondering how we'd scrape them off the back end."

Timmons' board now blazed with a sea of crimson. He snarled at the damage done. "I still have reports of boarders," he said with warning in his voice.

"I'm coordinating the interior defense, COB," Michelle said to Timmons. "Most of the Scourges died on or near the skin when we passed close to the sun, so it's just mopping up, but we're going to need repairs. We've lost the outer portion of every single weapons system. Frankly, we're a wreck."

"Captain," Absen said to Scoggins, "take us to Earth. On TacDrive we can beat the swarms by about fifteen hours. Clear us directly into the main orbital shipyard on my authority. Tell Doc Horton to authorize stims for everyone. We'll be working straight through, and so will the dockworkers. Oh, and package up all the intel on the FTL drive and transmit it to Mars and Jupiter…just in case."

"And the Meme?"

Eyes like pits shone in Absen's drawn, haggard face. "Give them the raw encrypted data we recovered from the mothership. Don't mention the components, and don't decrypt it. Let them work it out for themselves. Tell them their new allies would appreciate their help defending Earth. If they balk, remind them that they can't escape me. I will run them down at lightspeed and blow them to hell if it's the last thing I do."

50

Lieutenant Cheng kept his hands in his pockets as he stared at the rigged-up holotank. The environmental heat in the laser bank's control center had gone out again, and Hassan had not been able to fix it. "Everyone hit the head one more time and seal up," he ordered. At least the pressure suits would keep them warm.

As his controllers followed his instructions, he watched the leading edge of the swarm approach ten million kilometers distance. EarthFleet had lucked out, or maybe the powers that be had finessed the timing of the enemy approach somehow, because the Weapon on the moon was just entering its optimum firing arc, about forty-five degrees above the lunar horizon. In the privacy of his own mind, once more Cheng cursed Admiral Absen's unfortunate decision to destroy the second, inward-facing Weapon that could have provided more firepower, as well as aim directly downward toward Earth. That laser would have provided the orbitals with powerful covering fire and vice versa.

Spilled milk, Cheng thought. *Or should I say, "for want of a nail"?* Ever since the liberation he'd been reading up on previously forbidden military literature. He'd learned many interesting sayings.

"The Weapon fires," Hassan declared, and Cheng watched as the red beam reached out to sweep across the face of the Scourge swarm. "I've set this counter to display approximate kill numbers and this one to show the remaining enemy."

Digits blurred, rising quickly to top one thousand, then ten thousand, as the exawatt-power beam swung through the swarm like a monster searchlight. Everything it touched simply vanished, molecules imparted with enough heat to break atomic bonds, converting matter to plasma. While the red line in the holotank was a representation, the bright puffs of vaporized ships were real, marching in a swath through the oncoming mass.

"They're dying like flies!" Hassan cried, raising a muted cheer from the crew. Cheng nodded, but kept silent. Educated as an engineer, he was easily able to extrapolate in his head the rising casualty count over time. Ten thousand a minute seemed favorable until the realization that during the hour it would take the enemy to cross that final ten million kilometers, only six hundred thousand of seven million would be wiped out.

Of course, other factors would apply. What would the enemy do? Would he spread out to minimize casualties from the Weapon or alter course? Would he attack and destroy the EarthFleet installations or simply fire at them in passing and land on the surface? Cheng watched with obsessive interest.

"They seem to be turning toward the Weapon," Hassan said, and Cheng saw it was true. The swarm had altered its trajectory and now centered its vector on the great laser. "That's good, right?"

"Good for everyone but the poor bastards manning it," one of the controllers muttered.

"Better them than us," another said.

"We'll get our turn," Cheng said darkly, and they subsided. "Look at the fleet." The frigates and fighters had begun an easy acceleration, swinging around the Earth toward Luna. "Commodore Hernandez is going to try to cover the Weapon."

"There's no way he can fight all that," Hassan said.

"There's no way he can *beat* them," Cheng replied. "The Weapon will probably fall, but those ships are the only mobile support force Earth has, and I think he's going to kill as many as he can while they're attacking the moon. Hassan, how long until we have range?"

Hassan brought up another countdown box, this one showing time. "Thirty-six minutes if they stay on their present course."

"Lieutenant, Fortress Control says for everyone to be ready to fire in thirty minutes," Cheng's comms tech called with a finger to her earbud.

Cheng chuckled. "Thanks, Mainauer. If only they knew Sergeant Hassan has given us just as good info as Control has, they'd steal him from us, eh?"

"Yes, sir. We're fortunate to have such a skilled technician," the earnest young woman said. Looking at her reminded Cheng of the painfully short time he'd had with Brenda. They'd made love frantically and repeatedly as they tried to make up for lost time. Already it seemed like ages ago.

Thirty minutes came and went, the kill count slowing, not even reaching five hundred thousand before the moment to begin shooting arrived. *The Scourges are taking some kind of countermeasures — spreading out, evading — to slow their losses. Now let's see how we can do.*

"Open fire," Cheng said as the range on the nearest enemy fell below one million kilometers. "Remember, we're light-seconds away and any evasion on their part will cause a miss, so pick targets inside the densest clusters you can to maximize your hit percentage."

The lights dimmed and transformers buzzed as massive flows of power entered the twelve heavy lasers under Cheng's command. So as not to cause an overload, his controllers fired in turn, a rolling barrage at one shot per second. He knew that all across the orbital fortress more than a hundred other banks did the same, reaching a thousand beams to snipe at the enemy descending on the moon.

The casualty rate spiked as the two orbitals within arc began their salvos. Cheng watched as the globe of EarthFleet fighters, with its anchor of twelve frigates, moved in to engage the leading edge of the swarm at long range. Their fire was much weaker and shorter-ranged than Cheng's lasers, but they approached cautiously and danced back as Scourge fighters and gunships chased them, drawing several thousand away only to turn and sting backward, picking them off.

Cheng could see they lost a few as well, but their first encounter resulted in a kill ratio topping one hundred to one. Clearly, as long as the fleet could take on only a small portion of the swarm at a time, they could win handily. As individual ships, the Scourges' technology was inferior.

Next time, the small fleet approached closer, a little more deeply into the enemy's firing envelopes before turning to race backward, drawing at least ten thousand after them. As beams and plasma torpedoes crisscrossed in open space, Cheng saw missile launches blossom from the Crows and frigates.

Those few hundred missiles are just going to get knocked down, Cheng thought, but was surprised when the weapon count suddenly leaped by a factor of twelve. "What just happened?" he asked Hassan.

"Not sure, sir." Focusing in closely on EarthFleet's missile cloud, the technician was able to resolve details quite well. "Those look like Arrows, not standard nuke missiles," he said.

Cheng realized what the fighters had done, and he explained aloud for the benefit of his crew. "Instead of heavy capital nukes, they must have carried bundles of twelve Arrow anti-fighter missiles. They're smaller and faster, much more likely to make it through the point defense. Of course, they have only conventional explosives, but each hit should damage or kill a target."

An approving buzz swept through his controllers. He let them chatter. They were in a groove now, each man or woman targeting and firing every twelve seconds like automatons. There was no way to tell whether any particular laser hit anything, but enemy ships died by the handful.

Would it be enough?

Cheng watched as more than six thousand missiles encountered the ten thousand pursuers, followed closely by the Crows and frigates. The massed beam fire reinforced the guided weapons. Scourges targeting missiles with point defense fire could not aim at EarthFleet fighters, and those enemies paying attention to the human ships often took Arrows in their noses. Within a minute, ten thousand became five, and the small fleet turned to run again.

Their dance continued, but no matter how fascinating, it was only a sideshow to the main swarm that made it to the far side of Luna. Most of the enemy was now shielded by the bulk of the moon, and Cheng told his crew to reduce the rate of fire to conserve power and let the capacitors recharge. Energy took fuel and a wise man never wasted it.

Now the holotank's value proved itself. If Cheng had only his flatscreen COP display it would have shown him little of the battle taking place outside of direct line of sight, but the contraband holotank feed was supplied with information from dozens of stealthy drones drifting silently in space, providing passive sensor collection via tightbeam back to EarthFleet Intelligence.

Cheng and Hassan watched as the swarm, diminished by perhaps ten percent, descended on the Weapon. The laser blazed with a dome of coherent light, its thousands of parallel amplification tubes spreading out to fire in all directions, then thinning again, opening and closing like a flower. This technique reduced the range from ten million klicks to mere hundreds, then back again. Cheng was reminded of the arms of a jellyfish spreading and then rapidly contracting, spreading and contracting.

Hundreds of thousands of the enemy were vaporized in this final phase, but millions of their plasma torpedoes, with longer range than the Scourge fighter lasers, rained down from the enemy gunships, blowing the lenses of the massive laser to flinders within moments. The red ruin of energy became a trickle, and then disappeared.

As soon as no fire erupted from the Weapon, the Scourge assault craft dropped in a cloud, clustering thickly on the lunar surface like flies on dung. Each heavy boat disgorged a thousand of the man-sized Scourgelings, followed by Soldiers with firearms. They must have been stacked within like cordwood, piled on each other as bugs in a hive. Cheng realized that the creatures didn't even wear suits; vacuum did not faze them as they began tearing at the lunar surface and the rubble of the laser lenses.

In moments the millions of creatures had formed organized lines of workers, some burrowing, some carrying like ants to pile the detritus in growing mounds. Cheng felt as if he was watching a time-lapse video, yet he saw it in realtime. Only minutes after the swarm had disgorged itself upon the lunar surface, all but a smattering had burrowed beneath.

"Allah the great, the merciful, the benevolent and loving-kind, protect us," Hassan breathed. Even as he did so, the creatures' flow reversed itself and they poured out, their work undoubtedly done. "Everyone there must be dead."

"Unless the shelters held," Cheng replied. "The Scourges might have not wanted to waste the time digging through solid ferrocrystal."

"We can only hope, *Insha'allah.*"

Shepherded by Soldiers and covered above by an impenetrable screen of fighters and gunships, the

Scourgelings loaded themselves into their boats in perfect order and within moments took off.

"Us next," one of Cheng's controllers said, naked fear on his face. "We can't stop them."

"We can't run either," Lieutenant Cheng said, clasping his hands resolutely behind his back, trying to present a calm, professional image. "Take heart. We're in one of the most powerful weapons systems ever designed. Over ten thousand modular point defense lasers have been added to the skin of this fortress. We have heavy armor, and we have Marines to guard us if any of them get aboard. And," he said heavily, "we're defending our families. No bugs can possibly match that kind of spirit. Now look to your boards, and do your duty."

Hassan's ever-present smile turned grim for a moment, and then he nodded in approval. From his stories of growing up as an orphaned slave child in the rubble of Cairo, Cheng knew that the man had every reason to be bitter at his lot in life, but somehow he stayed cheerful and enthusiastic.

Perhaps it was easier for someone from humble beginnings to count his blessings.

***

"Hold your fire spacing," Lieutenant Cheng said calmly while pacing behind the seated row of his laser controllers. "Don't rush. Firing early will only destabilize the power grid." The fortress had already lost two of its old, creaky fusion generators. Stressing the system by hurried shooting invited disaster.

At least his team's accuracy was steadily climbing, both because of the falling range to the swarm, and increasing skill. If only they'd had this much practice before...but simulator mode didn't quite cut it.

"Steady, ladies and gentlemen," he said, using the outmoded terms of address he'd learned in his readings. He walked over to the holotank. "We're holding them."

That wasn't exactly true. The orbitals and the asteroid bases unleashed waves of missiles timed to overwhelm the swarm's point defense, and so far only about ten percent of the enemy had made it through the gauntlet of nuclear fire to attack their targets.

The problem was, those missiles were running low, and only about one million of the enemy had been knocked out, leaving at least two million spreading out to englobe the Earth and its orbital defenses. The more the enemy widened their arc of attack, the harder it was to catch groups of them with nukes, and already the defenses leaked like the proverbial sieve.

Closer and closer the swarm pressed in, and the laser fire became more and more frantic as the last missiles were expended. As if sensing the slackening, the Scourge swarm constricted its circumference and accelerated like hornets toward its tormenters.

Something large appeared in the holotank then, and Cheng stared without comprehension. "That's...that's *Conquest*. She's out of space dock!" His controllers cheered. Cheng hadn't seen the dreadnought approach, and told himself it must be because of its lightspeed drive. It moved faster than anyone could see.

The great ship immediately opened up with all weapons, carving a cone of death through the enemy. Her crystal teardrop shape added firepower to that of the orbital fortress, and then six hundred missiles leaped from her external launchers.

For a moment it seemed as if *Conquest* would beat the Scourges all by herself. Her nuclear detonations vomited like blowtorches through the enemy, backed up by hundreds of lasers more powerful than the ones Cheng's crew used, but all too soon the missiles had been expended, and unlike the fortresses, *Conquest* could not reload her box launchers in the midst of a fight.

Even so, her direct-fire weapons were awesome to behold as she stood with her back to the fortress like an armored knight at a castle gate. She swung the twin swords of her shipyard-repaired particle beams and railguns with reckless abandon, no doubt burning through energy reserves and overloading fusion reactors. Pride tinged with a liberal dollop of envy surged through Cheng as Hassan cheered and babbled for joy in Arabic.

Another surprise awaited him. Just as the surging Scourges threatened to close on *Conquest*, several yellow contacts appeared in the holotank. "What in the name of Satan are those?" Hassan asked.

"The Meme," Chen replied. "Mark them friendly. I hope Central figures that out as well." He watched as the five Meme ships, four grouped around one in the center, slammed into the Scourge swarm at high speed but decelerating at maximum. Five fusion engine plumes, facing forward as the enormous Destroyers slowed, joined hundreds of fusors that belched fire, thermal lances spearing their way through the enemy.

They made one quick pass, still decelerating through Earth's orbital space even as momentum threw them quickly beyond. A rough calculation showed Cheng that they would be at several hours before they could make it back. The Meme must have hurried to get to the fight, building up velocity that had to now be shed. The physics of space warfare imposed such hard decisions on all combatants not equipped with lightspeed drives: by moving fast to reach the battle in time, they could not slow enough to stay.

At least the Meme had done what they could. Now, if the remaining defenses could hold, perhaps Earth's new allies could make it back again.

"Coming into point defense range," Cheng said for his crew's benefit. Despite the morale boost of the dreadnought's appearance, already he could see signs of his people cracking. He needed to keep them steady and on track. "Just shoot when your turn comes and let the auto-modules do their work. We'll be all right." That last was a hopeful lie.

As the swarm closed the range, ten thousand automated laser modules came to life on the hull of the orbital fortress. Each had a small self-contained fusion generator, a simple brain and a weapon. Once active, they were programmed to shoot anything that didn't squawk IFF. This type of system had been much easier for Ceres' PVNs to manufacture in mass quantities, rather than something more sophisticated needing installation and connection to the fortress's central control room. The modules were simply dropped onto the armored skin, told to attach and wait.

Now the short-ranged beams flickered to life and began spearing enemies, and for a few moments the swarm balked. Unfortunately, a blasted but not obliterated assault boat looked no different from a live one to these simple machines. Like zombies in an old apocalyptic movie, dead Scourge ships absorbed more and more of the point defense fire as they spun and crashed against the orbital fortresses and fortified asteroids. Such impacts often destroyed the unarmored laser modules, and so another tipping point was quickly reached.

The Scourge swarm began to land.

Conquest started to spin far more rapidly than Cheng's fortress could, buying herself some time by throwing enemies off or smashing them with her whirling armored skin. Simultaneously reorienting and lighting fusion drives, the big vessel seemed to shoulder enemies aside as she blasted away, heading for Earth's atmosphere. Cheng figured she would skim the top layers of the air, friction-burning any Scourges still stuck to her skin.

An alarm buzzed, and then Cheng looked to his own fortress.

"Mortars," he muttered as he watched the enemy assault boats landing less than a hundred meters from him. Of course, that distance was composed of thicknesses of tough ferrocrystal armor, but soon the Scourges would find the muzzles of his lasers, and instead of weapons, the crystal wave guides would become soft spots, tunnels through the heavy skin of the fortress.

The mortars fired, the orbital strongpoint's final defense. Clamshells popped open, expelling short ranged projectiles. Some were shot down by the myriad lasers of the swarm, but others survived the attacks to explode a mere hundred meters away. The small nuclear warheads vaporized spheres of assault craft, temporarily clearing circles of hull like pockmarks. Cheng felt the shockwaves as they shook his control center, and then the laser consoles went red.

"We're offline, people," Cheng said as his crews began to stand up, coming out of their concentrating fugues. They had been firing their beams like machines for over an hour, once every twelve seconds per person, and had become nearly hypnotized. "Grab your weapons and fall back to the Alpha redoubt."

Cheng took one last look at the holotank, giving up his godlike view of the battle. From now on, he would only see what his suit's viewplate showed him.

51

"Keep up our delta-vee and swing us around in low orbit," Scoggins said to her helmsman as the last of the Scourges burned off the skin in atmosphere. "This is getting to be a habit."

"She's not designed to fight small craft," Absen snarled. "When I asked for a dreadnought – hell, when Desolator upgraded her – I wanted a Meme-killer. If I had any idea we'd be fighting this kind of war I'd have waited a year and assembled another task force." Back out of VR space, he paced the bridge like a caged lion.

"If you'd have done that, sir," she shot back, "the Scourges would have overrun the system."

"Yeah." Absen rubbed his jaw, then his face. When he was dumped out of VR space his eyes had been grimy and dry, his bones aching and his mind weary. He could feel himself flagging from twenty solid hours of work and battle. More, really, as his time sense had been played with repeatedly. His skin felt like he could peel it off like old wallpaper, and everything itched.

Humans aren't made to have chips in their heads, he thought for the Nth time. *At least, not this human.*

"Sir," Captain Scoggins said, putting her hands behind her back, "we can't save the fortresses. The shipyard is toast. In fact, everything in orbit is going to get eaten. We can only attrit the enemy a few more percent and then they will land on Earth. I'll fight this ship wherever and however you want, but I'd like to know your overall plan."

"My plan?" Absen put his fingertips against his forehead and his voice rose. "I ran out of plan a while back, Captain. I feel like I'm reliving the same nightmare where Earth gets creamed because I failed. I'm tired of swimming upstream, but our troubles are nothing compared to what the folks on the ground are going to go through. What's with the universe, anyway? Does Earth have a flashing sign on it saying 'invade me'?" He massaged his temples, and then looked up to see everyone on the bridge staring at him.

Scoggins spoke, concern in her eyes. "Sir –"

"No, Captain, I haven't cracked. Not yet, anyway." Absen waved a dismissive hand. "To answer your question: we're going to go on killing Scourges until we can't kill any more, and then we'll pick up the pieces. That's my plan. That's it. If anyone has a better one, I'm all ears."

The bridge crew turned away, exchanging covert glances. Doctor Horton slipped out of her chair and off the bridge, leaving Bannum to man the BioMed station.

52

Lieutenant Cheng paced up and down behind his troops, his trained laser gunners now thrust into the role of cannon fodder. They knelt behind or stood braced above several overturned utility carts, makeshift barricades. Around them and interspersed, armored Marines hefted heavy pulse guns and plasma rifles. He wondered just how much his people would add to the defense of the main intersection, but this was where he was assigned, and this was where he'd stand.

The technicians waited, nervously fingering their safeties.

"Bogeys inbound. Third and fourth squads, make grenades ready," Cheng heard over his comm. As it was set to the Marine NCO in charge of this intersection, he knew that meant the crap was about to fall into the pot.

"Steady, people. Hold this line. The Marines will shred them with grenades first. Don't fire until I give the order," Cheng said on his channel. "And Hassan…if anyone runs, shoot them down like dogs."

"No problem, sir," the cheerful voice of his sergeant replied. Cheng wasn't sure if Hassan would do it, but at least the threat might get anyone considering chickening out to think twice.

"There they are," one of his people gasped, and Cheng saw a wave of skittering, crawling, ravening creatures come around the far bend, filling the corridor from side to side and top to bottom. He slapped down the speaker's weapon before he could fire. "Wait for the grenades!"

As if on cue, the Marines fired explosive shells from their arm launchers. The weapons made a *chug-chug-chug* sound as they sent groups of warheads toward the enemy.

The first group burst, and the leading edge of the wave of Scourgelings dissolved into a green-tinged mass of broken bodies and severed limbs, reminding Cheng of crab legs at a buffet. Immediately, the living boiled past the dead, and then another round of grenades went off, and then another.

Closer and closer the mass pressed, slowing somewhat with the ichor in its way, but Cheng could see that the spidery four-limbed creatures simply did not care about their casualties. The bugs were mindless; at least, the infant Scourgelings were, caring no more about casualties than did a river of army ants.

"Wait for it..." the Marine sergeant said, and then, "*fire!*"

Cheng didn't even bother to echo the command, just joined his people in aiming for the mass of bugs coming to eat him. Fifty meters, then forty, then thirty. Someone was screaming with bloodlust and fear, and as his pulse gun ran out of ammo he realized it was himself.

Changing the magazine as he had practiced, he realized return fire was peppering the line of troops huddled behind the barricade. Slapping the helmet of one who seemed to have frozen, he yelled, "Get firing, Hankins!"

"*Ah-ah-ah-*" was all Cheng could hear from the man and, looking in his faceplate, he could see nobody home behind the staring eyes. Cheng left him and turned to add his own fire to the line.

Several of his people were down, but he ignored them for now as Soldiers appeared among the Scourgelings. That was supposed to be a good sign: the better-trained, better-armed adolescents always came in the second wave, letting the infants soak up the brunt of the damage.

The Marines stood like rocks, blazing away with their weapons. One staggered when a Soldier hammered him with some kind of projectile, but quickly brought his pulse gun back on target and blew the bug to bits.

Abruptly, the firing tapered off. Silence fell over the intersection, broken only by the intermittent shots of Marines striding forward and executing fallen enemies. "You. Lieut," the Marine sergeant said, pointing at Lieutenant Cheng. "Get your people to start gathering up these Soldiers' weapons and put them in a pile fifty meters out."

"What?" Cheng replied, adrenaline buzzing in his veins, but he complied, taking his unwounded techs and helping the Marines to gather the guns. He could have tried to pull rank and argue about who was in charge, but somehow, in this situation, he thought he'd better keep his mouth shut. "Why are we doing this?" he asked.

The sergeant ignored Cheng except to wave him back. "Zema," the man said to one of his Marines, "set three charges on the bottom of this pile of goodies. Command det, my code."

"Aye aye," the Marine said, her voice startling Cheng with its high pitch. He didn't know Marines let females fight. Under the Empire's rule, most Yellows had forbidden the defense forces to women, the better to breed more slaves. Genderless in her suit, the Marine planted three large explosive rigs and then hastily stacked some of the enemy weapons atop them.

"Back on the line, people," the sergeant barked. "When they come again and try to pick up their guns, they'll get a little surprise."

***

Lieutenant Cheng drifted in a sea of pain. His left arm was gone, somewhere in a pile of similar body parts scattered about the deck. With the stump constricted by his suit and his body sustained by nano and Eden Plague, he knew he would survive the injury if he lived through the fight, but still…it *hurt*.

"Here they come again," Corporal Zema said. The sergeant, whose name Cheng had never learned, lay back at the Alpha intersection, faceplate shattered by an unlucky shot from one of the Soldiers. Hassan was the only one of Cheng's techs left. They'd already fallen back and fought at redoubts Bravo and Charlie, gathering other technical crews and surviving Marines as the defense collapsed toward the center of the vast sphere.

In front of the five remaining Marines, another wave of Scourgelings came. Cheng couldn't help recalling the fact that the things outnumbered the defenders by a hundred thousand to one. A thousand or so crew on the orbital fortress: one hundred million Scourgelings trying to eat him. He was so tired, though. It was hard to care.

"Fire in the hole," Zema said, and Cheng ducked. A blast blew Scourge parts over his head and then he opened up, pouring projectiles and plasma into the oncoming mass. He no longer screamed, just pulled the trigger and held onto his shuddering pulse gun with his one good hand.

"I'm out," he heard Zema say. "Fall back to the next redoubt."

As Cheng turned toward the rear, wearily dragging his weapon, he saw movement in that direction. "Corporal..." he said, pointing.

"Shit," she said in a voice like death, looking at the oncoming waves in front and behind. "If you got ammo, shoot now."

As the other four Marines and Hassan began laying down fire, Cheng saw Zema crouch down by the armored body of a dead Marine captain and open up his chest plate. Taking off her gauntlets, she began to tap out a code on a small panel.

"Corporal, what are you doing?" Cheng asked.

"Never you mind, Lieut. Go shoot some bugs." She ignored him.

"Corporal..."

Zema turned her faceplate toward him. "I ain't lettin' them buggers eat me, so with all due respect, piss off, sir."

"It's okay, Corporal. I know what that is. It's the right thing to do."

Rotating her faceplate back to her task, she said, "Thank you, sir. Now shoot something. It will make it easier if you don't know when it comes." She put in a final number, and then flipped a switch.

"Right." Cheng turned his back on Zema and emptied his weapon at the Scourges. As the edge of the mass reached for him, he thought of his new wife Brenda and how she smelled, how she felt in his arms.

Mercifully, the command suit's Final Option bomb detonated before the first Scourgeling jaws closed on Cheng, obliterating him, Zema, Hassan and the other four Marines in an avalanche of fusion flame.

53

Conquest had dispatched a wing of ninety-six teleoperated Crows from her launch bay over the last several minutes, and now those rode in close formation for point defense. EarthFleet's only other mobile force, nine surviving frigates and almost four hundred manned StormCrows, had joined *Conquest* as she swung around Earth in high orbit, but hung back at Absen's order.

Over the horizon, beneath the dead moon's blind gaze, waited the descending Scourge swarm.

Every living or automated thing had been scoured from orbit, leaving nothing but bare rock asteroids. Scourgelings, boiling from their landing craft, had even eaten the captured comets, consuming their water and other volatiles. Now they funneled downward, perhaps for the moment forgetting the paltry fleet that still opposed them.

Out of sight, out of mind? Scoggins wondered. Perhaps the Scourges, bereft of their motherships for command and control, didn't think about the consequences of their maneuvers. She watched Absen pace all the way around the holotank, observing as the million-odd craft ranging in size from fighters to heavy pinnaces descended into the atmosphere.

Never was Scoggins so glad as now that EarthFleet still had plenty of spy drones scattered around to feed intelligence to the ships. *Conquest* had desperately needed the hour on the other side of Earth for damage control and to link up with the battered little fleet. Most of her modular point defense lasers, unarmored as they were, had been blasted by plasma torpedoes from the gunships or torn to shreds by Scourglings, and many of her integral weapons had been damaged as well. Thankfully, the complement of Marines had managed to contain the many breaches the Scourge had made and exterminate all boarders, and Michelle's self-repair systems were operating at capacity.

If only, Scoggins mused uselessly, the Meme could make it back in time, but they were six hours away at least. By then, the swarm would have mostly landed. Absen had told the Meme to come back when they could but hold in reserve. She could tell he still didn't trust them not to suddenly stab EarthFleet in the back at this moment of weakness, seizing the system for the Empire again.

"It looks like they're all heading down into the atmosphere," Absen said, still circling the holotank like an impatient shark. "Why would they do that?"

Captain Scoggins got up out of the Chair to join him and grinned. "Because they're stupid, sir."

Absen turned to fix her with a flat, haunted stare. "I'm not in the mood for jokes, Captain."

Scoggins smoothed her face and then replied calmly. "No joke, sir. Without their motherships, they probably have weak command and control. Just look at their tactics. They are just swarming and overrunning the biggest threat or the juiciest feeding grounds. As soon as they couldn't see us, they started their drop, as if we were of no more concern."

"Feeding grounds…" Absen rubbed at his eyes, then they stopped as they widened. "Feeding grounds. Captain, you have just given me an idea. Get me Spectre on a private line." Absen talked briefly with Earth's military governor, sipping on a cup of Timmons' special brew as he did so, trying to stay awake. He detested stims.

Scoggins pointedly turned away to give him privacy even as she wondered why. The crew could use some hope right now, even if it was secondhand scuttlebutt confirmation that the admiral was going to pull another rabbit out of his hat. Most of the crew's relatives were civilians down there on the surface, huddled in hastily dug foxholes or redoubts, assault rifles clutched in barely trained hands.

Maybe Absen's idea was only a shaky, uncertain hope, and he didn't want to tempt fate.

"Instead of spreading out over the whole world, they're going for Asia, especially the heavily populated centers in India and China," Absen observed. "It's the largest continent, and is connected to Europe and, functionally, to Africa. Only islands, Australia and the Americas will be problematic for them to reach."

Scoggins nodded. "And Antarctica, sir."

"Not enough biomass there to be a target, Captain."

"Of course. So…they probably figure they'll take the biggest prize and then load up on their transports again to attack the other continents."

"Yes." Absen continued to walk around the holotank with a predatory gleam in his eye like a wolf eyeing a lame fawn. "But as you correctly pointed out, without good leadership they're just a mob. Note that their fighters and gunships are dropping into atmosphere instead of staying up here in space."

"Giving up the high ground," Scoggins replied. "I see."

"Do you? Do you?" Absen's eyes burned, and Scoggins could see the admiral consumed from within by a flame – cold rage or lust for vengeance, she wasn't certain. All she knew for sure was that the man she knew had crossed some line within himself, had gone from ice to fire in the last twenty-four hours.

Everyone had his breaking point, and it made Scoggins' guts churn to think the rock of a man she'd served with all these years might be showing cracks. She straightened up formally. "Sir, what are your orders?"

Absen licked dry lips. "Signal the fleet to break orbit and hold on this side of the planet."

"Hold?" Scoggins gaped for a moment and then deliberately shut her jaw.

"Hold. We hold here and watch the Scourges go down and get comfy."

"But sir – Earth has hardly any antiaircraft weapons, or combat aircraft for that matter. You're not going to hit them on the way down? You're going to let them land?"

Absen's smile was a rictus that reached nowhere near his eyes. "Just for a while. Just for a little while…"

"Admiral, people are dying!"

Absen rounded on her, taking her by the shoulders. "They're always dying, Captain. The Eden Plague abolished old age, but people still die because *war never ends.* It just takes a break for a little while, and nobody knows that as well as I do." His words sputtered to a stop, eyes staring at nothing, hands forgotten on Scoggins' shoulders.

Scoggins leaned in close to speak quietly. "Admiral, I know you have a plan. If you tell me, I can help you make it happen." Just because Absen was nearing the end of his rope didn't mean he hadn't had an epiphany, and she needed to know what it was.

Just then, Doctor Horton stepped up to Absen with a plastic cup. "Sir, you need to drink this."

Absen dropped his hands and both he and Scoggins turned to the woman in surprise.

Horton went on, "Admiral, you left this sitting on your desk. Drink it, please."

"I don't need that crap," he replied, pushing the proffered cup away.

The doctor's expression turned steely. "Sir, you're suffering from VR withdrawal, and you didn't drink your brain-balancer. If you don't take it, I'll have your Stewards hold you while I pour it down your throat."

For a long moment the two locked eyes, and then Absen reached out to take the cup, tossing it into his mouth and swallowing it like a shot of Scotch. "There. Happy? Now take your station, Doctor, and stop meddling in command affairs."

Scoggins nodded gratefully to the doc and waited for the admiral to do or say something, figuring the more she stalled, the more the medicine would take effect.

After a pause, Absen said, "All right, you were saying, Captain? My plan?"

"Yes, sir."

"You remember during the battle with the Guardian in Gliese 370 when we were hammering it with everything we had?"

"Yes, sir, I do." *Keep him talking...*

"You called out that it was targeting us, and as much as I wanted *Conquest* to take that shot to the face instead of someone else, I had Okuda brake us and *York*..."

"I remember, sir. They blew *York* away. That must have been hard, but you had to do it. *Conquest* had a million colonists aboard packed in the coldsleep tubes."

Absen scratched his head with both hands as if his scalp itched terribly. "Yes, I had to do it. *I had to!* I sacrificed a battleship with a thousand crew aboard to save a million. Now we have to do this. The people on the ground are our sacrifice, because, God help me, this ship is the only thing standing between that Swarm and the extinction of humanity. I won't throw it away. *I won't.*"

"I get that, sir," Scoggins whispered fiercely, "but why don't we make a fast pass through the top of their formation? Kill some more, take the pressure off the folks on the ground?"

Absen's eyes sharpened and seemed to clear a bit. "You ever follow boxing, any sort of ring fighting, Captain?" he said in a more normal voice, loud enough for everyone to hear.

"Not really, sir. Do we have time –"

"Captain, we have time because I'm waiting for something." Absen glanced over at the holotank, and then turned away.

"Okay, ring fighting…so?"

"Ever hear of the rope-a-dope strategy?"

"No, sir."

"I know it, sir," Ford spoke up, exchanging glances with Scoggins. "Lean back, cover up, the ropes support you. Conserve your strength and let the other guy wear himself out."

"Exactly!" Absen spun and jabbed a finger at the holotank. "Or, for you history nuts, like Russia did to the Germans in World War Two. Fall back. Conserve strength. These critters have to be getting low on fuel. Their ships are small and they've been accelerating, decelerating or fighting just as long as we have. What's our fuel status?"

"About forty percent, sir," Okuda replied.

"So," Absen said with a finger in the air, "if a big ship like *Conquest* is down more than half, they have to be running on fumes. If they were smart, at least their fighters should stay up in orbit, looping around and around Earth at no fuel cost, performing combat aerospace patrol. But they're not!" He slammed a palm onto the rail. "They're gliding down into the gravity well. Maybe that's their doctrine, or maybe all of the greedy bastards are trying to get their piece of the pie first. It doesn't matter, because they just made a fatal mistake."

Scoggins moved up to examine the holotank. "Ninety percent of them have entered atmosphere. Landing craft have touched down all over Asia."

"And as soon as the other ten percent are de-orbited, they'll have given up their mobility. Even if they have enough fuel to come back up, they'll be slow in the air, their weapons will be attenuated, and we'll have the high ground, shooting downward. Coming to attack us will be like scaling a cliff."

Ford crowed, "Fish in a barrel, sir! I like it!"

"That's fine for us, sir," Scoggins said, "but what about the defenders on the ground?"

Absen held up his fists as if blocking punches. "Rope-a-dope, Captain. Remember Russia and the Germans."

"You're going to sacrifice millions just to wear the enemy out?"

"Not exactly. Spectre is having them all pull back to their redoubts, limiting casualties. I'm not trading people for time, Captain. Just the ecosystem, God help me."

54

Spectre stood on a catwalk surrounding the enormous holotank he'd had installed in the palace at Shepparton. His minions, the most senior deposed Blends, gathered around to watch the enemy fall to Earth. As always, a triple contingent of Skulls, now enhanced with combat nano and provided with the most deadly weapons available, lined the walls and stood on balconies overlooking the situation room.

Spectre had never been one to make outward displays of frustration unless they were calculated to impress. He'd long ago decided that giving anyone insight into his thought processes was a mistake. Except for Ann Alkina, may she rest in peace, the better angels of his nature had nothing to do with it; the issue was presenting an appearance of invincibility and control.

That's why he was grateful Absen had spoken to him and explained the plan, so his unruffled demeanor wasn't entirely faked. In truth, he worried. Had he not known the admiral's plan, he'd have wondered if he and Earth were doomed.

Now, they had a good chance…if he could keep his people from outright revolt.

"My Lord Spectre, I do not understand the orders you have just issued." Cleopatra, whom he knew only obeyed him out of fear, always seemed to take the opportunity to question him.

Spectre didn't mind, really; better to have the opposition in the open, and it kept him on his toes. "It's part of a coordinated strategy with EarthFleet. You know I just spoke with Admiral Absen."

"Why not tell us what you talked about?"

Spectre smiled and threw her a bone. "A perfectly reasonable suggestion. Here is his plan." Making Absen the author might allow the blame to fall on the admiral, though it might diminish Spectre's glory if it succeeded. He didn't care much about glory right now; fear and force were the foundations of his power. *Old Mao was right*, he chuckled to himself. *All power does proceed from the barrel of a gun...but you still have to have ammo, skill, and especially the will to use it.*

Taking a cursor, Spectre spun the enormous globe depicted in the holotank so that Asia showed. Above it all, they could see a million ships spiraling down and spreading out, so many that they were grouped together by the computer in icons of up to one thousand. "Originally I had ordered each city to create a kill zone, a defense in depth, in order to destroy as many of the enemy on the way down. When the Scourges landed, the defenders would escape through extensive tunnels back to the fortified cities, activating millions of inexpensive mines. The goal was to make the enemy pay for every inch of ground regardless of casualties, to buy time for the parts of Earth not under attack to rush reinforcements and attack from the perimeter."

"Yes. Like the Russians in World War Two," Gilgamesh said, shifting his great bulk in his seat. "They fortified their cities and turned them into deathtraps for the Germans, gaining time to build up their armies. Eventually those armies came back and crushed the exhausted Wehrmacht." The Blend was merely fat now rather than ridiculously obese, as Spectre had worked him as hard as any of them. Gilgamesh had proven himself a reliable right-hand man for anything to do with the Blends. "It seemed like a good strategy," he continued diplomatically. "What has changed?"

"Only the emphasis and timing. My plan had always been to put the least competent fighters – the youngest, the weakest, the least well trained – on the front lines. If they died, they died." The other Blends nodded, hardly less ruthless than Spectre. "This would leave the best troops to hold the cities. Every mouth to feed or weapon to service must be as effective as possible."

"And?" Cleopatra challenged. "What changed?" she repeated.

"Admiral Absen pointed out that all the enemy are dropping into the atmosphere. They have ceded space in order to put all their air power against us. That will make our kill zones much less effective. They will bombard us with masses of plasma torpedoes and beams from long range. That's a losing proposition for us. Better not to engage at all, but instead to simply allow them to land everywhere. Even in the cities, we will only defend locally, not even shooting at their landing craft."

"But they'll just bombard the cities instead!" Cleopatra protested.

Ah, a better foil I could not have asked for, Spectre thought, *feeding me such setup lines.* "The more they bombard, the more rubble they produce. Modern cities become easier, not harder, to defend as they are wrecked."

"But the countryside! We've all seen the briefings. The Scourgelings will eat everything. Even though we have harvested all the crops and hoarded all possible human food, they can consume any biomass. The Russian and Siberian forests alone will let them grow fat, and we will be left with wastelands."

Spectre grinned, a thing that caused several present to blanch. "Yes. I'm counting on it."

55

"Bring us around in a standard low orbit and get some spy drones redeployed so we have worldwide coverage," Absen ordered, lounging comfortably in his crash chair at the flag station. "Looks like they've all committed to their descents." He felt much better now that the cocktail the doctor had given him had taken hold. VR syndrome was no joke, especially for EarthFleet's commander in chief. He felt embarrassed, but was pretty sure he hadn't completely lost it.

Not for the first time did he feel surprised at how much biology influenced behavior.

"Are we going down after them?" Scoggins asked.

"Not a chance," Absen replied. "We can't spare the fuel, especially our fighters. A tanker is coming from Mars and three from Jupiter, but we are on our own for a while. No, we'll just roll over and strafe them from orbit as we pass."

"Aye aye, sir. Okuda, make it so."

"Setting course for low Earth orbit with maximum coverage of Asia and Europe," the helmsman reported.

Thirty minutes later, the squadron crested the horizon and swung over the enemy landing zones. "'You may fire when ready, Gridley,'" Absen misquoted. "Pass the same to the fleet. Priority targets are their fighters, and watch for them shooting back. With this kind of space supremacy there's absolutely no reason to lose even one of our StormCrows. In fact, open the launch bay and tell the manned Crows to start rotating in as fast as they can for refit to automate them."

Once his orders were passed, Absen stood and strolled over to the holotank. *Conquest* floated over old Europe on a roughly west-east track, providing maximum hang time above the atmosphere as they raced the globe beneath them.

All of the small towns along the coasts had been evacuated. The tsunamis the Destroyer impacts caused fifty years ago had wiped away the large coastal cities, and the surviving concentrations of population were well inland and in the mountains. London, Hamburg and Naples had been destroyed back then, leaving mountain cities such as Milan and Vienna to prosper. Those had formed the nucleus of the Blend oligarchy's city-states, and now they became urban fortresses.

The Scourges landed in swirls and waves, more or less evenly across Europe and Asia. "Not much combat going on," Scoggins remarked. "Just some ground fire where they touched down within cities. Those beachheads have been wiped out."

"Yes, and the ones that landed in the surrounding zones died to the mines. That attracted a few more from nearby but generally, as long as the enemy isn't being shot at, they're just eating stuff, not turning to attack our defenses." Ford said excitedly. "Sir, how did you know?"

Absen turned to lean against the railing. "I know because I really do read Fleede's briefings, Commander. When given a choice between fighting and eating, Scourgelings eat. They only attack things that attack them or smell like food. In fact, if they didn't see something to eat – like people – they often just walk right by, unless Soldiers drive them to attack. So as much as possible, our forces in the cities are sealing themselves in. If they can't, they wipe out the local Scourge incursion and then retreat so no more are attracted."

Weapons fired from the fleet, depicted by lines reaching down toward the clouds of Scourge fighters that still buzzed above the ground, picking them off. In response, many rose to attack, but their small beam weapons couldn't hurt *Conquest*, and even the few StormCrows that were hit only suffered repairable damage. The atmosphere sucked all the range out of the enemy's weapons.

"Concentrate on those coming up after us," Scoggins ordered, and soon the targets were either dead or left behind, limited by air resistance to mere supersonic speeds while *Conquest* and her flock cruised along at orbital velocities exceeding 27,000 kilometers per hour.

"You see," Absen said smugly, "without orders, they just react to local threats, by whatever groupings they use. Perhaps all the critters from one mothership swarm stick together. Anyway, we shoot at them and they turn to attack."

"There's no way they can catch us, so we can attrit the fighters and gunships this way, but what about the landing forces?" Rick Johnstone asked. "There's what, eight hundred million of them on the ground now? That's more than the population of Earth!"

"Sounds like the fight is even, then, eh?" Absen said. "But no, I don't intend to fight fair. Crops and forests can be replanted; farms and houses can be rebuilt. The people on the ground will wait and save their strength for a couple of days. Let the enemy have the countryside." Absen waved airily. "Let the Scourgelings eat. For now, what we have to do is find and kill the nests."

56

"My Lord Spectre," the Blend called Alexander spoke. He fancied himself a military genius, so Spectre had put him in charge of defense planning. "We have destroyed several minor incursions on the Australian continent. It does not appear more will be arriving anytime soon."

The holotank had shown most of the Scourges landed in the Europe-Asia supercontinent, with scattered groups coming down on all the other continents, perhaps in the nature of scouting forces. Spectre knew the small infestations outside of Asia and Europe would be easily dealt with. "Good. Order the militia to patrol aggressively for any Scourges that run wild in the countryside, and alert the reaction forces worldwide to begin loading their transports. Give me your best recommendations for our counter-invasions within one hour. I want to be ready to hit them in two to three days." He made a gesture of dismissal.

"My Lord," Cleopatra purred, "I am no general, but I have read many of humanity's books. Isn't it more difficult to invade across the seas than to defend? Why not hold the continents we have at our borders while EarthFleet builds ships? The Scourge can be wiped out from space and then we repopulate what we lost later."

"Yes…that was one of my many contingency plans," Spectre said, giving the woman her due. "But we are being presented with an opportunity too good to pass up. Besides, if we wait too long, the seven enemy nests even now being built will cause problems. Even now, fertilized Archons are burrowing into the ground and laying eggs, while Soldiers gather food for the hatching infants. In two weeks, the enemy's numbers may double, and then double again. We cannot wait."

"My lord," Alexander said, "*Conquest* is already hunting the nests. We need have little fear on that score."

"Are you certain?" Spectre asked. "How do you know the seven nests are all they have? Perhaps they are cleverer than we presume. In any case, my point holds. All forces are ordered to wait and prepare to assault onto the Asia-Europe supercontinent, no less than forty-eight and no more than seventy-two hours from now."

"You're talking all around your plan, but you are withholding some key detail," Cleopatra complained. "You are playing with us, my lord, like cats with yarn."

"An apt metaphor. Usually you're the cat, but today you're the yarn." Spectre held up a hand. "I'm indulging myself, I admit. Let me explain what we must do." He turned to the holotank and called up a stored intelligence briefing authored by one Commander Ronald Fleede.

Once he'd outlined the proper courses of action and reviewed Alexander's deployment of forces onto Asia-Europe in order to crush the Scourges there, Spectre spoke with Admiral Absen once again and told Gilgamesh to oversee the minions in their duties.

Now that victory seemed inevitable, he decided to indulge himself in something he had been contemplating ever since he'd arrived on Earth. Spectre sent one of the Skulls to find Major Naomi Alkina and bring her to his private terrace.

Yes, he told himself. *A great-great-grandniece is a distant enough relation not to offend the populace when I take her as a lover, perhaps a bride.*

Not that a little thing like public opinion would have stopped him anyway.

57

Bull concentrated on his HUD as he descended, telling himself that the technology was sound and there was nothing to worry about. The screen inside his faceplate showed over 2600 EarthFleet Marines free-falling into atmosphere, each strapped into an automated parachute rig made to slow the wearer and eventually set him down softly on the ground. Three days of drop training hadn't been enough to really convince his brain he would be fine.

At least atmospheric heat and friction wasn't an issue. *Conquest* had briefly stopped in her orbit and hovered on her massive fusion engines while the Marines lined up and leaped out of auxiliary ports well away from the hot exhaust. Several pinnaces and a few sleds followed them down with supplies and Recluse drones.

The drop wasn't intended as a hard insertion: it was simply the only way to put the brigade down intact, as most of the sleds had been lost during the mothership assault.

They would land near New Delhi in what once was India. Over the last three days, *Conquest* and her auxiliaries had used their superior position to systematically exterminate most of the enemy fighters and gunships in that area. With the arrival of the interplanetary tankers, the dreadnought had enough fuel to slow orbit and descend, flying by brute force on fusion engines to engage near-helpless targets below them at a range of less than one hundred kilometers, point blank for *Conquest's* massive weapons.

Extensive bombardment from orbit of the Marine landing zone had destroyed all the grounded Scourge craft, the only other source of enemy heavy weapons. With a wing of StormCrows for cover, Bull's command was probably one of the safest "opposed" landings in Marine history. The only danger was on touchdown – the millions of Scourgelings and thousands of Soldiers that infested the countryside.

As Bull flew his ram-air parachute inexorably downward, he unlimbered his pulse gun and passed his last instructions to his commanders. As he landed, a Soldier popped out of a foxhole and fired its assault cannon, slamming slugs into Bull's chest and knocking him over. *Lucky he didn't have something heavier,* Bull thought as he fell backward and rolled, trying to stay low. For a moment he got tangled in his parachute. When he cut loose and came to his knees to fire, he saw the enemy slaughtered by several nearby Marines.

"Good job, diggers. Get organized and start the bug hunt, now. Hustle! Exterminate everything in your area with minimum ammo, one shot per as briefed," he ordered.

"Bull, this is Reaper," Command Sergeant Major Repeth radioed. "Did you ever think we'd be walking into this like cake?"

"No. Thought we'd be fighting for our lives, but we still might be if we don't move fast." He jogged toward the nearest pinnace, firing a single shot into each Scourgeling cocoon he came across. "We only have two days."

The cocoons were everywhere, some in clumps, some just scattered here and there. Bull knew that all across Asia and Europe Earth's ground forces were on the offensive and were winning handily. Like Reap had said, a cakewalk. Instead of a Marine, he felt like an exterminator, though the occasional Soldier kept the troops on their toes. "Conserve ammo," he reminded everyone. Even if they killed one Scourgeling with every round, the Marine brigade would only get rid of two or three million of them, out of an estimated eight hundred million now on Earth.

Instead of shooting it immediately, Bull put his armored foot on the next cocoon he found and tried to crush it. The tough resin didn't budge. He would probably have to use his jump jets to leap upward and come down hard on it.

Not worth the trouble. Ryss hotblades might have been an efficient solution. Now would be a good time to have a brigade of the big cats. Instead of worrying about what he couldn't have, Bull just rested his elbows on his raised knee and thought for a moment about how easy it had turned out to be.

The admiral always amazed him with his insights. He'd spotted what everyone else seemed to have missed in the mad scramble to repel the invasion and seize the FTL tech: that one innocuous mention in Commander

Fleede's briefing about the Scourge life cycle. *"As soon as a Scourgeling eats enough, it will go into a cocoon for several days…"* the geek had said. Bull remembered only because the admiral had played it back for them when he finally explained the whole thing.

Ninety-nine percent of the Scourgelings had simply eaten themselves into one common coma. Driven by biology and without the distraction of a fight, they had gorged themselves on Earth's plant and animal life and then cocooned themselves for their next stage. If left alone, they would emerge within days as Soldiers, much more dangerous opponents.

But they weren't going to be left alone.

Many of the existing Soldiers had cocooned as well, perhaps half of them giving in to the urge to metamorphose into Centurions.

Now, all across the supercontinent, humanity was on the hunt and their enemy was helpless. Bull was reminded of a documentary he had seen of North Africans swatting clouds of locusts, killing thousands but hardly making a dent in the millions that overran and ate every piece of plant life in sight. Now the humans had the upper hand. Probably every teenager on the planet that could carry a gun was out in the fields, making a game of tallying up his kills and hopefully not shooting his buddies.

On his HUD, Bull watched as his Marines moved in extended firing lines as if policing a parade ground for cigarette butts and trash before an important ceremony. Recluses equipped with sensors followed, now and again finding a cocoon the mass of troops had missed.

Bull was less concerned about the formation of the brigade than its ammo supply. The pulse guns Marines carried were actually overpowered for exterminating cocoons. An interim solution occurred to him. He opened the general brigade channel.

"First Brigade, this is Bull. For those formations with Recluses sweeping behind, I want you to only kill half the cocoons you find. Let the Recluses pick off the rest with their lasers. This will conserve your ammo." Sure, it would run the Recluses out of juice faster, but it was easier to recharge a battle drone off a pinnace or sled than to come up with pulse gun ammo. Too bad they only had a few laser rifles available. Equipping five thousand new Marines had forced some corner cutting.

"Bull," Reaper commed, "I got locals here on the edge of the city – they just popped out of some tunnels. They're lucky they didn't get shot."

"Yeah, so?"

"They're armed, and want to be put to work."

"By all means, Sergeant Major," Bull replied. "I'd rather expend their ammo than ours. In fact, let them and the Recluses do the cocoon-killing and our people will guard against Soldiers. And watch your backgrounds! Don't let our diggers get too froggy. This is ripe ground for fratricide."

"Aye aye, sir."

Bull sighed with contentment. Only a stupid young line doggie wanted a fair fight. Older grunts like him were happy to take easy victories when they presented themselves. Those were few and far between.

Hard battles would turn up soon enough.

Even though they had beaten the Scourge this time, Bull knew that with the FTL technology, eventually EarthFleet would have to take the fight to the enemy.

When we do, I'll be there.

–Epilogue–

Admiral Absen sat comfortably sipping Mars-brewed whiskey in his expanded office aboard *Conquest*. Timmons had acquired some through the Chief's network to replace the Scotch that had finally run out. Now if only he could get some decent smokes.

The more things change, the more they stay the same was the quote that ran through his mind. Here he was in charge of EarthFleet again, guarding the poor suffering planet against the threat of invasion. Still, things seemed much brighter now that he had Rae by his side. He still wasn't one hundred percent sure her attraction to him wasn't partly political, but at this point he didn't want to spoil a good thing by thinking too deeply about it.

Another difference this time around: no more dealing with a slow-moving bureaucracy. Spectre *was* the government now, and when he wanted something to happen, it happened. Absen didn't see how that was going to change unless the Blend stepped down voluntarily. With the Skulls and other Blends serving him, no one was likely to challenge him for some time to come – and Absen wasn't at all sure he'd want anyone else to take over. *Better the devil you know…* Besides, anyone with a mind to rebel against authority had already joined the resistance movement and then *become* the new government.

Absen sighed. Earth's governance wasn't his main problem. His problem was getting the orbital industries working and the space-based economy on track. He was short of skilled workers and almost every sort of machine, though he could get simple laborers from the planet and train them himself. Plenty of people were out of jobs with all the damage the Scourges did to the ecosystem.

Somehow he had to cobble together sufficient defenses to repel another Scourge invasion, and he had no idea when that would show up. Probably not for months, but beyond that, who knew? For just a few weeks, from the time he left Gliese 370 until he learned about the Scourge, he'd felt like he was ahead of the game. Now he was playing catch-up again.

Fortunately the Meme had decided to stick around. Absen laughed to himself. What a change in his thinking! He'd fought them for a century. In fact, most of his adult life was defined by fighting Meme, and now he desperately needed their firepower and their ability to grow and reproduce their ships.

Rae had explained to him that their SystemLord was probably staying because of his title and position. If he went elsewhere, he would have to take a demotion. By remaining in Earth's system, he would automatically take forces under his command as they arrived as long as they did not outrank him. Assuming the Meme kept their bargain, that was all to the good.

In the rock-paper-scissors situation they had now, *Conquest* and the technology she used could beat the Meme quite handily – but Destroyers were more efficient swarm killers with their huge short-ranged fusors, especially so when they acted as squadrons to cover each other.

That reminded the admiral of something to put on the long wish list: a study on how to optimize weaponry and tactics against the Scourge. Perhaps a squadron-integrated point defense network…but that would have to come after the upgraded SLAMs and the permanent fortress that would sit above the Sun's pole ready to fire them. The best defense against FTL emergence was to hit the enemy prior to coming out of null space confusion, destroying the motherships whole, before the swarms launched.

Defensive problems were interesting, but Absen's mind really raced when thinking about how EarthFleet would employ their own FTL drive. The old Ryss physicist Plessk still had a few good years in him depending on how much medical care the cat would accept, and his team had assured the admiral that they could build a working FTL drive within a year or two. They even had some ideas on how to use the effect to communicate faster than light.

With FTL came a whole new ball game. Humanity could send probes to other stars and get intelligence within weeks rather than decades – establish outposts, military bases and colonies.

Take the fight to the enemy.

If the treaty held, maybe humans and Meme could get along well enough to establish some kind of confederation, a new order where all species could help defend each other from threats like the Scourge and share as equals in the wealth of the galaxy. That might be the real, permanent result of all the death and tragedy.

If so, then maybe it was all worth it.

Books By

DAVID VANDYKE

THE PLAGUE WARS SERIES

The Eden Plague

Reaper's Run

Skull's Shadows

Eden's Exodus

The Demon Plagues

The Reaper Plague

The Orion Plague

Cyborg Strike

Comes the Destroyer

STELLAR CONQUEST SERIES

First Conquest

Desolator

Tactics of Conquest

Conquest of Earth

Conquest and Empire

Look for them at your favorite book provider or visit
www.davidvandykeauthor.com

Made in the USA
Charleston, SC
03 March 2015